9-4-21

To: Michelle

Be blessed !

Celia

Tree
In Life Seasons Do Change

Calvin Denson

Yorkshire Publishing
3207 South Norwood Avenue
Tulsa, OK 74135

ISBN: 978-1-947247-64-2

Dedication

This novel is dedicated to my family, friends and South Park, Beaumont, Texas my number one fans. Thank all of you for believing in me during my transitioning to becoming the author I am today. God bless you and enjoy the book.

Introduction

H ey, Tree,

Your letter really surprised me because I thought I wasn't going to ever see or hear from you again. Thanks for your apology, but your words had me with mixed feelings for a second. Of course, you always knew the right things to say when you were in the doghouse. I'm sorry for all that you're going through. All I can say is everything happens for a reason, and I'll keep you in my prayers. As for me, I'm doing okay, and my mom is doing great too. I don't know if I ever told you this, but my mom has cancer, and I've been taking care of her since I left Houston, so please pray for her. The person you used to know is not me anymore, Tree. I go to church faithfully, I have a job, and I'm in college to be a veterinarian. As you can see, God is good and has opened a lot of doors for me. I'm not perfect, but I'm trying to do what's right because going to church has taught me a lot about forgiveness. Jesus forgave me, so I must forgive you. Please don't mix forgiveness with forgetfulness. *Need I say more?* I always thought we were going to live happily ever after no matter what obstacles came in between us, but you messed all that up, Tree, and it hurts because I invested four years in us. The money slip you sent me, I will mail back fifty dollars with it. I know it's not much, but that's all I can spare on my income. Thanks for writing and letting me know you're okay. Keep your head up, and never forget, God is in control of everything.

Sincerely,
Audumn Humphrey

"That's what's up," Tree said while tearing off the return address of Audumn's letter. *These cats in here can't be trusted as far as I can throw them. One slipup, and my girl will be getting a letter from someone other than me,* Tree thought as he put his letters with the rest of his mail. Life in TDCJ is starting to get too comfortable for Tree. Yesterday he had the whole world eating out the palm of his hands, but today he is confined to a corner of four men in a transfer facility.

His bunk mate was a guy named Bubblehead from Orange, Texas. Across from him was a cat they called Lil Third from his hometown, Houston. A Muslim by the name of Mouse slept underneath Third Ward. He was quiet and only spoke when he wanted to talk about his religion.

"I got next on the domino table!" Tree shouted across the tank.

"All right, we got you, but somebody better come and take score!"

"Say, Phat Fat, you want to be my partner because I got next!" Tree yelled from his bunk.

"It's all good, I'll run with you!"

Walking to the table, Tree thinks about his letter from Audumn. *Man, I wish things could have worked out between us.* "It is what is," he said to himself as he grabbed the pen and paper. Taking score, Tree looks around at the fifty-four-man tank and prays that this world he's living in won't be the last of what he was trying to become. All he wanted to be was the next Nino Brown, but that came to a halt when the police kicked in his door.

"Twenty!" one of the guys shout as he slammed the domino hard on the steel table.

The game is over, so Tree sits down to play his part in a race to one-fifty. He's 6'4", so his legs can't find comfort because the table is shaped like a stop sign and the seats are circular. Twelve inches is the diameter, so his butt cheeks hang off each side of the seat.

"Give me fifteen!" Tree yells to the next person up to play. "You betta ask the guards for some ice because you gonna have a lot of knots on your head trying to hold me, homeboy."

Five games are played, and Tree has won three of them. It's chow time, so the guards in the picket flash the lights to let them know their tank is next on the cement slab that leads to every building in the unit. The doors roll, and white cotton uniforms step on to what the penitentiary calls a bowling alley in an organized manner. All of the men have their hands behind their backs because it's a requirement in the handbook. Some have letters in their back pockets ready to be put in the mailbox at the cafeteria's door, but Tree has none because his next letter is going to take a lot of thought if he wanted to get his Audumn back.

The cafeteria is huge, and the temperature is seventy-five degrees. Winter is around the corner, so everyone enjoyed what is left of the heat. Summer was a beast and took a toll on everyone there, but what's up ahead is worse because nobody, not even the guards, were ready for it.

Wind in the cafeteria begins to circulate from the open metal doors throughout the tin building. It feels good, so no one complains as they eat their perfectly sliced pork chops.

"What's up, Tree, did you hear from your girl you always be yapping about?"

"That's how you gon' do your boy, Man Pooh! You act like I'm crazy about the broad or something."

Man Pooh starts laughing at his friend because Tree always gets roused up when you talk about Audumn. Even though they never hung out in the free world, Pooh knew him because they were from the same neighborhood.

"So did you, or did you not?" Man Pooh ask.

"Why you all up in my business for?"

"Cuz that's what I do."

"Whatever, but to keep your mouth shut, I didn't hear from her yet," Tree replied, putting his head down to finish his meal.

Man Pooh knew that Tree received the letter he was waiting on from his body language, and also Bubblehead told him when they were in the chow line. He didn't press the issue because he and Tree talked about everything. Recreation time is in a couple of hours, so he'll get the full details on the rec yard later.

"Row one!" an officer shouts, standing in the doorway.

Chow time is a rush because the guards gave you a specific time to eat as soon as you sat down. It's crazy because no one knew the time limit but them. With stuffed faces, each row gets up when called.

Man Pooh and Tree leave together and agree to meet in the rec yard, but before they split up, they shook each other's hands and snapped their fingers.

"Holla at you later!" Tree yelled as they parted ways to go back to their tanks.

1

"Rec time! Whoever's going to the rec yard needs to be at the door in two minutes!"

"Two minutes. These laws be tripping with these strange time schedules that they only know about." Tree is just getting out of the shower and drying his feet when the officer calls for rec.

Sliding his feet into his shower shoes, Tree stands and quickly falls to the back of the line for rec. More then half the tank has decided to go today, so the hour outside is cut short because it started when the guard said they had two minutes to get to the door.

The sun is setting as the inmates enjoy what's left of their time of recreation. Basketball, handball, and volleyball is being played on the overcrowded rec yard, and each race plays its own sport to keep confusion down. Blacks played basketball, Hispanics played handball, and the Caucasians played volleyball. All games were open for anyone to play, but no one ever participated in them unless it was only a few people on the rec yard.

Man Pooh's pod is next door, so he had to speak to Tree through the barbwire fence that separated the two tanks. Tree was there first, so he knew his friend had a lot on his mind.

"What's up, Tree? What's the gossip for the day?" Pooh asks.

"Gossip! Men don't gossip," Tree replied in a deep voice.

"We gossip if I say we gossip."

Seeing that the conversation is a dead end with no way out, Tree quickly changes the subject to what is on his mind. "Man Pooh, why is it that these females feel like they can just do or talk to us any kind of way while we are in here?"

"I guess it's because of all the bullshit we put them through while we were in the free world."

Reflecting on the past, Tree sees everything he's done to the love of his life as if it was yesterday. "You're right, Man Pooh, I did put her through a lot of bullshit," he said with a small chuckle.

"I already know. We all do, Tree."

Tree and his hood friend give each other the daily scoop until the whistle is blown and the rec yard lights begin to shut off one by one. Man Pooh gave his advice on Tree's situation, and Tree took it for what it is because his boy never steered him in the wrong direction.

"Don't stress behind her. Do your time and keep your letters to her respectful, and she'll come back to you."

"We'll see, and you're right about doing this time because I don't see nobody stepping up to do it for me. I hate that I got to go back to the county on another charge."

"Hey, you two by the fence, rec time is over unless you want to stay out here for the rest of the night!" a guard yells, walking on the outside of the fence.

"I'ma get up with you later before I tell these want-to-be police officers about themselves." Man Pooh stares at the CO through the fence.

"All right, Pooh, I guess I'll get at you tomorrow morning in the law library."

The dayroom is packed when Tree came in from his everyday meeting with Man Pooh. Tonight, no one is in their bunk, so all the seats are taken underneath the two televisions sitting high on the opposite sides of the tank. Standing behind a row of seats, he tries to block out all his worries and enjoy tonight's game. The clock is ticking, and he can hear each time a hand moves in it because tomorrow morning is the day Harris County comes for all inmates with charges pending.

With his fingers crossed, he says a silent prayer for another week of researching his case in the law library.

Roars and boos began to sound from the four rows of seats and bring him back to the jungle he's living in. Shaking the dreadful thoughts from his head, he focuses on the football game that he made a bet with Bubblehead the night before. If it wasn't for the bet, he couldn't care less on who won or lost the game because none of the teams were from Houston.

"What's up, Tree? You eating tonight, or are you going to watch Bubblehead take your money?"

"You already know I'm spreading tonight, Phat Fat. Do I ever miss a meal?"

"You show right about that. I don't know why I even asked that question."

"Are you cooking or am I?"

"I got it tonight because I know you got to watch your money."

"Thanks, Phat, I owe you one. Get whatever you need out of my locker."

"Count time! Count time! Everyone in their bunks!" Officer Briggs shouts, entering the dayroom with a woman officer named Ms. Williams.

All the inmates hustle back to their bunks as fast as possible so they can get their seats back underneath the TV. It's game night, and the guards know it because fifty-four men are not hard to count, but tonight it's difficult for some reason. Anger begins to fill the room as the lady officer counts for the third time.

"Count's clear, y'all can get up! I want towels out of the dayroom and the television volume down!" Officer Williams exclaims.

"Yes, ma'am, and please come back and visit us sometime!" a man yells from the shower covered in soap.

Laughter and muffled words of foul language come from the tank as the officers exit because a quarter of the game has passed, and the tension is higher than usual. Going back to their seats, everyone wishes they can see the guards that are not cool on the other side of the gates. But the offenders know that it's very rare for this to happen, so all of their eyes are once again glued to the two boxes that join the free world to the penitentiary.

The aroma from the noodles, seasoning, and meat packs causes Tree's stomach to growl. Phat Fat is in line for hot water, and he's two men behind. Two minutes are left in the game, and Tree is on the short end of stick on the bet he has made with Bubblehead. He knows that there's no hope in winning, so he takes his loss like a man and places twelve packs of noodles and a chili meat pack on his bunkmate's bed. With his locker open, he grabs a Snickers candy bar to satisfy him until Phat is ready to bless the small meal he's put together.

"Say, Tree, you eating or what?"

"Call me when it's ready because I'm thinking about something."

"Fool, it is ready! Now get your ass over here so we can eat!"

"I got your fool," Tree replied jokingly as he approached the table.

Everything Phat made was good, and tonight he has put together a chicken and cheese dinner. It's very seldom for them to have this meal because the chicken came from the kitchen on the random days they served it. Tree knew somebody who worked in the kitchen that didn't mind taking the risk in getting it back to the tank.

As they took their seats, Tree grabs his boy's hand and bows his head. "Thank you, Jesus, for this food we are about to receive. Amen."

A few minutes pass, and Tree's bowl is almost empty. After he takes his last bite, he laughs to himself because 70 percent of the time he manages to get Phat Fat to cook.

"What you smiling about?" Phat asks.

"If I told you, I'll have to kill you."

"Whatever, Tree. I cooked, so you have to wash the dishes."

"I know the rules. You don't have to remind me." Tree stacks the two bowls on the table to be washed.

"Act like it then and get to work."

Tree stood up and bumps into a Hispanic guy by accident. In the penitentiary, you can't show any weakness, so he looks down on him without saying "Excuse me." The Hispanic guy's name is Blake, and he runs half of the transfer facility unit they are on. Tree doesn't know him because he moved into the tank when he was in the recreation yard with Man Pooh.

"Say, *voto*, can you say excuse me?" Tree asks with a slight nudge from his shoulder.

"Excuse me for what? You bumped into me, homeboy."

"I don't care who bumped into who. But what I do care about is you giving me some respect."

"I got your respect, Mr. Tree, but I don't think you want it."

"We gon' see about that, *loco*, when the lights go off."

"We can see about it right now."

"I got too much on the line to smash on you in front the police. Meet me in the corner after last count."

"You ain't said nothing, homeboy, that I haven't heard before. Let the lights be the bell then."

Washing the bowls, Tree thinks about what his pride has gotten him into because deep down inside, he is a nice guy, but his circumstances wouldn't allow him to display it in jail. Usually his height and his weight made other inmates stay out of his way, but tonight, things didn't play out the way he wanted it to.

After drying the spoons, he leaves the wash area wondering how the new Hispanic guy knew his name.

The dayroom lights shut off at exactly 11:00 p.m. Count time was ten minutes ago, so Monday-night fights was about to happen as soon as the inmates by the door gave the clearance. Tree was a little nervous because he did some research on his opponent with Lil Third Ward. He was nervous because he heard a lot about Blake but never met him before. Tree was real good with his hands when it came to a boxing match, so losing wasn't an option. The consequences after winning is what he isn't too certain about because Tree did his time by himself. Blake, on the other hand, had God knows who ready to move when he gave the word. For all he knew, he probably had a hit out on him right now.

"Everything's clear. The guards are asleep in the picket. If ya'll gon' do it, now is the time," the lookout said in a loud whisper.

It's no turning back, so Tree wraps his knuckles with his face towel, and all the guys he associated with tell him that they have his back if anyone tries to jump in. With that in mind, he would worry about tomorrow later because tonight, he had some stress that needed to be relieved, and Blake is the one he is going to relieve it on.

All the inmates stayed in their bunks so that the fight wouldn't be so obvious, but Blake's bunk is in the corner, so he is already there with his shirt off. The smell of fear is scarce because they both are gladiators.

As Tree got closer to the corner, the Hispanics from around the tank started to stand to their feet, but Tree's eyes is only on his opponent, so he blocks out the fact that this could end badly.

No one is keeping track of the time when half of the lights turn on, and names begin to be called from the loudspeaker for tonight's chain. Everyone who is on the floor feels as if they were under a spotlight and try to run for cover. Officer Briggs notices that something was about to go down and shouts for Blake to put his shirt on before he gets written up for indecent exposure.

"Torrence Wingate, come your ass to the picket!" Mr. Briggs shouts in an angry voice.

The voice over the loudspeaker sends everyone in the tank in a loud frenzy while Bubblehead rushes over and secretly takes the face towel from Tree's back pocket.

Tree's mind is at ease as he walks slowly to the door because no one had a fight, and the evidence disappeared.

Opening the door, he walks out knowing he's in the clear. Mr. Briggs watched everything from his hiding spot in the picket, so he knew a fight was about to take place.

"Torrence Wingate, a.k.a. Mr. Tree."

"What's up, boss? You know you ain't got nothing on me."

"Did I ask you anything?"

Tree is silent as he stands in front of the picket while everything Mr. Briggs is telling him sounds like hogwash and goes in one ear and out of the other.

"Answer me when I'm talking to you!" Mr. Briggs screams as his face turned red. "Stop acting like a dunce and listen to someone for a change!"

"I didn't listen to my momma, so why in the hell should I listen to you?"

"You inmates think you're so smart when you can't even listen to words that come out of your own mouth. Now honestly, are you proud of what you just said?"

The officer's words made him feel a little ashamed, and he held his head down.

"Get out my face, and go get your shit ready because you're on the chain tonight."

All the lights are on when Tree turned around to go and pack everything he could possibly take back to Harris County. Opening the door, he sees Officer Henry taking inventory on another inmate. "Torrence Wingate, you're next, so be ready, or you'll be going back to the county with only your mail."

Tree knows that Officer Henry means what he says, so he bites his tongue and quickly packs his belongings. When inventory over, he is told to put his mattress in the hallway and go to breakfast.

"Yes, sir!" Tree said sarcastically.

"Now that's exactly what got you in here and exactly what you're probably going back to your county for." Officer Henry shakes his head in disgust.

Rolling his mattress up into his sheets, Tree says his final good-byes to his homeboys. His eyes began to open when he realizes that he is about to leave the facility he had grown accustomed to and because the men in his corner had become like roommates to him. Tension was constantly in the tank, but at the end of the day, nothing ever broke out.

Picking up the mattress by the tied sheet ends, he throws it over his shoulder and walks over to Phat to give him his address to his sister Gayriale's house.

"Holla at me when you touch ground. I got you," Tree said.

"That's what's up, now gone on and take care of that business so we can get back to the streets."

"Now that sounds like music to my ears, Phat Fat. Tell Man Pooh I'ma get at him when I get back from the county," Tree replied as he turns to go to breakfast.

2

G uards are everywhere supervising the chain going out Tuesday morning, and anyone who had something mischievous on their mind had
quickly disregarded all their negative thinking. Troublemakers and aggravated cases went first in the final processing-out stages because inmates
going to other TDCJ units went after them.

Tree's group is last because there are only two men going back to Harris
County.

The morning drags on, and inmates began to get hungry because breakfast was a boiled egg with a slice of bread. Everyone waiting to go to their
next destination started to become furious, so words of anger were out of
reflex due to their stomach's emptiness. Officers began to yank offenders
out of the holding cells and put them in solitary confinement until their time
to leave, but after seeing how the guards roughed those up who had bucked
the system, inmates' hunger pains seem to diminish as fast as they came.

"Harris County! All offenders going to Harris County, step to the gate
and show your wristbands!"

Two arms were placed in the open slot in the gate. With his clipboard in
his hand, the officer reads the names Chad Perkins and Torrence Wingate
Jr. off it. Looking down at the bands, he confirms the names and tells them
to step out to be shackled. After being shackled from head to toe, Tree
complains that the cuffs on his wrist are too tight.

"Be quiet, Mr. Wingate," the officer who put them on him said.

"Sir, my wrists are starting to swell up."

"Mr. Wingate, didn't you hear what Officer Gains just told you?" the
guard with the clipboard asked while getting into his face.

"Yes, sir," Tree mumbled to stay out of trouble.

"That's more like it. Officer Gains, will you please loosen Mr. Torrence
Wingate's handcuffs before he tells his momma on us?"

"Yes sir, Sgt. Tigner."

Everything is complete by noon because the process took about eight hours from the time Mr. Briggs told him he was on the chain until the time Sgt. Tigner said to roll out. Chad and Tree couldn't be any happier when the words fell from his lips that it is time to go, but saying the word *walk* was a lot easier than actually doing it. The cuffs around their ankles have only eight inches of chain in between them, so they have to take baby steps to the patrol car.

Getting into the patrol car is more strenuous than getting to it because his 6'4", 250 pounds stature couldn't find the correct angles to take a seat. After about five minutes, Tree finally figures out the best way to approach the puzzle that's before him. Taking a seat, he begins to laugh because he thought he would never be in the back of a police car again.

"What's up, I'm Lil C from Beaumont, Texas," Chad said as Officer Gains slammed the car door behind him.

"Beaumont, Texas. My girl is from Beaumont, Texas."

"What's her name?"

Looking him over, Tree says, "Audumn Humphrey" with a little hesitation.

"Audumn Humphrey," Lil C repeats. "Audumn Humphrey, who has a brother name Aubrie, but everyone calls him Brie."

"I think that's her. She did mention she had two older brothers and two younger than her."

"It got to be because Brie has three brothers and a big sister name Audumn."

"That's what's up. When was the last time you saw her, Lil C? Because she left me a while back to be with her sick mother."

"I haven't seen her in a minute. I think the last time I saw Audumn was about five or six years ago."

"I miss my baby. I hope when I get to the county, she'll come visit me because I'm back home now." Tree turns his head toward the window when Lil Chad replied to his last statement, but Chad's words only bounced off the car windows because Tree gave him a deaf ear.

The sky is blue and the grass is green as Tree looks at a pasture with cows staring at a white fence. Enjoying the peace that nature brings, Tree meditates on the charge he's about to go to court for because adding up the possibilities of what could happen isn't looking too good. Finally, he thinks he has an idea, but it vanishes when the earsplitting country music comes through the rear speakers.

Everything done up until this time was tolerable, except for the country music torturing them each time a new song came on. The speakers in the rear are the only two that works, and they are at its limit so the officers can hear the music in the front seats. Chad is asleep, but the old Westerns quickly opened his eyes when the sergeant pressed the power button to turn the radio on.

"What the fu— I mean, are you crazy? Can you please turn it down?" Chad shouted in anger.

"No, I will not turn it down. If your ass would stay out of jail, you'd be in your own car, controlling the volume the way you would want to control it. But since you're not out of jail or in your own car, you might as well sit back and enjoy the ride, Mr. Perkins," Officer Gains said while looking into his rearview mirror.

Chad and Tree's battle with the officers over the radio ended with the officers winning before it even began. All they could do is endure the next hour with hopes of them becoming tired of the country tunes.

Patiently waiting, Chad comes to the realization that the officers were sent from outer space to destroy their ears with their native music. Tree laughs as Chad continues to crack jokes on the country-listening chauffeurs in the front seat.

"Say, Tree, I feel like a superstar riding behind limo tint in this backseat."

"I don't know about all that, Lil C."

"For real though, I mean think about it. Two men dressed in black came to pick us up in a black car with tinted windows. On top of that, they opened the door for us when we got in the car, and I'm for sure they'll open the door for us when we get out."

"You stupid, Lil Chad."

"I wish it were raining so they could put on their little black hats." Chad burst out laughing at his own jokes.

Glancing out the front window, Tree sees Houston is only sixteen miles away. His time in the county will be short for all he knew because Harris County is known for sending you to court as soon as you get there. Good luck isn't in his favor, so all he could do is look for the worst and pray for the best.

Closer and closer they drew to Houston's city limits, and as he looks through the front windows, downtown starts to become bigger and bigger in the distance up ahead. His mind begins to boggle as he dwells on the potential outcome of what is to come for the second time. *God, I know I don't ask you for much, but please pull a rabbit out of your hat for me. By the way, this is Torrence Wingate Jr., if you forgot about me. Amen.*

The car stopped abruptly at the red light that changed from yellow at the last minute. Chad had dozed off, so the sudden stop sent his head into the gate that separated the officers from the offenders. Sgt. Tigner is in front of him, so he felt the vibrations from Chad's head in his back.

"After a bump like that, I bet you won't call this chauffeur company again for a ride." Officer Gains smirks while remembering Lil C's earlier backseat comedy show.

Like a turtle going into its shell, Chad doesn't respond because he thought his earlier comedy skit with Tree was strictly confidential because of the blaring music. Suddenly, they're surrounded by darkness, and the daylight from the rear seemed to become less and less as the officers waited for the police station's garage door to close behind them. A bright light in the garage then begins to turn on and blinds everyone as a loud buzz from the door being secured deafens them.

"You would think, out of all the money this county robs us for, they would have upgraded from the nineties into the twentieth century by now," Tree said sarcastically to break the silence.

"Torrence Wingate and Chad Perkins, please enter the door to your left and sit on the first row of blue seats!" Sgt. Tigner exclaims as Officer Gains opens the door through which they were about to walk through.

"I hate this place."

"Yeah, you and me both, Lil Chad."

"I shouldn't have never taken that last run with my boy Coop C."

"Yeah, and I should have listen to my girl and stayed my butt at home that night."

"That's enough talking for the two you. If you girls like each other that much, exchange numbers and go on a date when you get out," Sgt. Tigner said with a serious face.

Sgt. Tigner walked into book-in and handed their paperwork to the correctional officer in processing. Officer Gains took off their chains and told them to come back and see him sometime.

Chad responded by giving him an "I hate you" look. Tree, on the other hand, looked him straight in the eyes as if to say, "I'm not scared of you."

"Stand up and go to the back row so we can get you tough guys changed out."

Tree stood up thinking about how he used to play musical chairs in daycare, but a small laughter of disgust fell over him when he realized that he always lost that game because of his height. *I hope I don't lose in court like I did back in the day,* he thought as he began to take off his shirt.

"Put your damn shirt back on until you're told to take it off. Sgt. Tigner and I love to look at women, not men."

Yeah right, Chad thought.

Their escorting officers left as soon as Sgt. Tigner officially released Lil C and Tree from their custody. With his index finger pointed up, Officer Gains signals for the garage door to be open. "You ladies keep your hands to yourself, you hear," he said with a devilish look.

Sitting in their assigned seats, a black trustee by the name of Pookie comes out as soon as the door to the garage buzzed closed. He's a little overweight because the guards keep him fed to tell the unseen things that go on when their backs are turned. His orange uniform, shoes, and hair are well groomed, and the words he spoke from his mouth were as if he is the enemy. All the inmates in the county couldn't help but to obey him because everyone knew that the lieutenant gave him that job until his trial date came up. It's funny because he's been waiting to go to court for almost three years now.

"All right, inmates, I'ma need you to strip out of those whites and put on these orange county scrubs."

"Inmates! Who is this guy, Tree?"

"I don't know, but that orange uniform he's wearing sure looks like the one he's trying to give us."

"I don't need your mouth, Mr. Tall Guy. I get off in ten minutes, so just do it quietly."

"Well, I'ma grown man, and I don't appreciate when the chief sends Indians to do their jobs."

13

The look on Tree's face and the tone of his last statement made Pookie lighten up a bit. As they changed, Pookie handed them their housing papers and told them to step to the window to get their TDCJ wristbands cut off. The officer behind the window's words was short, and if you didn't catch what he said the first time, that was your bad. It's a rumor that an inmate sat in intake until the officer's shift was up because he was deaf, and the officer never repeated himself twice.

With the county's requirements out of the way, Pookie escorts them to the elevators to be housed. Chad's wristband reads C4/1-16, and Tree's reads C3/6-21 because their age difference is what put them on different floors. Since Chad was under twenty-one, he had to be placed with the youngsters on the fourth floor, and his face showed that he already knew what he had to overcome as soon as he stepped foot into the tank. Why, it's because no matter which tank on the fourth floor he resided in, he would have to fight as soon as he put his bags down.

"Looks like this is my stop, Lil C. and if I'm ever in Beaumont, I'll look you up."

"Yeah, you do that, and I'll help you find your girl when you come holla at me."

"Chad Perkins, right?"

"No, it's Lil C from South Park," he said, holding up four fingers, which is his neighborhood gang sign.

Tree smiled to himself and bumped fists with Lil C as he stepped off the elevator, ready for whatever the county had in store for him.

Standing at the picket, Tree hands his housing slip to the lady officer on duty.

After she looks him over, the CO hands it back to him with squinted eyes before pointing him in the direction in which he needs to go. "Grab a sack lunch from the room to your right."

Tree turns around and goes over to get his second meal of the day, but while he is bending down to pick up two bags, a floor trustee came up from behind him and says, "What's up, Tree?"

Tree thought it was an officer and dropped the extra sack lunch quickly. "You wasn't scared in the free world, so why you acting all scared now?"

At first Tree didn't catch his voice, but when he turned around, he saw it was his old high school buddy, Jiro.

"Jiro, what in the hell hole did you crawl from because this is the last place I thought I would have seen you." Jiro was somewhat of a model student growing up. He grew up in the hood but his parents always kept him in the house.

"I thought that too, until I graduated, and the real world wasn't as easy as I thought it was."

"You can say that twice. What you in for?"

"Robbery, kidnapping, and possibly murder."

"What were you thinking trying to pull a stunt off like that?"

"I don't know, I just did it," Jiro said as he walked Tree to C3/6. "Last year I held an old white couple hostage while their daughter went to the bank for the ransom money. I was caught, but shortly after the incident, the old lady died."

"Damn, Jiro, you put yourself in a hole with that one."

"It's all good because it's in God's hands now."

"You better hope so because they gone try to hang your ass when you step into that courtroom." Tree pushes the button on the intercom to his tank. "Especially with it being an old white lady and all."

"I know this may sound crazy, Tree, but can you pray for me tonight before you lay it down? I've been fighting this case for a year now, and the judge is not changing his mind about life without the possibility of parole."

"I promise I'll do that, if I remember."

Walking into the twenty-four-man tank, everyone stops what they're doing to give him a friendly stare. First things first, so Tree stares back, and everyone sees he's not the prey but possibly a predator. His wristband reads bunk 21, and all the odd numbers are bottom bunks, so he is happy that he doesn't have to climb to the top bunk later when he wants to chill by himself.

Placing his stuff underneath his bed, he lies down and realizes he's in front of the shower. *I hate the county,* he thought as he closed his eyes to think.

15

3

"Chow at the door!" an inmate shouts standing in the window of the tank.

Who in the hell is making all that racket? Tree thought, trying to tune out the noise of the twenty-four-man cell.

"Say, celly, you need to wake up if you want to eat," an inmate said, tapping Tree's foot.

"My name is Tree, not celly," Tree replied angrily, opening his eyes. "Look, homeboy, I'm not trying to make no friends up in here. Thanks for waking me up, but I'm tired from that long ride back to this hellhole."

"My bad, Tree, I just thought you were hungry because you missed breakfast and lunch. You know what they say around here, 'Sleep late, lose weight.'"

"You can say that again," Tree replied, jumping to his feet and stretching. "I'm sorry for snapping at you, but I didn't know it was last chow."

"It's all good. I forgot about it already."

The tank is quiet as the twenty-four men eat their last meal of the day. Inmates who don't have commissary eat their dinner in record time while Tree stares at the slot of pinto beans and wishes he was back in TDCJ. *This is ridiculous,* he thought. *At least I could get halfway full in the joint.*

"Are you guys finished yet, because we gon' need those trays," the trustee on duty asked from the hallway.

Eating the last bite of his sugar-free Jell-O cup, Tree hands his tray to the trustee through the opening in which it was handed to him from. Everything on his tray was eaten, and yet his stomach still felt like a bottomless pit. Walking back to his bunk, he feels sorry for those who have burned their bridges with their loved ones as he bends over to get a pack of beef noodles.

"I'm sorry, but what's your name again?" Tree asks his cell mate.

"TO," the guy replied, sitting up and letting his feet hang over the side of his bunk.

"TO, huh? You know, that was messed up when you left the Cowboys to play for Buffalo," Tree said, laughing out loud.

"My name is Tym Owens, not Terrell Owens. And besides, if I had half the money he has, I wouldn't be up in Harris County eating beans to survive." Tym looks down at Tree to give him his full attention.

"What's up with these cats up in here? Are they cool or what?"

"Everybody pretty much does their time to themselves, but every now and then, a fight or two will stir up because of the TV. Other than that, this tank is laid-back."

TO caught Tree up on everything that's been happening in H-town since he left for TDCJ. From politics, crime, and sports, they talked until daylight from the only window in the cell began to fade, and the second set of lights were turned on. Their long conversation finally came to an end, so Tree takes a break and sits in his bunk. As he tries to find some comfort in sitting, his height causes him to bump his head, and therefore, he has to hunch over to sit upright. *Damn, that hurt,* he thought, rubbing the back of his head. After he is forced to meditate in an awkward position, his thoughts are interrupted when a correctional officer yells his name for visitation.

"Visitation? How can I be getting a visit without feeling out a visitation list?" he said out loud.

Tree is tired because he still hasn't entirely caught up on all his rest from the long ride from TDCJ, and games are something he is not trying to play with the correctional officer. "I'm sorry, but you have the wrong Torrence Wingate," he complains.

"Explain it to someone who cares. Do you want the visit or what?"

"I know it's a mistake, but I'll accept it," he replies, only wanting to get out of the tank to stretch his legs.

His face towel is on the edge of his bunk, so he quickly grabs it and goes into the wash area to wipe his face. *This is some BS,* he thought, staring into the aluminum mirror, brushing his teeth because he doesn't know what to expect from this so-called visit he is getting.

As he is adding everything up in his head, a smile graces his lips because maybe it's Audumn coming to surprise him and tell him how much she still loves him.

"I'm ready, boss!" Tree shouts to the officer in the picket.

Guards are throughout the halls directing traffic when the door opens for him to leave his pod. The thought of whether his visit is fact or fiction continues to thrive in his brain as he walks straight to the visitation holding cell. The line is short for visitation, but somehow he finds time to take one last look at himself in a window to a dark room. After brushing the lint from his shirt and pants, he wishes he had more time to get himself together.

"Torrence Wingate," he said, waiting to be sent back to his tank.

"Torrence Wingate, you have a chaplain visit," replied the woman officer.

"A chaplain visit?" he asks, oblivious to why a chaplain would be visiting him. "Sorry, ma'am, but I just got here yesterday. Is there any way to see if this is a mistake?"

"Trust me, it's not a mistake," she said, telling him the number of the booth his visitation will be held at.

Looking over the booths, Tree sees his number and quickly walks over to tell the chaplain God is the last thing he's trying to hear about today. As he approaches the booth, he notices it's his father, Pastor Torrence Wingate Sr., sitting on the opposite side of the glass. A split second goes by as they both stare at each other, wondering what to say or do next.

Tree takes a seat and pauses before taking the phone off the receiver. He tries to muster up some courage by clearing his throat, but as he stared into his father's eyes, he feels sad that his father has to see him that way. Both of their words are hidden as they sit, bewildered by each other's presence.

"Hi, Daddy," Tree said, breaking the ice.

"Hi, son," his dad replies after saying a short prayer that this visit goes well.

They both feel as if they're looking in a mirror because Tree is a spitting image of his father except for the life he leads. Suddenly, both of them try to speak at the same time, but out of respect for his dad, Tree closes his mouth and lets his father speak first.

"Son, I'm here for you, and the life you live is not how I raised you, but that's the past, and everyone deserves a second chance."

"Daddy, I'm—"

"Be quiet, son, and let me finish," his dad retorted before Tree can complete his sentence. "Torrence, I love you, and it hurts my heart every day knowing that you're in this place. You are too smart to be letting your life go down the drain selling God knows what to God knows who. That mess you sell is destroying you and the person you're selling it to. When does it stop because that rope you're hanging from is only going to get tighter each time you call yourself making a deal?"

"Dad, I'm sorry for what I put the family through. That's why I only write once a month to let you know I'm still living and breathing," Tree explains.

"I know, son, but I'm your father, and you don't have to feel ashamed to ask me for anything. When you were in the streets, it was hard for me to watch what you put all your knowledge into because you didn't know whether you were going or coming. That's why I wouldn't answer your phone calls or allow you to come to our house."

Tree sat and listened to every word his father spoke, and his words of wisdom sunk into his brain as he thought about living a life with no worries. His heart is the heart of David in the Bible, but his mind only allowed him to see dollar signs every day he opened his eyes to start a new day. Pastor Wingate assured him that everything is going to be okay as long as he kept his eyes on the cross.

The visit went according to the way his father had prayed the night before. Every day Pastor Wingate asked the Lord for a chance to talk to his son without the both of them blowing up and turning their backs to one another. Today his prayers were being answered, and all he could say is, "Thank you, Jesus."

Torrence Wingate Jr., on the other hand, finally heard his dad out, and he made sense to him. "I hear you, Dad, and thanks for not judging me," is all he can say as he tasted the salt from his tears brushing against his top lip.

"Wrap it up! Visitation will be over in five minutes!"

"Son, we have to cut this visit short for now, but your mom, sister, and I will be back next week to see you again. Before you go back to your tank, I would like to pray for you."

"Yes, sir." Tree closes his eyes and bows his head.

"Dear heavenly Father, we come to your throne of grace, mercy, and truth with bowed heads for my son, Torrence Wingate Jr. Before we petition you on his future, we ask that you forgive him for his past. Only you know what is up ahead for my son, so we pray that you keep him in your bosom on this journey he's on. Today, I stand in the gap for my son, asking that you keep his mind focused on what is real and not fictitious dreams. He has so much potential, Lord, and he needs to know this. Please give him the knowledge and understanding to see what we know he's capable of being for your kingdom. In Jesus's name we pray, amen."

They both stood wishing they could give each other hugs as they hung up the phone. His father places his hand to the glass and says, "I love you" as Tree reads his lips.

I love you too, he thought, hanging his head because of the constant pain he's put his family through.

"So how was your visit?" the lady officer asks, checking his name off her clipboard.

"It was all right, I guess," Tree answers, wondering why the officer is meddling in his business.

"I'm sorry for prying, but it's a pleasure to finally meet Pastor Wingate's son."

"Huh?" Tree said, not understanding the purpose of the conversation.

"My name is Mrs. Magee, and I go to your father's church, Let It Shine. Every Sunday for the past six months, your dad has asked the congregation to pray for you, and to be honest, it's an honor to see my pastor's prayers being answered today. God is good, Mr. Wingate. Trust him and listen to your father because he really loves you."

Officer Magee's words were sharper than a double-edge sword because he never knew how much his father had cared about him. All his life he pushed against his father's teachings, and most of all, he hated walking in his dad's shadow. Everyone always told him how great his father was while growing up and how he is going to be a powerful preacher just like him someday. Tree never once asked to walk in his father's shoes, but so many people he encountered prophesied miraculous things over his life, and Tree didn't want to fall short of the mark of expectation. Fear of what he felt he couldn't do made him decide to become Tree and not Pastor Torrence Wingate Jr.

As he walked back through the halls, inmates stared at him because his face showed frustration. His childhood played in his mind like a video on repeat, so all he could see is his mother teaching Bible study, his sister Gayriale in the choir, his dad preaching the word of God, and him ushering. He put God on the back burner a long time ago, and today, his presence was surely being felt because conviction is slapping him in the face every step he takes. *Leave me alone, Lord, I'm not ready!*

The door to his pod rolled open and slammed hard behind him when he stepped into the tank. Glancing toward his bunk, he notices the guy who slept in the rack next to him have company. Tree is not in the mood to be around anyone, so he takes a seat under the one TV that no one seems to come to an agreement on.

"What's up, Tree, you all right?" Tym asks, sitting on top of the table.

"I'm straight, TO. Just thinking about my old man."

"I know we not cool like that, but if you want to get something off your chest, holla at me. You know where I'm at." TO walks off, thinking about their earlier confrontation.

Tree shakes his thoughts by focusing on the television, but the intro to *Cops* comes blaring trough the speakers, and a third of the tank rushes over to get any open seats available in the sitting area. "Bad boys, bad boys! What you gonna do! What you gonna do when they come for you!" Listening to the introduction song irks his ears, and Tree tries to comprehend why so many people in jail want to watch someone else go to jail. "What has this world come to?" he said to himself, pounding his fist softly on the table before getting up.

Time flies by faster at night in jail for some reason. Lying in his bunk, Tree reads 9:40 on the clock over the picket and realizes he has only twenty minutes to take a shower. He knows that the guards don't play when it came to count time or rack time, so he quickly grabs his towel, soap, and shower shoes. From the time his eyes opened until now, his day hasn't gone accordingly, and he didn't need the guards adding anything extra to what is running through his mind.

The showers in the county only last for one minute on each push of the button that turns it on. One push and it's freezing cold, and another push, it may be scorching hot. Every now and then you may get sixty seconds of warm water, but tonight is not that night, so he has to play double Dutch with the low-pressure mist and wait for the right time to jump in.

Standing behind the trash bag shower curtain, Tree dries off, thinking about the visit with his father, and feels like Tony Montana again. *This is jail, not church. And I must be Mufasa, not Simba, if these fools in here are going to respect me,* he thought as he slid the trash bag to the side on the shoestrings that held it up.

Tym is sitting up in his bunk drinking coffee and cherry Kool-Aid mixed with crushed Jolly Ranchers. The smell of the cherry and coffee mixture travels down to Tree's bunk.

"Say, Tym, what's that you drinking on up there?" he asks.

"A pretty I whipped up before they had shut off the lights," TO answers while sipping the hot syrup.

"You must be trying to ride all night because you fixing to be wired up drinking all that caffeine and sugar."

"Here, Tree, taste this. Who knows, you might try to keep my cup." Tym passes the cup down below carefully.

Talking among themselves, the coffee and sugar starts to run through their veins as words begin to spew from their mouths between each passing of the cup.

"TO, I've been hustling now for nine years, and I don't have shit to show for it. I ain't gon' lie, I did shine when I was out there, but it wasn't worth it now that I'm in here," he said, feeling like an ass.

"I feel you on that, Tree."

"When I was out there, TO, I was Ike, and my girl Audumn was Tina, and together we were out there getting paper. When I first got hit, I had just dropped my girl off at her job Magic City when the laws rammed in my door and made me eat my carpet. I was in there cooking some dope one minute, and the next minute I was hog-tied from head to toe. I never experienced anything like that before, TO, and it was like my dreams of becoming Scarface went down the drain in the blink of an eye. This last time those laws ran down on me, I was high on that PCP and outran them for a good little minute. I almost got away, but my girl was in the car screaming in my ear to stop. On top of that, while I was in the county, I was served a secret indictment because my so-called homeboy, Blue, set me up with some undercover laws a couple of weeks before the incident. Shit, if it wasn't for Blue's fraud ass, I'd be in the penitentiary doing my time like a real gangsta instead of back in the county on a bench warrant."

"Damn, Tree," Tym replied, picturing Tree's short legacy.

"It's crazy because when I get out, I'm going to try one more time to be successful in the dope game. If I fail, I'm through, and I'm going to see what my dad's talking about," Tree said, lying on his cracked plastic pillow. "I'm out, TO. Holla at me in the morning."

Replaying the conversation, he thinks about how he didn't pick Audumn up from work on that dreadful night the police kicked in his door. The stories of Ike and Tina's strange love affair made him want to do better in his relationship with Audumn because Ike and Tina was a perfect couple when it came to making money and music, but their love life was another story. At the end of the day, everyone would agree that Ike loved Tina but expressed his love in the wrong way.

"I love you, baby, and I'm sorry," Tree said to himself, thinking about the song "What's Love Got to Do with It."

4

T he lights turned on at three thirty this Thursday morning, and soon after, names began to be called for 10:00 a.m. court. Tree knows he's on the list the officer has in his hands because he checked his court date on the computer every day since he got back to the county.

Falling to his knees, he says a short prayer for deliverance and says "Amen" as he stands to his feet, ready to face the music in Judge Gis's courtroom. Disregarding all the rumors about Judge Gis, Tree holds his head up high and says, "Let's do it. I'm ready." before walking to the lavatory to wash his face.

"Court out the door! Court out the door! All stragglers will have to go on Monday because Friday is a holiday!" an officer yells, standing in the entrance of the pod, logging offenders off his list as they walked by.

Today's courtroom docket is extremely larger than usual because of the holiday. All offenders on the third floor are groggy, and the elevator is taking forever because it picks up the offenders on the top floors first. After about twenty minutes, the doors finally open.

"Wake up and get the hell off my floors!" the officer shouts, shocked to see all the offenders sleeping.

With his foot in the door, the officer herds thirty orange uniforms into the elevator and presses B for basement. Their masculinity is soon tested as they touch one another from being pressed so close together. The bell rings, and a loud sigh bursts into the basement as a gust of air rushes inside, allowing everyone to take a deep breath.

"It's about time," an inmate said, stepping off the elevator first.

Two by two, they are paired and told to keep their mouths shut while they are walking through the underground passageway to the courtroom. A few of the inmates decide to ignore the officers' wishes and began to talk among themselves about their cases and what they're possibly facing. Half of them are lying and a quarter of them are telling truth, but the rest just want to hear themselves speak.

Tree ignores the conversations and prays silently, hoping he can get another five-year sentence to run concurrent with the one he already has.

Everyone suddenly stops at the yellow line beneath the courthouse. Tree isn't paying attention and bumps into the offender in front of him and says, "Excuse me." At a podium in front of the loud crowd, an officer begins to call off holding cells for specific courtrooms. Offenders who don't know Harris County system stand dumbfounded against the cemented walls, but the officers are not in the mood for babysitting, so they quickly pick out the rotten apples and tell them to get with the program.

The officer at the podium shouts, "Torrence Wingate, court room 146, holding cell 3!"

After hearing his name, Tree steps out of line and walks up the ramp to the podium. The officer seems impatient, so Tree extends his arm and shows his wristband before any unnecessary comments come out of his mouth. Everything checks out according to the court list, so he points him down the ramp toward holding cell 3. Tree shows no hesitation because he's ready for whatever the judge has in store for him.

Holding cell 3 is packed because inmates are standing in the door conversing with the other holding cells next to them. Tree divides the pack and squeezes through, looking for any space available on the iron benches along the walls. He sees there's no hope in finding a seat, so he turns and stands, waiting for his court number to be called.

"Tree!" a familiar voice yells from below. "Tree, down here. It's me, Lil C from Beaumont, Texas."

"Lil Chad, why in the hell are you lying on this disease-infected floor? Boy, you got to be crazy." Tree maneuvers around offenders trying to get to Lil C.

"Man, I'm tired, Tree. You already know we riding all night every night in C-4."

"I bet you ain't got a wink of sleep since we got here, huh, Lil C? Every day them youngsters be wilding out like there's no tomorrow up in there."

Chad nods his head yeah and changes the subject. "So what it do? You got a lawyer, or are you going to roll with a court-appointed?" asks Lil C.

"A court-appointed, so I'm prepared for the worst."

"Don't sweat that court-appointed talk because some of them court-appointed lawyers be getting down for you. It depends on your case and attitude, so be cool when they talk to you."

"I feel that, but this ain't my first time walking through these doors. I know how to handle myself."

Lil C and Tree find an open corner and reminisce on all they were missing in the penitentiary. The food, the weights, respect for your fellow man, and the small things you can get away with every now and then. At the end of their travels down memory lane, they both couldn't wait to see the judge so they can catch the chain back to TDCJ as soon as possible.

Before they knew it, an hour had passed, and it is going on 9:00 a.m.

A trustee steps inside the holding cell and pushes the overcrowded inmates back as far as possible. As the trustee begins to call courtroom numbers off his list, everyone stands, praying that they're first on today's docket because otherwise, they could be in the holding cell until 3:00 p.m.

Tree's last name is Wingate, so he remains seated when hearing the names are in order.

"Chad Perkins and Torrence Wingate!" the trustee shouts. "Fall to the back of the line! You guys are bench warrants, so you two will be first!"

An officer lines everyone up at the end of the hall and tells the offenders not to talk, or they would be sent back to their pods. Everyone zipped their mouths shut and walked quietly because they couldn't bear repeating the chaos from this morning again. Standing at the metal detector, three women officers pat the group down quickly and permit the offenders to proceed through. The maze of hallways leads to a round desk with a Texas star engraved in it, and behind the desk is a tall husky Caucasian woman who could probably start for the Chicago Bears. Tree and Lil C are told to come to the front of the line while the rest of the group is divided in half because half of them are going with Tree and Lil C.

After putting the guys who were left in a holding cell, the officer locks the door to the cell and walks Tree's group to the elevators around the corner. Her hands are full of papers, so she uses her elbow to push the button for Judge Gis's courtroom while she patiently waits to hand the offenders over to the officer who is working the elevator for the day.

"I'll take it from here, Sgt. McDonald," the officer on the elevator said as he is handed a folder of papers with the offenders' names on it. "So who's ready to stand before the iron fist!" the officer exclaims jokingly as he pounds his fist into his hand.

The inmates remain silent staring at their reflection on the elevator doors because Judge Gis has their future in his hands, and no one seems to think anything's funny.

"Trust me, it's not that bad, and besides, the judge is in a good mood because he has a three-day weekend after today."

Stepping off the elevator, the inmates follow the officer to a holding cell behind the walls in which the judge sits. Most of them know the procedures, so the officer cuts his speech on do's and don'ts in the courtroom down to a few sentences.

"Yes, sir!" comes from all the inmates at once before the officer locks the door behind him.

"Is there a Mr. Torrence Wingate in here?" a Caucasian guy in an expensive blue suit asks through the opening of the attorney visitation glass.

"Tree, I think that lawyer's calling your name." Lil C. nudges Tree on the shoulder.

Tree gets up praying for the best. *I hope this court-appointed lawyer is talking my language because if not, he's fired.*

"Good morning to you, Mr. Wingate, and my name is Attorney Kent Johns. The reason why I'm here is because your father asked me to do him a favor and see that justice is served on your behalf today. Last night I looked over your files and noticed that that you have an extensive drug history from the time you were a juvenile up until now. All morning I've been speaking with the DA, and we came to an agreement of four years running concurrent with the five years you are already doing. I feel that this is a blessing, I mean a great offer considering your track record, Torrence. And if you refuse, I don't know how she would react when you come before her again after turning down her generosity."

"I'll take it," Tree replied quickly before his lawyer can say anything else.

Mr. Johns is overwhelmed that Tree has accepted the only offer because the DA recognized his name on the docket from the five years he received nine months back and told Mr. Johns to take it or leave it. She wanted to start at seven but changed her mind when his lawyer assured her that Tree made bad choices in life, and he's learned from his mistakes.

The officer who escorted the inmates into the holding cell unlocks the door and comes in with chains for their wrist and ankles. After shackling the inmates, he then adds a separate chain that combines the handcuffs to the ankle cuffs. These tactics has always been around but never enforced until last year when an inmate threw a chair at a judge. Since then, all measures of safety have been at bay for the sake of order in the courtroom, but the downside of these measures falls on the inmates because it makes them look like monsters before the judges and the jury.

Tree steps inside the courtroom a happy man because he knows he is getting one more chance at being the king of the streets. As he looks around, he notices his sister Gayriale and his mother Lovey sitting on the front row behind the banister. Tree smiles but soon turns away when he sees the anguish on his mother's face. His dad felt that he did all what he could have done to help his son, so he made it his purpose not to see him stand before a judge.

Lil Chad is the first to be called before Judge Gis because he copped out for three years running concurrent with the two years he already has. The judge and court-appointed lawyer went over his new sentencing, so he signed his John Hancock on the line with the X and whispers to Tree that he'll be out in a year on good behavior.

"The court calls Torrence Wingate Jr. to the stand," the DA said, handing the bailiff his record and a documents stating the four-year agreement.

After handing the document to the judge, the bailiff tells Torrence to step to the podium in front of him, so Tree takes one step forward and plants himself like a tree. Motionless, he stands listening to his past while thanking God for Mr. Johns intervening and not getting the maximum sentence of ten years. "Yes, Your Honor" and "No, Your Honor" is all he can say until he is asked if he agrees to the sentence they've came to an agreement on.

"Are you Torrence Wingate Jr.?" Judge Gis looks down over the top of his reading glasses when speaking.

"Yes, sir."

"Are you in your right mind today?"

"Yes, sir, I'm fully in my right mind."

"Were you pressured in any kind of way to sign the terms that you, your lawyer, and the district attorney have agreed upon?"

"No, sir, I wasn't pressured in any kind of way."

"Do you agree with these terms?"

"Yes, sir, I agree with these terms," Tree answers while smiling in the inside.

"After examining the offender, the court agrees that Torrence Wingate Jr. is sane and competent to the terms he has signed for and sentences him to four years running c.c. with the five years he is currently doing in TDCJ." Judge Gis slams his gavel to finalize his judgment.

Tree signs the agreement, and the pressure of his future is released off his chest. "Thank you, Judge Gis!" he blurts outs while shaking his attorney's hand.

Mr. Johns tells him to stay out of trouble because his next drug offense will label him a habitual criminal. His excitement ceases when thinking about his possibilities if he had to stand before the judge or this DA again.

Taking small steps, Tree stops before leaving and slightly waves at his mother while saying, "I love you" as silently as possible. His sister and his mother are sad to see him go but are overjoyed in knowing that his feet will someday touch ground again.

Court is now adjourned, so his family watches the back of his orange jumpsuit until he disappears into the hallway to the holding cell. *Please, Lord, let your angels watch over my son,* his mother prays as she exits the courtroom holding her daughter's hand.

At the entry of the holding cell, Tree's mind is in shambles because he knows that it was only God who delivered him from the green mile. Ashamed of his actions, he promises to do better and try to walk straight from this day on.

Lil C doesn't know what to expect when Tree takes a seat next to him. His face is blank, his head is low, and his lips are pointing downward instead of upward.

"Tree, what's up, why the sad faces? Did the judge hang you out to dry, or are you just messing with me?"

Tree lies down on the steel bench and puts his arm across his forehead. "I'm good, Lil C, I got four years ran c.c. with my five," Tree replied, sounding as if he got the chair.

Court is over for their group, and at noon count cleared, so everyone who has seen the judge or got a setoff is allowed to go back to their pods.

"Stand up, it's time to get you guys back before they call a recount, and you'll be in here till God knows when!" the officer bellows into all the holding cells of the offenders who are done.

Lil C taps Tree on the leg and says, "Let's roll, I'm hungry and dying for a pack of chili noodles." As he is helping Tree to his feet, he hands him a ply of toilet paper with his name, address, and phone number written on it. "Look me up when you touch ground because you're real, Tree, and I need someone real in H-town to score from if I decide to play in these streets again."

The two of them talked all the way back to the elevators in the basement. Mostly their conversation was about doing things different when they get to see daylight again, and they both agreed to get a job to cover up their hustling next time around. Chad's company is cool because Tree loved to talk about the dope game, and that's all Lil C wanted to talk about. Every drug Lil Chad asked the prices on, Tree answered each question by adding his taxes to each product. In the elevator, Chad finishes his jailhouse interview with Tree, and Tree tells him he'll give him a call if something comes up. Before the doors open, he reminds Chad to look up Audumn when he gets out and tell her that he still loves her.

"I gotcha, big homey. Just look out for me when you fly this coop, all right?" was Lil Chad's reply as the doors closed on the tiled floor of C3.

Back in his bunk, Tree lies down eating a cold leftover tray. The burrito is hard as a rock, but he chews it as if it's fresh from Taco Bell because beans have been the main course for the past week. After finishing off his Mexican entrée, he thinks about his mother and smiles because she's never washed her hands on him despite all the negative things he's done in life.

"Torrence Wingate, come to picket. You got mail!" a guy's voice over the loudspeaker yells.

Mail! Who in the world could be writing me? It must be some late mail from my mom telling me she will be here today when I go to court.

Tree takes his time walking to the picket because he's been up since 3:30 a.m., and it's starting to take a toll on him. Dragging his feet, he stops at the door, and the officer opens it with the push of a button. "What's up, boss, you got some mail for me?" he asks, speaking into the speaker on the picket. The letter is given to him through the mail depository, but his heart stops and his hand shakes when he reads Audumn's name as the sender.

Walking back to his bunk, he flips the letter over to open it but can't because of fear of what she might say. As he takes a seat, his butt sinks into the cushionless mattress, and he smells a sweet fragrance rising from the envelope. *Not right now, Audumn. My day is going too good to let you spoil it,* he thought, lying on his side, anxious to read what the love of his life has written him.

5

I'm too young for this. I should wait. Tree's palms are sweaty, and the top button on his collared shirt feels as if it's choking him. Today is a day he's been waiting for all his life, and yet he's all alone in a back room. His stomach feels like a pot of boiling hot water as he paces back and forth, wiping the beads of sweat from his forehead with his sleeve. *What were you thinking, Tree?* he asks himself while looking in the mirror.

"Tree, unlock the door!" Man Pooh shouts while twisting the doorknob, hoping that it will miraculously pop open. "Everyone's waiting for you! We should have been in the church fifteen minutes ago!"

"I'm sorry, Pooh, I'm calling it off. I can't go through with this."

"Oh, yes, you are! Especially since I paid $140 for this suit! Now open this damn door before I break it down!"

Unlocking the door, Tree takes a seat in a folding chair and hunches over to rest his head in his lap. Man Pooh steps inside with Tree's cufflinks and closes the door behind him. "Tree, it's time. Your dad needs you in the sanctuary so we can get this show on the road. Audumn loves you, and we all know you love Audumn. All this you're doing is nonsense because you're afraid of letting Tree go."

Finally, Pooh's pep talk has gotten through to his head, and he realizes that this is the best day of his life. He knows he's running late, so he asks his friend to help him with his tie while he puts on his cufflinks.

"Finished," Man Pooh said while brushing Tree's shoulders off.

"Thanks, Pooh. I don't know what I'll do without you."

Tree steps in the hallway and sees his boys Lil C, Phat Fat, Jiro, and TO praying that they didn't waste their money on the tuxedos they were wearing.

"Are you done whining? Because if not, I'm going to the liquor store to get me something to sip on," Lil Chad said with a look of exhaustion.

The church is full to its capacity when the six of them came from the back. Tree can feel anger and impatience from all directions as he takes his position next to the communion table with his friends. His mother is proud of her son when she sees him standing handsomely in his orange vest in front of his father. A small clap travels from pew to pew when Man Pooh falls in shortly behind him. Pastor Wingate Sr. steps to the microphone, and the audience becomes silent when the pianist begins the song of all songs that is played at this specific event.

Everyone's heads turn and focus on the glass double doors to the rear of the church because two ushers have entered and are holding each door open for the guest of honor.

Audumn's bridesmaids wait for the signal from the director and start to walk down the aisle on their precise note. Tree's groomsmen meet them when they reach the specific mark they had set on the floor and escort them to the opposite side of the altar. His youngest niece follows them in a replica dress of Audumn's, holding a light-brown square pillow. Two gold bands shine brightly in her hands as she smiles as if it's her day to get married.

Everything is perfect and not a beat is missed as everyone involved has performed their part according to practice the night before. Suddenly, darkness falls over the pews, and the aisle is lit from the pastor to the back of the church. Patiently, the guests wait as ten minutes go by on their wristwatches, and words begin to be murmured through the stillness of the building seeing that the bride hasn't made her entrance. The ushers begin a search throughout the sanctuary only to find an envelope taped to a colorful bouquet in the room Audumn put her dress on.

The bouquet of flowers is brought to Tree in front of everyone present. Looks of disbelief are on the audience's faces as he unfolds the letter and reads, "I'm sorry, Tree, but I can't marry you" before the small note slips from his fingertips.

XXXXX

"Torrence Wingate! Wake your ass up! You deaf or something? I've been calling your name for over twenty minutes. Pack all your crap. You're being transferred to C2/6-1."

"What for? I haven't gotten in any trouble," Tree replied, waking up in a pool of sweat.

"Damn it, boy, I don't make the rules around here. Pack your shit, and I'll find out for you by the time you come get your transfer slip."

Tree got up, thanking God for taking him out of that humiliating nightmare. He knows that it was only a dream, but his heart feels like Cupid ripped his arrow from the center of his chest. It's been eight days since he read Audumn's letter, and since then, he's never left his bunk out of fear of getting into trouble. The letter stated that she's been thinking about his welfare and that she is coming to visit him this weekend with his sister, Gayriale. It was only a few sentences, but Tree has read it over and over every hour on the hour.

Throwing all his belongings in his sheets, Tree grabs all four corners and ties them in the biggest knot you've ever seen. TO is still asleep when he tosses his knapsack over his right shoulder to leave. The two of them have become cool over the past week, so he decides to tell him good-bye. "I'm being transferred, lil homey, to C2. You know where I'm at when you get from behind these walls. It's Northborough 4 Life!" Tree bumps TO's fist and puts up the *H*, which is the hand symbol for Houston, across his chest.

"What's up, boss? What hotel do I check into next, and will this transfer affect my visit this weekend?"

"You're being transferred to the kitchen."

"Kitchen? How in the hell I'm being transferred to the kitchen, and I'm on a bench warrant? I'm sorry, boss, but I ain't working in no hot-ass kitchen!"

"Are you refusing? Because Harris County can make your stay here very unpleasant."

Tree thought about the one-man cell without a window and snatched the transfer slip because his time in the county was already hard without any activities, and being in solitary confinement would only make it worse.

"Snatch something from my hands again, and you're going to wish you were in the hole after I'm finished stomping my foot in your ass!"

I can't believe they got me working in the kitchen. I barely want to cook for myself, and now I have to cook for these fools, he thought as the elevator doors open for him to get off on level 2.

The walk to the main picket is only a few steps, so Tree puts his mouth to the speaker hole and angrily tells the correctional officer he's a new transfer from C4. The woman officer disregards his attitude and takes the transfer slip and puts it in her log-in box. "Your new housing arrangement is down the hall and to the left."

"But I didn't sign up for a job."

"We know you are a bench warrant, but your record shows no violence in your Harris County jail history. Please bear with us until we can find you a replacement, and if you refuse, it could follow you back to TDCJ and look bad when you see parole."

"Yes, ma'am, I guess, but please get me off this job as soon as possible. I didn't work in the free world, and I'm damn show not trying to work up in here."

"I'll see what I can do, but in the meantime, you will be staying down the hall and to the left. Good day, Mr. Wingate," she said, handing him a slip with his job schedule on it.

The county always trying to get a brother to do some cheap labor. What's next, shoe shining at the courthouse? Tree thinks with a small chuckle.

Entering into his new house, he quickly gives the tank an unfriendly stare. Some inmates look and a few glance before returning to their daily routines because it's very seldom that anyone tests his "I am not the one" face. Tree's mind becomes curious upon seeing the lights are off at 1:00 p.m., and everyone in their bunks is still under the covers. Bunk 1 is his new housing arrangement, so he scans the room, trying to find the empty bunk, and then realizes that the bunk he is looking for is right next to him.

After getting situated, he takes off his shoes and socks because his feet are hurting from carrying everything he owns. Lying down, he tries to catch up on the rest he was cut short on from this morning, but his slumber is quickly interrupted when a male officer steps in and shouts for kitchen quad 3 to be ready to roll out in ten minutes. Tree is not trying to hear that, so he covers his head with his sheets to finish what he started.

Peace is throughout pod 6 when kitchen quad 2 comes in like the million-man march and changes the atmosphere. Everyone on quad 3 is still underneath their sheets, so they get up to brush their teeth for work while quad 2 hollers back and forth to one another for dibs on the showers. The inmates watching television act like they don't hear how the noise level went from a 3 to an 8 on the Richter scale because this is an everyday routine for the working tanks.

"Damn, a brother can't get no rest around here," Tree mumbles, trying not to open his eyes. "I went from being in the library to the Super Bowl in a matter of minutes."

"Tree, is that you over there lying down like a whale sunbathing?"

Whoever this is, I pray he knows Jesus because today is not the day, Tree thinks, pulling the sheet from over his face.

"Tree, wake up. You act like you can't holla at your boy or something," Jiro said, standing in front of his bunk. "Hold up, something's wrong with this picture, and why are you working in the kitchen? I know you ain't tripping when it comes to making commissary."

"Jiro, you are either stupid, crazy, or just a plum lunatic for disturbing my sleep. You lucky you're my homeboy from day one because I was about to let this Tree fall on your ass. You feel me?"

"Yeah, I feel you. Sorry about that, Northborough." Jiro laughs and pounds Tree's fist.

"Naw'll, you good, Jiro. You know I was just messing with you."

Sitting up, Tree gains his composure and tells Jiro about his dreadful day because up until today, he has skated by in the system with a lame excuse on not to go to work. In the penitentiary, he told the nurses he had lower-back problems and gets migraine headaches when being in the sun for long periods of time. This morning, his mind wasn't at work when the officer woke him up because he thought it was a computer error due to the fact he is on bench warrant. Now he me must pay the price and play the hand dealt to him the best way he can.

"Kitchen quad 3 to the door! Anyone not ready will be given a disciplinary!"

Jiro is leaving Tree's bunk when something tells him to ask Tree what quad he is on. Tree shrugs his shoulders, but Jiro knows that the kitchen doesn't play when turning out for work, so he tells Tree to ask the officer if his name is on the list. Tree replies by saying he doesn't care.

"Say, Tree, you really need to ask if you have to turn out because if you don't, you're going to be written up. The county doesn't care if you just got in here today, so if I was you, I'll do what I have to do to make sure I don't lose my commissary or visits."

Tree walks to the officer knowing he's in a no-win situation because he has to abide by the rules if he wants his weekend to go according to plan. The officer is checking inmates off his list as they exit out the door, so Tree stands on the side of him, waiting for the last three people to call off their names. He looks over the officer's shoulder as the line come to an end and sees his name handwritten at the bottom of the computerized sheet. *Damn!*

"Why are you over me, inmate?"

"Sorry, boss man, I was just trying to see if I was on your list."

"Well, I think you need to ask instead of hovering over me like some bees on honey."

"Yes, sir."

"What's your name, inmate?"

"Torrence Wingate."

Guiding his finger through the names, the officer comes to his name and replies, "Suit up! I'll give you five minutes to be at the door, or I'm giving you a case for failure to turn out for work."

"But I just got in here twenty minutes ago."

"Explain it to the lieutenant," the officer said, leaving to pat the other kitchen workers down.

Tree is pissed, but he still goes to his bunk to make sure everything's in order. After making his bunk up, he stuffs everything that's left out in his locker. "This is some bullshit for real, for real," he said, slamming the door and putting an old toothbrush in the hole where the lock is supposed to go.

Falling in line, he looks down on the officer as he checks his name off his list. "Smart decision, Mr. Big Guy."

Tree looks away because he wants to punch him in the face.

"That's right, inmate, respect my authority. Everybody roll out because we have a lot of work to do, and we're behind schedule! You can thank Mr. Wingate for that when you get back to the tank."

Working in the kitchen is the first time he worked since high school. His first and last job his dad got him was in a supermarket bagging groceries. It's sad to say, but the job only lasted a few months because he was caught on camera taking a pack of gum out of the candy section. With his last check of honest income, he scored his first fifty-dollar bag of crack with his child-hood friend, Blue. As soon as they divided the package up, a smoker asked him for forty dollars' worth, and Tree saw how easy it was to make money, so he never thought about working honestly again.

Everyone in quad 3 knows what to do but Tree, so he follows the other guides and puts on a plastic apron and a one-size-fits-all mesh cap. *What in the hell am I doing? I got to find a way out of this masquerade,* he thinks, feeling ridiculous.

"Torrence Wingate, you have a visit!" the kitchen leader shouts.

"Now that's what I'm talking about." Tree quickly rips the apron off and snatches the mesh cap off his head before running out the door to visitation.

He is all smiles as he sat down in the booth to see Audumn and his sister Gay. Gayriale has a smile on her face too because before Tree's court date, she hasn't seen or heard from her brother in almost two months. Audumn is happy as well but doesn't show it because the pain of all he's put her through is still in her heart, but the love in her mind makes her wait patiently for him to pick up the visitation phone to speak.

"What's up, sis, and thanks for coming."

"I'm only doing my sisterly duties because the Bible says that we are our brother's keepers."

"Hey, baby, you look just as beautiful as the day I met you," Tree said, staring at Audumn's milky skin and curly brown hair she got from her mother being white and her dad black.

"Please don't call me baby, Tree. You know where we stand in this relationship, and I'm only here to show my support." Audumn looks away.

Gayriale eases the tension with a joke. "How's life been treating you?"

Tree laughs and tells her that God doesn't like ugly.

"Whoever said that, big brother, would have changed that statement if they would have met me before they said it." Gay is feeling herself and smiles at her chocolate reflection in the thick glass.

Their visit is good, but the sixty minutes given to them went by in a blink of an eye. Gayriale never left the two of them alone because Audumn asked her to stay the entire visit before they walked in. Tree apologized and asked for forgiveness three times, and each time, Audumn replied that she isn't here to talk about the past. After hearing that, Tree felt like he still had a chance at regaining his love's heart because he knew Audumn loved him, and with hard work, he would someday have her back in his arms again.

"I know you don't want me to call you baby, but, baby, I love you, and I promise that I'm a changed man. All I ask is that you let me be your friend because this five years I'm doing will be over soon, and I'm going to need your help to get me through this. You may not believe me, but your letters and visits will give me something to hold on to while I'm in here."

"Tree, the life I live now is not the life I used to live when I was with you. You really slapped me in the face when I found out you were cheating on me with my classmate Chikora from the county jail. I forgave you because that's what my Bible teaches me to do, but forgetting is something that can only be cured over time."

"Baby, I'm sorry."

"I know you are, Tree, because you've said it four or five times already. All I can say is that we'll see what happens," Audumn replied, thinking about her long-distance relationship with her old friend Secorion.

Audumn and Tree hang up the phone gazing into each other's eyes, wishing they could hold each other one last time. The lady officer over visitation tells him to hurry up before his visitation privileges are taken away from him, so Tree kisses his hand and places his palm to the window when hearing the outcome for going over his time limit.

Audumn puts her hand on the opposite side of the glass and says, "Be careful in there." Tree doesn't know what she said, but his spirit feels it wasn't anything bad.

Distance is in the eyes of Audumn, and he can feel that she's moved on but savors the moment, disregarding what he knows has happened in her life. After winking at his sister, he leaves, telling himself, *I'm through with the dope game forever because I finally see that I love Audumn too much to lose her again.*

6

"**P**eas on line 1!" The serving pan clings at the sound of the big spoon scraping the bottom. A week has passed, and all Tree can think about is how selfish he was during his visit with Audumn. Audumn's mom has cancer, and he didn't show any concerns for her mother's health, not once. His first chance to make a good impression, and he blew it by talking about himself again…as usual.

"Peas on line 1!" Tree yells again to the guy working backup. Ever since Audumn came to see him last week, his mind frame of thinking has changed. His attitude has changed as well because everything that used to get under his skin doesn't faze him as much anymore. No matter what circumstances may come his way, Tree has decided to do the opposite of what he used to do until he's back in her arms where he belongs.

One is accepting his job in the kitchen so that he can get an idea on how to work with others. Being a kitchen worker is also teaching him how to bite his tongue when it comes to authority and the people around him. His apron is tied tight today, and his mesh cap is tied in a knot to the back of his head. It's probably the reason why his brain feels as if it's in a vise grip. His uniform isn't much, but Tree wears it proudly.

"Wingate!" the male supervising officer shouts. "What was the count on that pan of peas?"

"Ninety-six, Officer Durant, sir!"

"Ninety-six is not going to cut it," he retorted angrily. "I know you're a new boot, but we need 112 scoops out of each pan if we're going to feed your buddies today. I want level scoops from now on, you hear me! That goes for all of you!" The officer adds a pitcher of water to the fresh pan of peas that was placed inside the steam table.

Be quiet, Tree, and finish working, Tree thinks as he levels off his spoon on the inside of the pan's wall.

41

The county had more inmates than usual this week, so the plastic tray carts were empty a little after an hour. Styrofoam trays are what completed the job when they ran out of plastic trays, and except for the outburst, the day went smoothly, and the two hours of hard labor were due for a break.

"Line up. It's chow time!" Officer Durant yells after today's task is finally complete.

Kitchen duty doesn't pay well in the county unless you're in the penitentiary. So in order to get the portion you deserve downtown in Houston, you had to be a cook, kiss ass, or steal it. If you're neither one, you only get two servings while the rest is thrown in the trash in front of you. Tree isn't a cook or a kiss ass, so if he wanted to get his wages due to him, he had to take it back to the streets. Up until this moment, he's been doing well by only taking Little Debbie snack cakes every now and then, but turkey is the main course today, so it's time for a little payback.

"Cougar James, you ready?"

"You already know, Tree, I'm down for whatever, especially since it's turkey day. Is you ready is the question you should be asking yourself?"

"Last time I look, the game didn't stop cuz I went to jail, Coo Woo."

"Now that's what I'm talking about, Northborough."

Cougar James is Tree's new kitchen buddy, and lately he's been showing Tree the ropes on their new job. He's been in the county for eleven months appealing a twenty-year sentence, and his family doesn't have anything to do with him because he's in for killing a seventeen-year-old girl. He was identified by his South West tattoo on his neck, but he swears he's innocent and that his entire neighborhood has similar tattoos. Since his family disowned him, he prefers to go by Coo Woo. It means wanderer, so he says.

"Tree, somebody's snitching up in this kitchen because lately, Officer Durant has been eyeballing me like crazy."

"Say no more. I got you, Coo Woo. Just look out for your boy while I show you how it's done."

"Cool," Cougar James said, walking to the front of the line to cause a distraction.

Cougar James cut the line knowing Officer Durant and Officer Thibodeaux would stop serving the inmates to jump down his throat. The other kitchen workers keep their mouths shut, hoping they can nab something during the commotion.

Standing in front of the line, Cougar James complains that he should eat first because he stacked the trays, and the weight of them has made him hungry. Officer Durant threatens him by saying, "Fall to the back of the line, James, or I will nail your ass with a case that will kick you out of the kitchen for good!"

With no one in sight looking, Tree makes his move and takes two handfuls of turkey meat from the heating oven.

"Officer Durant, could you come to my office please?" the sergeant asks over the loudspeaker, opening the blinds.

"Give everybody one serving till I get back, Mrs. Thibodeaux."

Officer Durant steps inside the sergeant's office and closes the door. Their words were short because they both came out in less than a minute, pointing in Tree's direction. Officer Durant nods his head to confirm the right suspect and walks over toward Tree, shaking his head with an "I told you so smile," on his face.

Tree and Cougar James are sitting in the dining area destroying all the evidence, and nothing is left but a wishbone when Officer Durant and Mrs. Thibodeaux come over to search him.

"I hope you two are full because, Wingate, you're being written up for stealing out of the kitchen."

Cougar James and Tree picked up the wishbone and pull it apart. Tree gets the bigger half and replies, "Today must be my lucky day, Coo Woo, because I could've sworn you needed evidence to make a theft case on someone."

"Stand up and face the wall, Wingate! You know what comes next."

Tree stands and assumes the position to be searched. Mrs. Thibodeaux pats him down while Officer Durant yells in his ear all the negative things he is thinking about him. White teeth and one dimple is the only answer Tree gives off as nothing is found on his person.

"What's next, a strip search?" Tree jokes to Officer Durant.

"What's next is that Sgt. Hadnot saw you take the meat out of the oven, so evidence doesn't matter. Get out my face, Wingate, you disgust me. By the way, Sgt. Hadnot wants you in his office."

Sgt. Hadnot is standing behind the blinds watching Tree's body language as he spoke to the officers, trying to con his way out of a theft case. *He has another thing coming if he thinks he can con me,* he thinks, waiting for Tree to step inside with his lies.

"Close the door behind you, Mr. Wingate."

Tree steps inside with a smirk on his face and closes the door with a slight force, causing the blinds to swing from left to right.

"Step outside my office and try that again with a little more respect next time."

Tree steps outside the door and reenters with a change of attitude when realizing he's speaking to someone who has the rank to strip him of all his privileges.

"So what makes you so special than the others that you can take or eat what you want to when you want to in the kitchen?" Sgt. Hadnot calmly asks with authority.

"I don't know what you're talking about," Tree replied, putting his hands up.

"Stop right there and listen because it's two things I hate and one thing I can't stand. One is a thief and two is a liar. Now that's what I hate, Mr. Wingate, but what I can't stand is someone who disrespects me by not showing me some respect, and you, Mr. Torrence Wingate Jr., number 1052181, just committed all three."

Standing with his hands loosely to his side, Tree says, "I don't know what you're talking about, Sgt. Hadnot" with a dumb look on his face.

"Put your damn hands behind your back before I get one of my officers to do it for you!"

Tree puts his hands behind his back when seeing how rapid the conversation went from him being on the offensive to the defensive. Sgt. Hadnot didn't allow him to say anything but "Yes, sir" throughout the ten-minute disciplinary meeting, and Tree is asked to sign a disciplinary action for theft and lying to an officer. The case made him think about how much he had tried to be a square during his first week in the kitchen, but feeling foolish, he accepts his faults like a man and signs his name on the carbon paper.

"I apologize, Sgt. Hadnot, for my simpleminded behavior," he looks back and says as he exits the sergeant's office.

"What's up, Tree, what happen?" Cougar James asks, waiting on some crates of dry cereal.

"Sgt. Hadnot caught me red-handed, Coo Woo."

"Did he let you make it because he let me slide a couple of times?"

"Hell na'll, he didn't let me make it! He hit me with a theft and lying to an officer case." Tree hands Cougar James the yellow copy of the offense.

"I didn't know he was even here today because today is his off day. If I'd did, I would've told you to chill, Northborough. That's my bad, Tree. I should've known these laws were going to be policing this turkey with an eagle's eye."

"I ain't tripping because I did that, and I can't change nothing now. I'm just mad that I'm going to lose my privileges behind a piece of meat," Tree replied, throwing his apron and cap in the trash. "If they put me back in population before gym rec tomorrow, holla at me in the free world, Coo Woo."

"Real talk, Tree, I got a cousin that live on the north side of Houston. I'll look you up when I go visit her."

The elevator ride up to the second floor is quiet and lonely because for the past week, his kitchen buddies would pile inside trying to get back to the tank quickly so that they can take a shower first. Laughter would echo off the elevator walls from all the jokes they would continuously crack on one another about how they performed at work during the day. Disappointed in himself, he wishes he could do everything over again because it's his first chance at trying to change, and he failed over something stupid and menial.

Everyone is looking out the corner of their eyes when he pushes the button to take a shower. Tree can sense that the tank is wondering why he is back so early, so he closes his eyes and tries to wash off his delinquent behavior. After four minutes of letting the water run over his head, he realizes that soap cannot cleanse away what he's constantly going through in life because the only solution that can wash away failure is change.

A puddle of water has started to form due to the poor drainage system, so Tree has to brace himself against the wall before stepping out the shower. He tries to tiptoe in his shower shoes, but he slips and curses out loud because lately, nothing seems to be going his way, not even a simple shower.

As he sat on his bunk to dry those hidden places, his shortcomings began to pop into his mind one by one. Erasing them with the days in which was good, Tree realizes those were the days he prayed and God answered.

"Lord, what's wrong with me? All this week I tried to be like a normal person, and yet I still allowed mischievous things to clutter my thinking.

Is this where I'm supposed to be for the rest of my life?" he asks, looking toward each corner of the pod. "Walking straight is hard when you're a gangsta. I don't know if I can change, and I don't know if I want to change. Tree is me, and I'm finally accepting that. If I'm wrong, Lord, say something or do something. Hell, do anything. I don't care what it is. Amen."

The dayroom lights are the only lights on when he opens his eyes from the nap he didn't see coming. *What time is it?* he thinks, looking for a window to see if it's dark or not outside. Tree closes his eyes and tries to go back to sleep but can't, so he sits up and watches TV. Jiro is at his bunk reading the Bible when he looks up and sees his friend wide-awake because earlier today, he had to go to court, and he's been anxious to tell his high school buddy the blessed news.

"Hey, Tree, I'm sorry for bothering you, but I would appreciate it if you would join me in the prayer circle tonight."

Tree disagrees for a second, but Jiro said God told him to wait for Tree to wake up before he called it.

"Prayer call! Prayer call!" Jiro shouts. "Prayer call! If anyone wants to pray, we'll be in the back left corner in five minutes!"

Tugging on Tree's pants leg, Jiro asks him to get up and come pray with him again. Tree's curiosity leads to him saying yes because Jiro is facing a life sentence and is glowing as if the sun is shining in his face. Something definitely happened in his life today, and Tree can tell he wants to share it with the whole world.

"How's everyone doing tonight?" Jiro asks the small congregation, grinning from ear to ear. "My name is Jiro, for those who don't know me, and this morning, somehow my name got on today's docket, and I was called out to court. The crime I committed was a crime of stupidity, and I regret the day I forced myself into that family's house to rob them. Everyone in this tank knows that I've been offered a life sentence without the possibility of parole, but God said something different today inside that courthouse. I used to be a college student and a hardworking man until I decided to fall in love with a beautiful woman who would later become my downfall. This woman I speak about desired the finer things in life and knew the right things to say to me to make me get them for her. I was charged with kidnapping, robbery, and murder."

The crowd stood listening in amazement to Jiro's miraculous courtroom experience in today's judicial system. His murder charge was dropped on behalf of the old lady's age because her medical history showed severe heart trauma from previous heart attacks. The autopsy revealed she died of natural causes and not from anything he could have possibly done.

"God is good and listened to my prayers." Jiro picks up his Bible. "Standing before the judge, I listened as he dropped my sentence from life without the possibility of parole to sixteen years in the state penitentiary." Pausing, he turns his Bible to 2 Corinthians 11:14 and 15. "Tonight I would like to read a scripture that caught my eye earlier when I was doing my Bible study. It reads, 'Satan himself masquerades as an angel of light. It is not surprising, then, if his servants masquerade as servants of righteousness.' What this means, fellas, is that Satan can make himself very pleasing to the eye to get you to do wrong things. He can use a car or a house. He can use money or your own family. In my case, he used a woman. Whatever it may be, he uses it to his own advantage because he knows what makes you tick. Sixteen years is a long time, but I deserve every day I do on it because it's time for us to change, guys. The Bible says that the devil comes in many ways and that he can disguise himself as an angel of light. If Satan can do all these things, people, how then will we know when it's God and not him? You can't! At least not on your own. That's why we need to pray and ask God for guidance daily so that we can recognize the wicked one when he comes with his evil schemes to get us to do wrong."

Jiro points his Bible at Tree. "Like I said before, God is good, and thank you for coming out tonight. Please bow your heads so I can pray."

Jiro prayed his heart out for the first time in front of his cellmates, and his words were truth and flowed into everyone present. When their eyes opened, the mixed crowd was hand in hand, saying, "Amen." Some of the men hugged one another, and a few guys asked Jiro to pray for them one-on-one.

Tree on the other hand felt the presence of the Holy Spirit and walked off cleansed white as snow because he asked the Lord to forgive him for all of his sins.

"Wingate, you're on the chain tonight back to TDCJ! Meet me in the dayroom in twenty minutes!" the officer shouts after seeing the prayer circle dismissed.

7

Vacation time is up. Three months have passed since Tree left the county, and the daycare transfer facility he was sent back to has finally shipped him off to his assigned unit. As he looks over the rows of fields that he would soon be tending, he thinks about his boys, Phat Fat and Man Pooh, he had just left. Pooh left about a week earlier to another unit while Phat Fat was classified on the transfer facility.

I wish this guy would scoot over or something, Tree thinks as he squirms for some air next to the 5'9", 220 lb. Caucasian.

The ride to the Wells Unit is only an hour, and Tree is feeling every minute of it. His left wrist has a ring around it from the handcuffs that cuffed him and the guy next to him together. The pain is excruciating because it has traveled up his arm and caused his forearm to fall asleep. Tree never thought that seeing a unit would put such a big smile on his face as he stares through the gated windows and lets out a small sigh.

"All right, ladies, we're here!" a guard shouts, unlocking the small gate that separated the driver and the piece officer from the rest of the bus. "You see that door over there?" he said, pointing to his right. "I want you inmates to line up in a straight line in front of it quietly."

Everyone on the bus stood and followed orders, not wanting to be on any of the officers' hit list. Two by two they walked down the one-foot passageway with their ankles cuffed. The time it took to board the Bluebird is a lot shorter than the time it took to depart from it because their legs are stiff from being so compact.

"My back is hurting," the Hispanic guy behind Tree tells the offender he's handcuffed to. "TDCJ makes billions of dollars off us, and they can't even give us decent buses. Someone needs to write the person in charge and tell him to sign a contract with Greyhound," he said, laughing as he jumped onto the slab.

They all stood at the door waiting for the officers inside to open it and begin processing them. As Tree waited, he thought about the rumors of the Wells Unit. Drugs, cell phones, and gang violence were on the top of the list as he said a breath prayer for God to watch over him. When he said *amen*, he remembered his mom taught him that God will never put anything on you that you cannot bear.

Stepping inside, the offenders are told to stand on the three rows of yellow lines and hold out their wrist with the cuffs on them. One officer took them off while another went around and unlocked the ones on their ankles. When free, everyone stretched but were quickly told to be still.

"Don't act like you don't know what comes next because if I have to show you, you're going to be in a holding cell butt naked freezing your tails off until tomorrow!" an officer shouts, handing a trustee a large linen bag. The inmates are moving slow, so the sergeant becomes pissed. "Damn it, strip! If you need some help, act like there's a pole in front of you or something! I have another chain coming in about thirty minutes!"

Tree looks around, and all of the offenders are hesitantly taking their uniforms off. This isn't his first rodeo, so he decides to be the first to show everyone how to ride this penitentiary bull. Finally, in a record of eight seconds, his black cheeks are out, and he thinks, *Ain't no shame in my game* while cupping his hands over his private parts.

A black officer steps in front of the offenders and tells them to raise their hands as if they're reaching for the sky. "Row one, step forward and raise your arms as high as you can!" They all follow instructions carefully except for a few Hispanics who claim they don't speak English. "With your hands still in the air, wiggle your fingers and lift each leg while wiggling your toes!" the officer shouts a little louder with his authority. "At ease, inmates. You can put your hands down now."

Row one puts their hands down and prepares themselves for their privacy to be violated. "Turn around, spread your cheeks, and squat!" Turning around, they all squat, spreading themselves, waiting for an officer to come and check their third eye. As the officers go to each one of them, the inmates are told to cough two times to prove there's nothing in there. Finally the embarrassment is over, and everyone has gone through the grueling procedure, swearing the officers are homosexuals.

"Next time get some women up in here to do this. I don't feel right giving ya'll a striptease for free," an offender said, standing straight up.

"Who told you to open your damn mouth? One more outburst out of you, inmate, and I'll put you in a tank with some guys where you gon' have to sleep with one eye open." Standing in the offender's face, the officer grins. "Yeah, they gon' really like you in there. Especially with that big pretty mouth of yours."

Chill bumps begin to form over their bodies one by one because the gigantic vents are open, and the breeze is cool due to the season changing. Shivering, Tree is suddenly on the other side of the gates, waiting for Audumn to pick him up from work so they can go to his mother's for dinner. After numbing his body with positive thinking, he thanks God because no matter what he endures while incarcerated, his mind will never be behind bars.

"All offenders from the transfer facilities, step forward and throw your old uniforms in the linen bag to your left! Afterwards, the trustee will give you a new uniform, boxers, socks, and TDCJ-issued shoes. When you finish, step to the desk to complete processing."

Reality is back, and Tree's vision vanishes into thin air. After he tosses his old rags in the linen bag like he is told, a trustee hands him a new white uniform while a correctional officer shouts for him and the others to put on their boxers. Following instructions carefully, he steps to the desk and is handed a handbook, toothbrush, and some baking soda for toothpaste.

"Nice to have you back, Wingate," the lady officer behind the fenced window said, looking over his file.

"It's nice to be back," he replied, thinking about all the uncooked beans he ate in the county.

Row by row, benches of white uniforms started to fill slowly after the officers decided to pick up the pace a bit. Inmates who had finally been processed wondered why the officers always claimed to be so behind but took their time on doing everything. Talking among themselves, the offenders came to the conclusion that all the officers needed to get a life.

Everyone is finally finished, and the benches seem to be becoming harder by the minute. It's lunchtime, so the officers leave the offenders to go and get something to eat from the officers' dining room. The chain that came after them are put in four 10' × 10' holding cells, and all of them become hungry when they see the trustees start throwing johnny sacks to the chain Tree came in on. A dried-up hot dog and a hard biscuit sit like rocks at the bottom of the paper bag, and the outdated milk didn't help anything better in washing it down.

Lunch time is over, and the officers are moving sluggishly from all the food they ate in the officers' dining room. Tree looks over to the gated holding cells and feels sorry for all they are about to endure the next couple of hours. A smile curves at the corners of his lips as he thinks about the softest mattress he is going to find in the pile he will have to choose from. *When I get to my tank, I'm not doing nothing for the rest of the day but sleep, sleep, and more sleep.*

"Chain 1, if you're finished being processed, go through the blue door in front of you and sit on the benches in medical," the woman officer said from behind the desk.

"Medical? Why are we going to medical when we did all that at the transfer facility?" an inmate asks from the back row.

Talking back to the women officers is not tolerated in the penitentiary at all. A husky officer from the SWAT team hears the back talk and comes over to ask the offender to repeat himself. Usually the woman officer would sit back and enjoy the show, but it's shift change, so she motions with her hand that she can handle the situation.

"Excuse me, but what's your name, inmate?"

"Kelvin Battles."

"Well, Kelvin, since you enjoy holding everyone up with your questions, I'll answer you this time, but please note that this will be your first and last time talking without permission."

"I apologize, miss."

"The reason why you have to go to medical, Mr. Battles, is because it's flu season, and the state of Texas has issued a notification for all offenders to be vaccinated."

"Oh," Kelvin said, running his fingers over his lips as if to say he's zipping his mouth shut.

The flu shot needle felt like it touched the bone, and afterward, Band-Aids were given to the inmates to cover the red punctures on their arms. As they got up, all of them followed behind one another to get their housing arrangements.

"Torrence Wingate," Tree said, holding out his wristband for verification before being handed his housing slip.

Exiting, Tree is not focusing on where he is walking and bumps his head into a glass window because the guy in front of him didn't hold the door for him. His new housing arrangement is A3-16, and it's at the end of the bowling alley. Placing his hands behind his back, he falls to the back of the line on the cement slab with a group of men heading in his direction. His hygiene, bedsheets, and extra uniform swings behind him in a bag as he prepares himself for the unexpected in building A.

Building A is the only building on the Wells Unit for drug offenders because the rest of the unit consists of child molesters, murderers, robbers, and rapists. Usually TDCJ places you in units that fit your crime and sentence, but in his case, it's different. It's different because his file states that his first offense was in a school zone, so the court has labeled him 3G, which means aggravated, in a sense.

Standing on the outside of the rusty metal door, the small group waits for the guard in the picket to press the button to open it. Daylight fades away as they walk inside to hand the officer working the floor their housing slip. In haste, he calls their names, floor, and cell numbers off the list while pointing to the steps for those on upper levels. Tree sees level 3 is no cake walk as he looks at the steep steps he's going to have to climb every day for chow.

"Doors rolling, row three!" the officer shouts. "All hands, legs, and any other limbs will be broken if they're in the way!"

With their bags in their hands, Tree and another guy walk, looking for the number of their cells on the cells. Some inmates are doing push-ups, some are cooking, and some are writing letters to the free world, but all of them seem to be distracted from the new faces that have entered their dwelling place. Sixteen is read over the cell as Tree looks back and sees the other guy has disappeared into his cell already.

"What's the hold up, offender? My break time is in ten minutes, and I don't have time to watch you stand around lollygagging all day."

Confrontation on his first day is the last thing he needs, so Tree proceeds, ignoring the CO's comments.

"Doors rolling!" the officer shouts again when both of his feet goes inside the cell. "Fresh meat, fresh meat!" the officer yells in laughter. "We have fresh meat in cell 4 and 16 on level 3!"

Two bunks stacked on top of each other are in the small 6' × 6' cell, and the one on the bottom is occupied by an offender with his back turned, sleeping. The lockers below are not marked, but one has a pencil in the locker hole, so Tree puts two and two together and places his belongings in the one adjacent to the marked one. The cell is clean, and whoever the guy is below is a tidy person. A shelf in the back left corner has a cup with a toothbrush in it. Colgate toothpaste is in front of the cup, and Tree wishes he can use some of it because he can't go to commissary until his funds are unfrozen from the transfer facility. Baking soda is the only thing he can taste as he thinks about his morning and night brushes before he starts his days and end his nights.

After making his bed, he sees he doesn't have a pillow and curses to himself. He wants to use the bottom bunk for a step, but decides not to out of respect for his new celly that he hasn't gotten acquainted with yet. The toilet is the only thing close enough to support his weight, so he uses that for a ladder until he can figure out something.

As he sat at the foot of the bed, he notices the twelve-inch television is at eye level and in a reachable position. For once he feels like something good has happened today in his favor for a change because when you're locked up, everything counts to help your stay better, even the little things.

"Who are you, and where are you from?" the guy asks, still with his back turned.

"Who am I is not the question," Tree replies. "Are we gon' do this the hard way, or the easy way is what you really want to ask me?"

"I'm not even on no shit like that, homeboy, because I'm on my way to the house in six months. On top of that, I'm very plugged in around here, so stepping outside of your boundaries with me would be devastating, if you know what I mean."

"I ain't never been scared of nothing, but I do respect that you're on your way home to see your people though. You have my word that I'll stay out of your way so you can see the other side of these walls again."

"Thanks for keeping it real because that'll go a long way here on the Wells Unit. By the way, I'm JU from Texas City." JU stands to his feet, holding out his hand.

"And I'm Tree from H-Town."

Tree is exhausted, so he lies down and stares at the cemented ceiling while reading every gang message written on it. Lightning bolts and Nazi symbols are what stood out the most to him because the harsh words and jokes that were written beside them were for people of the African American gender. His first mind tells him to write his thoughts about the racist remarks, but his second mind tells him not to because racism stops with us.

"Torrence Wingate, fall out!" The officer in the picket rolls the door of cell 16.

"What now?" Tree asks out loud because he had just gotten comfortable.

"They probably about to give you your job assignment, celly."

"Job assignment?" *Oh Lord, please don't let them put me in the fields.*

Tree is handed his job assignment and is highly disappointed when seeing that he's in Hoe Squad 1. Entering back into his cell, he asks JU how to get a job transfer, but JU answers him by telling him everyone goes to the fields until all their paperwork is put into the Wells Unit's system.

"I'm not going to no fields because I have a medical clearance for my back and migraine headaches."

"I'm sorry, big homey, but on this unit, you have to be cleared by their medical staff."

"We'll see about that," Tree replied, trying to figure out how he's going to outsmart the doctors. Nothing comes to mind, so he rests his head on his arms and stares through the bars over the facility from level 3. The indoor rec yard between buildings A and B is down below, and it's empty because in a few minutes, the buildings are about to turn out for chow time. Pigeons fly throughout the structure because they know it's time to eat as well. As the birds wait for their daily feeding, a big fat one with a purplish emerald green chest sits in an open window in front of his cell. The calendar in his head calculates the months he has ahead of him, and the bird's wings make him wish he could trade places with the pigeon just for one day.

8

B reakfast in the morning came late because second-shift kitchen workers had to be called in on behalf of first-shift kitchen workers were under investigation. Reason being is because a knife was found stashed in the
dishwasher, and the warden wants to know who put it there. But as usual, no
one on first shift owned up to the blade, and as usual, no one saw anything.

Everyone on the unit is angry because the theft could have put them on
a maximum lockdown for a month had it not been found.

Words are murmured among the inmates in the bowling alley today as
they exited the chow hall. On the way back to the building, Tree listens, not
wanting to get too in-depth into the gossip because he's not here to make
any friends.

As he is enjoying the early morning sunlight, someone yells, "Torrence
Wingate!" from the line going to breakfast. The sunshine is fluorescent, so
Tree has to squint to see who in the hell has put his government name in
the air. His eyes begin to search throughout the line going by him, and he
becomes astonished when he sees Blake going into the chow hall he just left
from. Tree continues in his direction without responding because he doesn't
want to dig up the past with the influential drug lord.

"Here I am trying to start over, and I bump into this cat again. I can't win
for lose with this dude," he said, looking up at the clear blue sky.

"What's wrong, Tree, you straight?"

"I'm straight, JU, besides the problem I see that I soon must deal with."

Back in the cell, JU wants to know what has changed his cellmate's
demeanor because a forest fire has stirred up in Tree's mind from the few
minutes he had to think on the bowling alley. Meditating on how to handle
the unfinished business with Blake causes him to forget how far he's come
in the last couple of weeks.

"Talk to me, Tree. I told you I'm plugged in around here, and as long as
you are in this cell, you ain't got to worry about nothing."

"You ain't got nothing to do with this, short-timer. I can handle my own."

"Whatever, H-town, but if it affects my business, then I have a lot to do with it."

Tree's nerves are sprinting because he wants to make peace with Blake or bash his face in. Whichever one, he's ready for whatever Blake chooses to do. Just in case things don't go accordingly, Tree starts to do sets of fifty push-ups so he can be physically ready if things get out of hand during their next encounter.

"What's up with you, Tree? I can't help you if you don't holla at me."

"It's nothing, JU, but old loose ends I should have tied up with a Mexican name Blake a few months ago."

Hearing who he has confrontation with makes the hairs on the back of JU's neck stand because he is the main distributor to the blacks on the facility, and Blake is his supplier. Friend or foe, money comes first in the drug lord's eyes, and with Tree entering the equation, JU doesn't know how to add up the problem on his imaginary blackboard. Business before honor is the code you have to live by to be on Blake's team, so hopefully, JU can think of something to convince Blake that this controversy will affect his pockets with the blacks. But an apology will have to be said if the beef they have is amendable.

"I ain't tripping on apologizing, JU, because I was in the wrong when this BS started on the transfer facility. If some simple words will cause my stupidity to be rectified, I'll do it so I can just do my time and go home like everybody else. At the same time, jail or no jail, I'll never let nobody play me for weak." Tree stares at his physique in the aluminum mirror.

"I got you, Tree, so don't stress too much about it. Tomorrow I'm meeting with Blake at church, and hopefully, I can clean this mess up between you two," JU replied, doing his own set of push-ups when Tree steps to the side. "I want you to do me a favor in the future and don't bump into anyone by mistake again without saying, 'Excuse me.' Respect is all we got in here, and you're playing with it like it's a game of marbles or something."

The call for church came roaring through building A from the lower levels the next morning. Tree's eyes are wide-open because of everyone coming out of their cells, but JU's bunk is empty when he looks down to tell him the doors are rolling for Sunday morning service. *Where in the hell is he, and how did he get out of here without me knowing it?* Tree thinks, jumping down quickly to get himself together for God's house.

Inmates are all over the bowling alley while building A waited at the red line for their signal to go to church. Last week and the weeks before that, building A was first to go into the sanctuary, but numerous I-60s were written to the warden, and that stopped them from going first all the time. This morning they are last because Lieutenant Harris called himself, making things fair by rotating dorms for service from now on.

Tree steps inside the church but is quickly reminded that the building is a gym. Weights, basketballs, and other recreational equipment are locked in a tall fence behind rows of folding chairs full of inmates seeking an answer from God. A white wooden podium with the Texas star on it sits in the front of them, waiting for someone from outside of the gates to give the word of God. The inmate setup crew notices that the doors are closed and turns on a gospel CD to wake the morning zombies up. Stragglers are told by supervising officers to be seated as the music causes the offenders who came wholeheartedly to feel the presence of God.

The overhead projector is turned on, and the back wall becomes its screen. Casting Crowns' lead singer's voice begins crooning through the speakers, and the words "Jesus, can you show me how far is the east is from the west" is on the transparency, so inmates can join in with the singing. After two or three songs, the offenders who sang from their spirits feel reassurance because the past week was full of malice and strife.

A minister from the Fifth Ward Baptist Church is the Wells Unit guest speaker today. The church is at its capacity because the unit knows that the Fifth Ward Baptist Church tells it like it is without sugarcoating a thing. As the man of God speaks, his words begin to make the offenders feel like they're looking in a mirror because nothing is hidden as God's word helps them see their faults in their past and in their everyday lives.

Every word spoken falls on Tree's mind, body, soul, and spirit as he listens on, praying that his new outlook in life is the correct choice in the course he's currently on.

The sermon is full of power and authority, but Tree can't stay focused because of the low whispers coming from behind him. The Aryan Brotherhood is holding a meeting on what their next move is going to be, and Tree can hear everything they're saying. Not wanting to get involved or get caught listening, Tree turns around and tries to get back into the spirit. His attention span lasts only for a few seconds because when he sees Blake and JU in the corner looking toward him, anger is stirred up inside of him all over again. *I want this shit over with today because if it's on, let's get it over with,* he said to himself, waiting for church to be dismissed.

Church is over, and the letter *A* is on the overhead projector screen for them to line up on the bowling alley, but Tree disregards the rules and walks over to Blake. "Say, Blake, I ain't on that bullshit no more. I should have said 'Excuse me' when I bumped into you on the transfer facility, but I didn't, so I'm sorry."

Blake listened to his apology and looks up at JU, nodding his head. "I have no beef with you, Tree, and everything's straight between us. Holla at JU if you need anything from this day on," Blake replied, thinking about the agreement he and JU just made.

Tree is at peace with himself when hearing the drug lord's remarks because since the day he entered TDCJ's system, he vowed never to show vulnerability. A change has definitely been made in his life, and it feels good knowing it.

As he catches up with his group, he smiles when thinking of how Audumn and his family would be so proud of him for what he did today. Standing at the back of the line, he looks at the entrance of the church and thanks God for the sign of hope toward burying his arrogant ways once and for all.

A few weeks pass, and Tree receives his first letter of many from the one person that matters most to him in his life. He thought the letter was from his mother or his dad, but the return address read Audumn Humphrey. Staring at the date in which it was stamped, a quick jolt of joy engulfs him because she had to have written him back as soon as she received his letter he last wrote her. No matter what the letter reads, he knows she still loves him because of the rapid response and the sweet-perfumed fragrance undeniably jumping off the envelope.

It took him an hour to read what she wrote him out of fear of what she might say due to his current conditions. Her name on the envelope is good of enough for him until he feels ready to see what she had to say. Finally the time has come, and he opens it with expectancy before he can think twice about opening it. He reads it word for word and sees that Audumn holds no grudges against him for his past or his present situations. A feeling of glee changes his curiosity to a big smile because she wrote that he looked like the Tree she met five years ago and that she's sorry for being so nonchalant at their visit in Harris County. She also said for him to stay out of trouble because she heard that troublemakers do 85 percent of their time. The last sentence he reads seals what he was looking for. "I'm here for you, Tree, but you have to promise me that your old life is over with. Love, Audumn."

"I promise, my love," he said in a whisper so that JU would not hear him from below.

"What's up, Tree, you said something?"

JU's voice catches him off guard and causes him to leave the land of happily ever after. "Nah, JU, just talking to myself about this chick who wrote me today."

"Whatever, Tree, sounds to me like you're in love," JU said, dragging out the word *love*.

"Love? Ain't nobody in love, JU. I mean, I ain't gon' lie, I do have feelings for her."

"Whoever she is, celly, she sounds special, and besides, there's nothing wrong with being in love in this place." JU looks up at a picture of his girl Tanya taped to the bottom of Tree's bunk.

Sitting up, Tree's mind is racing over Audumn's closing sentiment. *Price is Right* is on, and usually, he enjoys seeing the expressions on the people's faces when the show's announcer yells, "Come on down!" but, *Love, Audumn* is the only thing he can see today as he stares through the 12" tube with a heart full of rose petals.

"Dayroom open!" a guard shouts, rolling the cell doors.

Jumping down, Tree slides his feet in the Bob Barker name brand canvas shoes the state has issued him. After splashing some water in his face, he grabs his face towel and follows JU out the door. The dayroom is already packed from levels 1 and 2 as Tree looks over the railing at all the white uniforms down below. *I feel sorry for whoever falls or is pushed from up here,* he thinks, trying to figure out how many feet it is between the ground and someone's fate from where he is standing.

"What's up, T. Loc, you brought that down for me?"

"For show, for show," T. Loc said, shaking JU's hand while secretly handing him a balloon full of narcotics.

"Good looking out, hometown, because things were looking a little shaky on the rec yard yesterday. I don't care what Blake says, somebody snitching up in building A."

"I feel sorry for whoever bumping their gums around here, JU," T. Loc replied, shaking his head because he is loyal to the code of "snitches get stitches."

The three of them sat down to play a game of dominoes while JU and T. Loc have their daily Texas City meeting. Besides Tree being his friend, T. Loc is his boy from the free world and his fall partner. The police pulled them over on 45 South on the way back from Houston and found 150 lbs. of marijuana in the cab of JU's Uncle Pop's truck. In the county, T. Loc fought his case because the police didn't have probable cause to pull them over, but JU knew he was dead to the wrong and signed for three years. T. Loc on the other hand got five years because he lost in trial when the police showed the video of the truck's license plate lights being out during the time of arrest.

As the day goes on, T. Loc and JU hustle until the dayroom slowly becomes empty. The guards on duty know what's going on but keep quiet because they enjoy the extra pay at the end of the week from Blake and whoever else is doing what they're doing on the side. T. Loc hands JU all the stamps and cash he was paid for the drugs because it's time to re-up, and Blake will not do business with nobody but him when it comes to drug deals.

"Give me a couple of days, Loc, and I'll have us right before you know it," JU said, stuffing T. Loc's money package down the crotch of his pants.

At the stairs, an officer walks up and hands Tree a lay-in before he can take the first step. JU is on his way up but looks back to see what has his boy stopped in his tracks. The lay-in is from parole, and he has to be there in thirty minutes, but fear is present because of the new charge he just came off bench warrant for. Step by step, he walks to level 3 thinking about what to say, what to do, and what parole is going to think of him.

Back in his cell, Tree brushes his hair while looking in the mirror and asks God to remember him when the board of parole makes a decision on his release.

The lay-in for parole is in the main control building that sits in the center of the bowling alley across from the officers' dining room cafeteria. The windows have a slight tint on them so that the ranking officers can see all movement on the slab without being noticed. Tree is not the only one under review today. so he goes in and stands against the wall behind the four guys in front of him. Butterflies fly endlessly in his stomach as a bead of sweat runs down his forehead.

"Good luck and God bless you," an offender said to the other offenders waiting as he is exiting the office. A big smile is on his face when he walks by because he feels as if all went well before the board of the parole.

Tree's next, so he goes in and stands next to the only vacant chair in the room. He knows the board wants to talk to Torrence Wingate, so he puts Tree to the side for this special occasion. Two men sit at each end of a table, and a woman sits in the middle. As he stood there, he could feel different vibes from each of them as he sits, waiting for someone to speak. For a minute, it's hard for Torrence to gain his composure because it feels like he's under interrogation for something he didn't do.

"Hi, I'm Mrs. Bennett, and these are my colleagues, Mr. Arceneaux and Mr. Cooks."

"Hello," Tree said as he sits in the only vacant chair in the small room.

"How are you today, Mr. Wingate?" Mrs. Bennett asks, writing something in her notes.

"Blessed."

"Blessed? And why would you say you're blessed?" Mr. Cooks asks, as if he's heard the statement many times before.

"I'm blessed because God allowed me to see another day, and I'm blessed to have this parole hearing so that I can possibly go home to my loved ones someday," Tree replies with a cool indifference.

All three write something in their notes after hearing his answer.

"I see here that you have an extensive drug history and that you evaded arrest in a motor vehicle when the police tried to apprehend you. If the board of parole were to grant you your release, how do we know that this pattern of behavior is not going to be repeated in the future?" Mr. Arceneaux looks straight into his eyes from across the table when he addresses him.

"The man in your files is not the man that is sitting before you today. Why, it's because I'm not proud of what I've done in the past, but I am proud of who I've become. Being in TDCJ has taught me that my life affects others and that a life of crime only adds up to being behind bars or six feet under in a grave. I hope someday I can put this learning experience behind me and move on with my life in the direction God desires me to be on. If that time is coming soon, praise the Lord, but if it is not, so be it. Whatever happens, my father taught me that I must pray that God's will be done no matter how I feel things should have played out. With that in mind, I do ask that the board will show me some mercy and give me another chance to make it in society. Thanks."

The three of them continued in awe, meditating on all of Torrence's remarks because not once did he slip up in what he wanted the board to know about him. His dialect is clear, and his vocabulary sounds like a doctor or lawyer as he put all the good things about him in the air before the board of parole.

When the meeting had come to an end, everyone felt that he handled himself like a man who is ready to walk out the front gate today.

"Well, Mr. Wingate, we appreciate all that you said here today, and we will turn in our recommendations to our supervisors on what we feel is best concerning your rehabilitation," Mrs. Bennet said. "Thanks, and you will be receiving an answer in three to five months."

"No, thank the three of you for listening." Leaving the office, he is relieved that his new charge wasn't brought up and confident that his words have possibly gotten him his release.

9

H is parole answer came a day before his third month of waiting. Winter is here, and Tree's day felt as if it is without ending. Because of the season change, Hoe Squad 1's last day of work is today, so that meant they had to till the cold ground until it was reduced to only dirt.

Tree had just came in from his tiresome day in the fields when the officer on duty handed him his mail. As he looked over the mail from those who cared, his hope for tomorrow falls from his hands when he enters his domain. Pausing, he picks it up, praying that his performance before the board of parole got him an Academy Award for his release. Without thinking further, he tears the envelope open because if he had waited any longer, the seed of fear would have been planted inside his brain. *Torrence Wingate Jr., the state of Texas hereby grants you parole,* he reads as his anxiety of going home or not is buried forever.

Not paying attention, the doors begin to roll shut while he is standing in the doorway. The iron cell bars almost clip him as he steps inside his cell to read the best mail he has ever received since he's been incarcerated. "Yes!" he shouts because he can't contain himself, but the inmates throughout the building yell back for him to shut the hell up. Staring at the new man he's becoming in the mirror, he says, "Thank you, Jesus" while tuning out all the negative remarks from around him.

After fully reading over his answer, he sees his parole release came with stipulations. Tree was granted an FI-9 with a release date of 5/1/2011, but upon being released, he must complete a pre-release program called Changes and get a certificate in a state-issued drug class. He thought the classes were worthless, but his drive to do whatever necessary outweighed his thinking. Reverse is the opposite direction in which he is trying to go, and being in neutral is the devil's playground.

JU comes in shortly after he got his exciting news. The energy in the cell is different for some reason, and JU can feel it's coming from his cellmate.

He neatly folds his state-issued uniform on his bunk and glances over at Tree doing number 2 while reading the Bible. From the first day they met until now, JU didn't know his cellmate even owned a Bible, so his curiosity rises at the change in his celly's behavior. Suspense runs out the door when he notices that Tree hasn't taken his eyes out of the book of life since he stepped inside their cell.

"So why the sudden change, H-town?" JU asks, interrupting Tree's study.

Tree laughs at JU's comment and replies, "Last time I checked, sudden change was better than no change."

"I ain't trying to hear all that philosopher talk today, Tree. What's up with the Bible reading all of sudden, and why are you so cheery today? You act like you're the one going home at the end of next month."

"I might not be going home at the end of next month, JU, but I will be going home three months after you." Tree is full of joy when he hands his cellmate his parole answer.

JU scans over the letter and verifies Tree's merriment. "That's what's up, and congratulations, celly. Looks like we both gon' be in that free world together. Before I go, I'm gon' shoot you all my info so we can link up on the outside."

Tree gets up and wipes himself, wishing his day for release is tomorrow while JU pours baby powder in a sock. "Excuse me, Mr. Happy Guy, but you need to definitely do something about the nasty odor that's lingering," JU said, handing him the homemade air freshener he put together. The cloud of baby powder refreshes the smell to something tolerable as Tree swings the sock around, trying to cover up the smell as much as possible.

Everything is good in Tree's life. His letters home showed maturity and made his parents accept their son as a new being. Calendar days turned into weeks and weeks turned into months as Tree watched the days practically fly by. Audumn came every other week to visit him, and each time she saw him, his love for her chipped away at her heart. She knew her relationship with her friend Secorion had come to an end because the sight of Tree is what truly touched her soul. Her heart is divided in two between the two guys, but Tree's side is a lot bigger.

Finally, the month has come for JU's time inside the joint to come to an end, and Tree is three months behind him.

"Jon Joesef, you're on the chain tonight to the Walls Release Unit. Get all your things together before eleven o'clock," the guard said through the bars as he checks JU's name off tonight's chain's list.

The sound of JU's real name gave them both a scare, and it took a minute for the two of them to regain their composure. Afterward, they both were on their feet, excited that in a few months, cell 16 wouldn't have any recognition of neither one of them being in there.

"All right, Texas City, you be careful out there. You know them laws want to see us locked up in this cage, so stay on your p's and q's when you're making business deals." Tree picks up JU's mesh bag of mail and hands it to him.

"I'ma be straight, Tree, because when I touch ground, I'm chilling."

"Now that's what I want to hear, my boy. I got your info, so I'll be hitting you up in May."

"Why don't you do that, H-town," JU said as the doors roll for him to leave. "Looks like that's my cue, Tree. I'm out, and do what you have to do in here so you can go home on your release date."

"I got this, JU, and thanks for being a true friend," Tree replied as he watched the back of his cellmate walk down level 3 for the last time.

JU was a little sad when he left cell 16. He was sad because the time had come for him to own up to his part of the agreement with Blake. Tree kept it real with him since day one, and it hurt that he had to do the unthinkable to keep Blake from doing him in.

As he pours his stuff onto the table to be processed out, JU looks up at his old cell and hopes for the best for his Houston friend. Blake gave him his word that Tree would be okay if he does what he is told until he goes home. Thinking about the past years of business he had with Blake, he recalls that Blake's word is gold. "Forgive me, Tree," he mumbles, hanging his head, disappointed with himself.

The next morning, Tree's mouth is parched and his stomach is empty from missing breakfast. After pushing the button on the sink for some water, he remembers that his alarm clock left the night before because JU never missed a meal and made sure that he didn't either. At the beginning of his sentencing, Tree told himself that he was going to do his time by himself, but that was before he was sent to cell 16. JU never lied to him and always had his back from the time they called a truce, so all he could say is, "Keep your head up out there, brother, and thanks for keeping it real with me."

Tree's mind is boggled as he transfers his sheets from the top bunk onto the bottom bunk three days later. His time is growing shorter by the days, and he doesn't know who the state is going to put in cell 16 with him. Before, he wouldn't have cared less who his next cellmate would have been because he'd handled the situation with his fist if that's what it came down to. The month of May is what he's looking forward to, so he prayed for a celly with a goal of going home just like him.

A loud bark from a dog on level 1 grabs his attention as he rises to his feet. With his face almost through the bars, he tries to look and find out why a K-9 is in the building. Whistles and yells of "One time," which is the code name for *police*, cry throughout the cells as the dog sniffed each level in order. Level 3 is next, and he can hear SWAT coming up the stairs because faint patters of footsteps start to become louder by the second. Tree is not worried in any kind of way as he sees the nose of the K-9 pass cell 13.

Closer and closer the dog approaches, then begins to bark and goes into a delirium at cell 15. SWAT stops in front of the cell as if to check it, but for some reason, they yell to roll 16. Tree is asked to step out for inspection, so he does so kindly. The K-9 eyeballs his every move and growls as Tree carefully goes around him. The Wells Unit drug team tears Tree's cell apart inch by inch, looking for what they already know is in there. As they rip the sheets from off his bed, they flip the mattress over and find a slit on the side of it. The commanding officer reaches his hand inside of the slit, and two balloons are pulled out and placed in the sink. After cutting them open, the SWAT team finds packs of ecstasy, cocaine, and heroin.

"Book him," the gang sergeant said with a grin. "We found what we're looking for."

Tree's eyes are wide-open and his mouth has dropped to the ground when replaying what has just happened in his mind. It's like he's here but not here because he can't believe what the gang sergeant has in hands. "That's not mine!" he screams as they spin him around onto the railing to handcuff him. The clicks on the cuffs start at one but stop at six, and the pain from their tightness is unbearable as he moves while they are slapping them on his wrist.

"Tell it to the lieutenant Monday when you go to court," one of the SWAT members said, pushing him roughly toward the stairs.

SWAT and their commanding officer are relieved that the bust was a success. Everything that Blake told them down to the drugs being in the mattress turned out to be true and gave the underhanded officers leeway to collect more money from the offenders. It's been a while since they had a major drug bust on the Wells Unit, so the warden started to come down on his staff because of the void in disciplinary actions. This morning the gang sergeant got a word from a birdie that cell 16 had narcotics hidden in the mattress. Moving quickly, SWAT handled their tactics according to procedure and apprehended Tree, just as their unknown source had promised them.

Being handcuffed for a new charge is something Tree never saw coming. The only thing he can think about is losing his parole and hurting Audumn's heart with his foolishness again. Gloominess surrounds him on the bowling alley as he walks to the main control building to be housed in Ag-Seg. The sun is rising and the ice chips are melting away off the grass, but Tree can't enjoy God's creation because he can only see darkness as he looks for a door that's not there.

How and why me, Lord? he thinks as he listens to the iron key turn to open the steel door to main control.

Ag-Seg is quiet because the offenders are still asleep this early in the morning. The cell doors are locked heavily on both sides of the hall as he walked handcuffed through the octagon tunnel. Lights are scattered throughout the dark passageways, so his pupils have to adjust quickly to the lighting around him, or he could possibly trip and fall.

"Stop, we're here, Wingate," the officer to his left said in a low voice.

As the cell door is unlocked, Tree could hear every sound of the door creaking off the masonry walls when it is opening. Staring into the dungeon, he pauses because he's gone from some of his best days of his life to the worst day of his life in a matter of minutes. A slight nudge to his back makes him step in, wondering, *How in the hell am I going to get myself out of this mess?*

Over the past year, daylight has kept his mind sane because he knew that same daylight shined on Audumn. Some may think he was crazy for always staring into the sky, but frankly, that's just how he did his time. It wasn't much to hold on to, but at least he knew that when Audumn looked to the heavens, they both saw the same thing for a split second. Now his daylight is limited to one hour a week, if that.

Darkness is the only thing around him, and darkness is how's he's feeling. An atomic bomb has been detonated in Tree's diaphragm and has blown through his mouth with words that shouldn't even be spoken or thought of. Swinging endlessly through his dim-lighted cell, his fist hits a wall at full impact. Blood comes streaming from his knuckles down to his fingertips, and he does nothing but let it drip. With his back to the wall, he slides down into a corner, shaking his head toward his friendliness with JU. *I can't believe JU left that dope in his mattress. A few days earlier, and it would have been you, JU, in Ag-Seg instead of me. I can't put my finger on it, but something ain't right with this bullshit.*

The mattress is flat, and Tree feels like he's lying on nothing. The pressure valve in his brain has been released, so the color in his face has returned to normal. Everything is obscure, so he closes his eyes to fall asleep and try to wake up out of this nightmare. Thirty minutes into the land of no coming back, a voice calls and breaks his slumber.

"Get ready for showers!"

Tree gets up and steps to his cell door when hearing the doors throughout the tunnels opening. Ag-Seg is heavily secured, so handcuffs are not needed unless an offender has to leave the building. Stepping into the center of the octagon, showers are lined up along the walls and down the center. Straight inmates wait for a shower along the walls to become free while those on the kinky side wash in the middle. Body odor lurks throughout the inmates because most of them can't afford hygiene products, and half of the rest of them don't bathe but once a week.

Tree took a shower yesterday but takes another one because of all he's endured in such a short period of time. All he can say is "Thanks" with a face of gloominess as he's handed a bar of soap from a trustee.

The shower helped cleanse the trash off his mind and body. He didn't know what chapter he was on in the book of Tree, but at least he didn't feel like Oscar on *Sesame Street* anymore. He wished he could stay in a little longer, but the peep show in the middle between the gay inmates started to get ridiculous.

As he steps over the ledge that held the water in, a trustee hands him a towel to dry off with. After unfolding it, a small note falls to the floor like a feather, so Tree picks it up discreetly and tucks it away in his shirt pocket on the bench.

"Showers are closed! Everyone line up at the door, and make sure your towels are thrown in the linen bag, or you'll be written a case for contraband!" an officer exclaims, putting on his gloves for a quick pat down.

Back in his cell, Tree takes a seat on his bunk and pulls out the small note that fell into his possession. He doesn't know what to expect as he unfolds it, but his curiosity makes him want to read it because for all he knew, it could have been a map to bust out of prison.

What's up, Mr. Tree. I know you're probably mad at the world for what you're going through, but that's life. JU is gone, and my pockets are not going to be the same if I don't find somebody I can trust to work building A for me. He told me I can trust you to take his spot if I did him a favor by letting you live for disrespecting me. The shit you're going through is just a little collateral on my investment in you. This could all be over with as soon as tomorrow morning if you agree to these terms, but if you don't, you will have to face Lieutenant Harris Monday morning and lose your parole. I'm sorry it had to come to this, but my money comes before everything. Let the trustee working the floor know what you're going to do, and hopefully, I'll see you in church Sunday morning.

Business before honor,

Blake

PS: Look around, Tree. I'm a very powerful man, so don't play with me or try anything stupid.

Tree balled up the note in pain because his hand is swollen from his earlier fistfight with the wall. Standing to his feet, he takes his paper baseball and pitches it at the cell door at 70 mph. As he paces throughout his cell, he murmurs underneath his breath what to do next. "Why, JU? I didn't need your help. I came into world by myself, and I'm damn show was gon' leave the same way. This ain't over with, lil homey. I promise you that."

His mind is empty as he tries to think of the best possible solution to get out this predicament he's in. Blake is too powerful to snitch on, and more importantly, he's too powerful to deny his proposition. Looking around the dark cell, Tree turns his back on God and says, "Sorry, Lord, but in the real world, the devil's way out is a lot faster and easier than Jesus's way out. It's time to do things my way. Holla atcha when I go home in May," he said, signaling for the floor trustee so that he can give Blake his answer.

10

"Class dismissed! Torrence, I would like to speak with you before you leave."

Everyone in Changes rushed out of class while laughing at Tree for having to stay after. Ms. Guidry constantly stayed on the offenders about life after being released from prison, but none of them listened because they felt the free world had nothing to do with the inside.

Tree didn't mind staying after because his freedom is only three days away. "Here I come, Ms. Guidry, but can you hurry this up because I got business to take care of?"

Everything she said was brief, and every time Ms. Guidry asked Tree about his future plans, he brushed her off by saying, "I got this" because he believed that his life is his life, and he must live it. Three months ago, he made that decision when he went into business with Blake. After seeing how Blake made his moves and how he was cutthroat when it came to respect, Tree begin to admire him in a weird way. The wrath he vowed to come upon JU was thrown into the trash after seeing the power Blake had in the penitentiary and in the free world.

"So, you mean to tell me 'I got this' is your answer to making it in a society that's very strict on felony offenders!" Ms. Guidry snaps in anger while taking off her glasses to look him in the eyes.

"Maybe I said it wrong, Ms. Guidry. What I meant was that I'm going to do everything possible to survive in a system that's designed for people like me to stay in bondage."

"Is that's what you think this is all this about?" Ms. Guidry asks. "The penitentiary is designed for whatever you make of it, Torrence. I've seen offenders come, and I've seen them go. I've also had numerous updates on offenders who've used this setback in their life to regroup and move forward to becoming better men than they could have ever imagined."

Looking over Ms. Guidry's shoulder at the clock, he says, "Is that it?"

"Yes, that's it, Mr. Wingate," Ms. Guidry replies, knowing that Tree would be back. "Here's your certificate of completion for Changes. Torrence, you have the whole world before you when those doors open for you at the Walls Release Unit, so please make the right decisions, or you'll be just another number behind a brick wall."

"Thanks, but I'll be okay," Tree replies, exiting.

"Torrence."

"Ma'am."

"Everybody knows what you do around here, *Tree*," Ms. Guidry said, emphasizing his nickname. "I say that because that mentality of surviving is not going to get you anything but more time in TDCJ. Good luck, and be careful out there."

The bowling alley is motionless, and Tree is the only inmate on the cement slab. Trying to hurry to building A before count time, the horn sounds loudly, causing everyone wearing a white state-issued uniform to stop. If this was last week, he would have been pissed at being caught in count on the bowling alley, but his time is too short to get mad.

An officer comes by and tells him to go to main control to be counted.

Count cleared in record time today, and Tree walks back to his building with a grin on his face because for the past twenty months, he's been taking orders from power-stricken officers. Some were cool, but at the end of the day, they were wearing gray, and he was wearing white.

As he signaled to be buzzed into building A, he thinks about Ms. Guidry's heartfelt conversation and feels a little ashamed on giving her the cold shoulder.

Entering the building, he hears the doors on level 1 are rolling as he prepares himself for the steep steps to level 3. It's recreation time, and all the offenders are coming out of their cells for their daily fix because every-one knows its Tree's last day of hustling.

T. Loc is waiting on the steps of level 2 when Tree comes down and hands T. Loc half of their latest score from Blake.

"What ya'll boys got for me today?" a Caucasian inmate asks, shaking hands with T. Loc while secretly giving him a twenty-dollar bill.

"Whateva you want, Sweet Al, we got you."

"Just give me the usual, T. Loc, and don't make me late, babe," Sweet Al replies, ready to get high.

Business is good because all the inmates knew he is on his way to the house. Everything his clientele had, they spent as they waited their turn to get the hookup from Tree and pay T. Loc. The guards' eyes are purposely covered as transactions are made right before them.

"Say, T. Loc, I'm through with the dope game because I didn't want to go down this road while I was in here. The rest of this you can have, but I do want the cash money made today so that I can bring it home with me Monday."

"I can feel that, Tree. Here, it's about $210." T. Loc pulls the money from his sock. "You think you can hook me up with Blake?"

"I already tried, and he won't do it because he's going home in July. If I were you, I'd chill, T. Loc. JU was right when he said someone is snitching around here because Ms. Guidry told me after class in so many words. Besides, you don't want to hustle around here if you don't have Blake backing you."

"You know I go home in October, and six months is a long time to chill, Tree."

"Six months and be free, or a new charge and do some extra time. You're not stupid, T. Loc, do the math," Tree said, handing him two balloons of narcotics.

"Rec time is over! Everyone back to your cells!"

"Finally, it's over," Tree said aloud with a sigh. "Handle your business right, T. Loc, and watch your back because it's a lot of cats in here ready to drop a dime on you for nothing."

The weekend went by as if it never came at all. It's Sunday night, and the last meeting with Blake at church went well earlier. Blake apologized in a roundabout way for how he recruited Tree on his team, but Tree wasn't tripping because it all worked out for the best. Money was exchanged, and Blake promised him that by the time he got home, he'll have his cut of what is coming to him. Tree gave the Hispanic drug lord his house number to assure that Blake's end of the agreement is fully met.

"Say, Tree, you ready for tonight?" his cellmate asks from up top.

"Yeah, I'm ready, Band-Aid. Just a little displeased at how I got this second chance at the free world."

"You gone be all right, Tree, if you keep your nose clean and leave that PCP alone."

"I'm through with that bullshit, Band-Aid, because I already know that drug is going to throw me off the mission I'm trying to achieve. Plus, Audumn promised she'll drop me like some flapjacks in the chow hall if I smoke that mess again. I'm flying straight this time, lil homey," Tree said while carving his nickname into the steel of the bottom of the top bunk.

Band-Aid gave Tree his advice on life as he understood it, and Tree listened to every word that came out of his celly's mouth. To others, Band-Aid's advice may have sounded senseless, but if they had listened carefully, they would have realized that his conversation had some meaning to it.

Band-Aid is a youngster and has been through a lot during his twenty-two years of life, so when he spoke, his voice displayed a lot of pain as he talked about his rough childhood. All Tree could do is be silent and let him vent about staring your demons in the face, but when he began to run on about the same thing, Tree tuned him out by thinking how his demon was the love for smoking PCP.

Later, Tree is called out for the chain to the Walls Unit, and to him, riding to the Walls Unit was the best ride of his life. Even though he is handcuffed from head to toe, it didn't disturb the joy he is feeling in kissing Audumn tomorrow evening. Looking over the fields, he remembers the first time he laid eyes on the endless rows of dirt and thanks Jesus that another chapter of his life is behind him.

As the unit grew smaller by the mile, he glances back one last time and faces forward, looking toward his future.

Only three inmates are being released from the Wells Unit tomorrow, but that doesn't change the fact that the state of Texas has scheduled other offenders' release with the same discharge date as them. Hopping off the bus, officers escort the three of them to an overcrowded gated holding cell outside until the offenders who have gotten there earlier are processed in and housed.

Tree's handcuffs are unlocked as he enters the outside cell, and the heavenly locked gate is slammed behind him. He shivers as he rubs his hands together because a gust of wind has blown through the early morning with nothing stopping it. Blowing his warm breath into his fists, chill bumps start to pop up one by one, covering his arms. He tries to withstand standing alone, but the chilly air makes it unbearable. After looking for anything to block the wind coming from all directions, Tree finds himself in a huddle, basking in the warmth of the other offenders' body heat.

The hour and a half outside made everyone being released appreciate May 1 even more. Their fingers and toes are a little numb as they are herded into the gym for the next stages in being processed out of the system.

Dropping his bags on the floor, Tree's hopes of this going quickly diminishes as he looks at the hundreds of inmates in line at the numerous tables throughout the rugged gymnasium.

"Next," an offender said, not giving Tree any eye contact as he grabs a release form to document his belongings. "Please put everything you want to keep on the table and everything else in the garbage can to my left."

Tree's hungry, so he dumps his mesh bag onto the table, hoping it will speed up the procedure. After sifting through everything he thought he wanted to keep on the Wells Unit, he decides that the state-issued stuff he is trying to keep needs to stay with the state. By the time he is finished with processing, he had thrown everything in the trash except for his letters from Audumn, his hygiene, and his Bible.

"Johnny sacks will be handed to you as you leave to be housed for the night. Please have a seat in the gate with your last initial on it."

It's almost over, Tree thinks as he ponders on the eight hours he has left in captivity.

As soon as he sat down, all the offenders are told to stand and listen for their housing arrangements. A guard finally gets to his name, so Tree takes a sack lunch and falls in line to go to the release side of the Walls Unit. Walking into his temporary cell, Tree listens to the cell door close behind him, and a sigh of relief leaves his lungs.

"What's your name, youngster?" an old man asks, rolling over to see who his new cellmate is.

"Tree, and who are you, old school?"

"It's funny you called me that because that's what they call me around here."

"What?" Tree asks, trying to figure out what the old man's name is.

"Old School," he said, extending his hand as a peace offering.

"Oh, I should have guessed that," Tree replies, shaking his hand.

Stepping onto the toilet, Tree climbs to the top bunk without even making his bed. As he lies down, he takes an orange from his johnny sack and begins to peel it while looking through the bars over the unit. The unit is old, and it's no secret because the doors are manually rolled instead of electronically like the Wells Unit. It's rumored that Clyde Barrow was once housed here during his legacy of rampage with Bonnie throughout Texas.

"Say, Old School, what do you have planned when you touch ground tomorrow?"

"Touch ground? I wish I was touching ground tomorrow or even the next day after that," the old man answered quickly. "Hell, I won't touch ground until 2016."

"2016? What in the world did you get yourself into?"

"Everything besides murder and rape. Tree, you probably won't believe me, but I've been in and out these jail cells practically all my life. When I was thirteen, I stabbed a man two times to get into a local gang and ended up doing five years in a juvenile facility till I was eighteen years old for attempted murder."

"Damn, Old School, you were out there at a young age." Tree leans his head over the side of the top bunk to give his celly his full attention.

"Ever since then, I couldn't shake the system no matter how hard I tried. As of right now, I'm being expedited to Chicago for a case I've been slipping through the cracks on for the past twenty years. I just did a full ten-year sentence in Texas, and now this. I say I'm going home in 2016, but actually, I really don't know what them white folks gon' throw at me when I get to Chi-town."

"Old School, you just got to chill out and do things different when you get out."

"Don't call me that," the old man blurts out.

"Huh?"

"I never told nobody this, but I hate being called that because I'm not an old school but an old fool!" he exclaims as his voice echoes off the wall. "Tree, you're going home tomorrow, and if you don't change your life today, you'll be an old school in here just like me. After these twenty-six years behind bars, I realize something. What I realize is that we are never to play another man's game because he didn't invent it for us to win. I say that because that dope game you're playing is only a two-way street. One side of the street ends up in this place, and the other side of the street I don't have to say because you already know. Don't end up an old fool like me,

Tree. It's not worth it. Remember that tomorrow when that fifteen-foot gate opens for you."

Rolling over, Tree closes his eyes and later opens them to his name being called from the other side of the bars. Jumping out of bed, he brushes his teeth and grooms himself as best as he could with the tools before him. The cell door rolls for him to step out, so he reaches under his mattress for his mail while purposely leaving his Bible. "I'm gone, Old School, and thanks for that knowledge earlier," he said, stepping outside the cell.

No one seemed to miss breakfast this morning because their focus is on booze, clubs, and girls. As they moved slowly through the lines, the guards begin to shout for them to pick up the pace and put the stale-smelling Goodwill clothes on. Everyone listens and started to dress in haste, not wanting their morning release to be pushed back to the evening.

Tree looks down at his attire and chuckles because for some reason, he wants to dance down the seventies *Soul Train* line.

"Torrence Wingate," he said while at the window, waiting for the state-issued TDCJ check that was supposed to help you get your life back started.

"Torrence Wingate," the female officer repeats, looking through the envelopes with *W* stamped on them. "Here we are," she said, placing it in the window. "Sign here, and you are to report to the parole office on West Thirty-Fourth by 8:00 a.m. Tuesday morning."

"Thanks," he replied, holding up the check for $50.

The motor on the fifteen-foot gate closing is the last thing Tree heard as he began to walk through the streets of Huntsville to the Greyhound bus station. His one-way ticket to Houston is in the envelope he received from the clerk, so anything else he might need can wait until he reaches his hometown.

Some of the guys cashed their checks after being told the bus didn't come for another half hour, but Tree had no need to because he still had a few dollars left over from his books. Dairy Queen is the only thing in walking distance that can account for their half-hour delay, so he decided to get something to eat with the rest of the crowd.

Smoke filled the air as the men watched the bus pull into the station. Their stomachs are full, so all of them unbutton their tight pants to take deep drags. The cigarettes gave Tree a few dizzy spells, but after the third or fourth one, it is as if his lungs embraced the smoke openly. He finishes his cigarette and then flicks it onto the pavement as he is boarding his free ride to the house.

On the bus, he finds a seat vacant near the rear and flops into it and says a short prayer of thanks as the bus begins to roll out. After saying *amen*, he opens his eyes and notices that they were almost out of Huntsville. Yawning, Tree is tired from all he's endured in the last forty-eight hours, so he closes his eyes again in glee after seeing a sign stating Houston is only sixty-five miles away.

11

It's pitch-black, and Tree is clenching Audumn's left hand in hopes of not stumbling. Waving his other hand endlessly through the air, he concentrates on the daylight that seeps through the cracks around the blindfold. After a stumble here and a stumble there, he finally finds his hand on the step rail going onto the porch of his mother's house.

"Just a few more steps, Junior, and you'll be inside," his mother said, grabbing his free hand to guide him into the door.

"Don't let me go Audumn," he said, dragging his feet across the porch while taking small steps.

"I got you, baby, I promise."

Everything seems so unreal to Tree. His mother is proud of him, his dad has turned the other cheek on the shame he's brought to the family, and Audumn is by his side, giving her all in his new outlook on life. And to think, yesterday he was surrounded by a bunch of men who could have cared less whether he lived or died. As he steps over the threshold, *God is good* crosses his mind more than once as he squeezes the love of his life's hand to make sure he isn't dreaming.

"Welcome home, Tree!" his family and friends shout at the top of their lungs as he enters. Tree's mother takes off the blindfold and greets him with a heartwarming smile, but in Tree's eyes, he feels no one has ever did anything for him, so he goes mute with hesitation for a second.

"Thanks, Momma Love, for never giving up on me" comes to his tongue after realizing that his mother has always been there for him no matter what.

Hugs are everywhere as he tries to make a path through his loved ones into the dining room so that he can finally eat some real food. Tree accepts them wholeheartedly even though it makes him feel uncomfortable because of the twenty months he has just done. Audumn sees that his family wants to give him words of encouragement, so she gives him some space so that everyone can say what they have to say to him. After a few minutes go by, he notices she has left his side and quickly finds her because even though the people in front of him are his blood relatives, Audumn and his mother are the only two people he truly calls family.

"Lovey, do you have anything to say before we say grace?" his father asks to his mother as everyone pulls their seat up to the table.

"Yes, love, I do have something to say, and thanks for asking," his mother replies, looking across the table at her husband. "Today, family, is a joyous day for me because today my beloved son has made it back home in one piece. As I look over and see my son not behind those bars, all I can say is 'Thank you, Jesus' for Luke chapter 15. For those who don't know the scriptures, it's a story about a son who went out and did his own thing in life, but realized that the way of life he was living was not the way he was raised. After being beaten up by a superficial lifestyle, the son looked to the heavens and realized the way he was raised wasn't as bad as it seemed. When the son returned home, his father told the rest of the family in verse 32, 'My son was lost but now he is found.' I love you, Torrence Wingate Jr., and welcome home."

"Would anyone like to say grace? Because if not, I will."

Audumn raises her index finger and surprises Tree. "I'll say grace, Pastor Wingate, if no one else wants to."

Audumn began to pray, and everyone gave their undivided attention. Her words showed that she is serious about church, and most of all, her words showed Tree that the Audumn sitting next to him is not the same Audumn that hustled marijuana in the streets with him before he went to the penitentiary. When she said *amen*, Tree knew in his spirit that Audumn was genuinely trying to walk straight with the Lord.

Everyone is hesitant before digging in to the meal Popeyes Louisiana Chicken has prepared for them because Audumn's blessing over the food has made Tree's family look at her in bewilderment. Pastor Wingate and Lovey are proud to see Tree has someone who loves God standing in his corner. And his sister Gayriel is overwhelmed to see how much Audumn has grown in the Lord since she invited her to her church two years ago. Two thumbs up is the gesture she gives as she smiles at her sister in Christ from across the table.

"I's show is hungry," Tree said, trying to sound like the little boy on the movie *The Color Purple*.

"Everyone can dig in," his father said, still in awe at how much Audumn has grown up since his son brought her home to meet his parents.

Tree is the guest of honor, so he gets the special treatment of being served first. As he pulls the long strip of white meat from the breast, he remembers how he wished for a piece of Popeyes Chicken while on the inside. His wish is granted as he places the tender meat in his mouth and swallows.

"Baby, I didn't know you can pray like that."

"I've learned a lot since you been gone, Tree."

"How's your mom been doing with her cancer?"

"She's cancer-free and back to her old self again," Audumn replied with excitement.

"I'm glad to hear that, and please forgive me for my selfishness during your mother's sickness," Tree said, truly sorry for his incompetence and insensitivity.

The meal hit every spot he dreamed about during his time of incarceration. Afterward, his mother told everyone to go into the living room because the family had a surprise for Tree. His father humbled himself and gave his son the master seat so he can feel at home, but before he could settle into the chair good, Momma Love handed him an envelope with a $500 gift card to Macy's inside of it. As he opened it, Audumn whispered in his ear flirtatiously that she saved the best gift for last.

Tree's family and friends gave their full support in making him feel at peace in today's society. His body language is adapting slowly, but his reactions are stiff like a robot because the rules of TDCJ still have him second-guessing his judgments. Audumn can feel his tension and rubs the back of his head. Her sweet touch loosens him up a bit and gives him the courage to mingle freely.

"It's getting late," Pastor Wingate said, looking out the window at the sunset that's fading quickly. "Sorry, but party's over, and I'd like to thank everyone for coming. My wife and I are very grateful for all you have done to help us achieve what we desired for my son's first day at home. I know my son is grateful too, and the love he's received from all of you today will not be forgotten. Good night, and drive safe home."

After saying their final good-byes, Tree showed his gratitude by shaking everybody's hand as they left. When the crowd was reduced to only his immediate family, he locked the door and gave Audumn a kiss she would never forget.

"I love you, Audumn Humphrey."

"I love you more, Torrence Wingate Jr.," she replies, staring deep into his passionate eyes.

"Okay, break it up," Momma Love said, really not wanting to interrupt them. "Junior, your father and I have decided to let you stay in the guest-house. You know how he is when it comes to following the Bible, so please respect your dad's authority. Audumn is the only company you are allowed to have back there, and it took weeks for me to open his eyes to the reality of you two. Anyone else, you must have them meet you somewhere other than here, son."

"Yes, ma'am, and thanks again for the coming-home party. I love you, Momma."

Momma Love gives Audumn a hug and Tree a peck on his cheek. Pausing to grasp her son's freedom, she tells them, "Everything you need is in the closet in the bedroom, and don't stay up too late. Junior, you know you have to meet your parole officer at eight in the morning, so, Audumn, please make sure he gets there on time."

Audumn awoke early the next morning for who she feels is her future hubby. The past is right before her as she sits up and looks at the man who stole her heart almost six years ago. *What am I going to do with you?* she thinks, pushing Tree's head for the past pain she has forgiven him for.

Pushing all the negative thoughts from her mind, she gets up and heads for the kitchen to make breakfast. The smell of pancakes, eggs, and bacon begins to travel through the guesthouse, and Audumn is over the stove in her T-shirt and panties, preparing Tree's breakfast to perfection. She knows his favorite meal of the day is the one in the morning, so the first home-cooked meal her baby is going to taste in the free world will be from her hands and her hands only. Putting down the spatula, she smiles while pondering on the two of them becoming one throughout the night.

Tree's eyes opened from the aroma rising up his nostrils down to his stomach. After looking for his better half, he realizes Audumn is the one who's causing his stomach to grumble. The smell is unbearable as he floats through the air, following his nose as if he's Toucan Sam. He kisses her on the back of the neck, and she turns around and says, "Good morning, baby" while rubbing her hands across his muscular chest. He wasn't big on working out before he went to jail, but the endless free time gave him the initiative to work on his body daily. Making the muscles in his chest jump, he brags about his physique he's worked on day in and day out.

"You like that, huh, baby?"

"You all right, baby, but you should have worked on that swollen head of yours."

"Whatever, Audumn, and don't hate me because I'm beautiful."

"Oh Lord, first you're Arnold Schwarzenegger, and now you're Keri Hilson," Audumn replied sarcastically while seductively putting his breakfast on the table. "Hurry up and eat, baby, because your parole visit is in an hour, and I want to be there early."

Cherry, which is Audumn's nickname for Tree's Cadillac, is in the garage waiting for her true master to get behind the wheel because during Tree's time away, Audumn has been driving the car and keeping the maintenance up on it.

Tree takes a seat, and before his body can feel uncomfortable from Audumn's adjustments, he presses the number 1 button on the panel of the door. The seat slides backward, and the back of it reclines until it reaches his comfort. As he watches the steering wheel tilt upward, he presses a code in the radio, and "What's up, Tree" comes from the speakers.

"Dat's my girl," he said as he taps the dash before backing out.

Driving to the parole office, he hopes to God that parole is nothing like the probation he was on before he was incarcerated. In TDCJ, offenders told him before getting out that parole is more lenient than being under the eagle's eye of probation. Also, the $18 a month versus the $120 a month probation fee is a $102 difference that already made him look at parole as something not too stressful to do.

After placing his car in park, he looks at Audumn and says, "Thank you, baby, for sticking by my side. I don't know where I'd be without you."

Tree made it to the entrance first, and before opening it for Audumn, he looks through the glass door and sees ex-offenders are lined up along the walls, and the rest are seated in the overcrowded seating area. Stepping inside, Audumn and Tree maneuver their way through the impatient men and women waiting to be seen. The clerk at the front desk slides her window back and hands Tree the log-in sheet for the day while she calls his parole officer and tells her Torrence Wingate is present and on time.

"Please have a seat, Mr. Wingate. Ms. Liberty will be out shortly to give you your orientation."

The wait is tiresome, so Tree dozed off twice, waking up periodically within the hours. Audumn took naps with one eye open so Tree wouldn't miss his name being called. Finally they got a break around 11:50 a.m., and Ms. Liberty came out and called Tree's name with six other ex-offenders.

Audumn is relieved the first steps of today's visit is in motion as she watches the wooden door close with a loud thud behind Tree.

Walking through the maze of halls, Ms. Liberty stops at a conference room and tells everyone to go in and have a seat. "How are you guys doing this morning? Or shall I say this afternoon," Ms. Liberty said, glancing at her wristwatch. "Sorry for the delay, but after today, you will not have to wait this long again. Since today is everyone's first parole visit, you will have to watch a twenty-minute video on the do's and don'ts while on parole. After watching the video, a twenty questions questionnaire will be passed out to signify you understand all the stipulations required of you. It's a very simple test, so it's no need for you to get all tensed about it. If it makes you feel any better, I've never seen anyone fail it."

Everything required of them is finished in about forty minutes, and as the ex-offenders turned in their questionnaires, Ms. Liberty saw each of them in the back of the room. A bag of condoms, a list of jobs, another check for $50, and an appointment card with their next parole date stamped on it is handed to them after being told to pay the fee of $18 at the cashier's window.

Everyone left and did what is told of them while thinking Ms. Liberty is up-front, and the only thing that could violate them are themselves.

Audumn is waiting, looking as beautiful as the first day he met her at the corner store in his neighborhood. When she saw Tree, a smile of relief cracked the corner of her lips because of how he is finally trying to change for himself. Cashing the check for $50 slipped his mind the day before, so Audumn paid the $18 fee until he cashed it. A receipt is given to them, and before he can ask what to do next, the cashier says, "See you next month."

The wind is blowing a little harder than usual today and causes the papers from the parole officer to sway endlessly in his hand. Audumn has the keys, so she quickly opens the doors and jumps behind the wheel after taking a beating to her hair.

Tree gets in the passenger seat and reclines his seat to relax. Thinking about the day, he opens the bag of condoms and pulls out a red one. "Look, baby, it's my favorite color."

Laughter drowns out the music as they both joke about having safe sex while he is on parole.

Before driving home, Audumn stops at an Ace check-cashing place so Tree can go inside and cash his two checks. Stupidity of his past actions comes to mind when Tree is handed a $100 bill from the teller. "This is crazy. A hundred dollars for twenty months of hard labor," Tree said to the cashier before walking off. Shaking his head, Tree thinks, *I've got to be crazy or just plumb dumb if I go back to the penitentiary to work for less than 20¢ a day.*

Tree asked to be dropped off at home so Audumn can go visit her best friends Kizzy from New Orleans and Diana who is Houston bred from birth. Both of them never did like Tree because of all he put Audumn through over the years, but no matter what, Audumn always stood up for him when they talked down on her man. "I'll be back later, baby, and don't look so down because we're going to get through this together."

Sitting on the foot of the bed, he looks at the list of jobs and sees a few gigs that he wouldn't mind working. The pay rate doesn't add up to the corners of Northborough, but at least it's not 20¢ a day.

After placing the list on the nightstand, Tree kicks his shoes off and lies down, staring at the ceiling. Silence surrounds him as he picks up the list of jobs to scan over them for a second time.

As he meditates on tomorrow, the conversation he had with Old School before getting out of prison sounds in his ears as if he is still underneath him. His words of wisdom about the dope game won't stop playing in his head, so he reaches for the phone and begins to call the numbers on the list.

"Hello, my name is Torrence Wingate, and I'm seeking employment," Tree said, grabbing a notepad to take down the first job's information. When hearing the skills needed for employment, reality sinks in, and he realizes his fast-money days are over.

12

Today was the first argument for the 2011 Romeo and Juliet. Tomorrow will make two weeks since Tree has been released, and work is something he has not yet found. The frustration from being turned down for his felony is starting to get under his skin, so he decides to scratch it by yelling at Audumn.

"Baby, I'm back, are you ready for church?" Audumn asks as she enters the guesthouse from her early morning drive from Beaumont. Tree is already up when she gets there, thinking about all the cash he made each time he used to pass go in the dope the game. Ignoring her voice, he rolls over because she's the one who has been upholding him during his financial crisis, and dependency is not something he's used to.

"Baby, what's wrong, and why aren't you dressed for church?"

"Church? Why should I go to church? God doesn't do anything for me unless someone else prays for it!" Tree exclaims angrily. "He wasn't there for me my last six months in the penitentiary, and he's damn sho not here for me now. I mean, look at me!" Tree shouts as he stands to pull out the inside of his pockets of his pajamas.

"What are you talking about, baby? God loves you. I know times are hard for you right now, but I'm pretty sure everybody you left back on the Wells Unit is praying for one day in your shoes beyond those gates."

"Yeah, that's easy for you to say because you have a job at your fancy clothing store in Beaumont, Texas. Maybe if you were here in Houston, I'd probably be working by now and not catching the city bus all over H-Town for nothing. I bet you enjoy driving my car and me asking you for money, huh?"

"Baby, please don't spoil this beautiful Sunday morning. I've been gone all week, and during that week, all I did was think about you. It's summertime, and I could have taken extra classes to get ahead on my veterinarian degree, but I didn't because if you're not right, then I'm not right. Please, baby, let's talk about this after church."

"This is not over with, Audumn. I'll go, but only because everyone seems to be on my case about not going."

Dressed and groomed, Tree rides to church staring out the window, giving Audumn the cold shoulder because nothing has been going according to his plans. Pressed for cash, he starts to allow negativity back inside his brain by thinking about all the things he used to have in the past. The thoughts he is having he can't seem to shake, so he turns and confides in Audumn.

"Audumn, I think my empty pockets are making my mind drift in the wrong direction."

"Baby, I understand what you going through, but everyone who gets out of jail has it hard at first. While you were in there, I did some research on ex-offenders, and mostly all of them went through what you're going through. Some of them made it, and some of them didn't, but they all agreed that their struggles made them a better person at the end of the day. Those thoughts you're having is only the devil trying to dismay you from what he knows you're about to become. I'm not perfect, but what I do know is that I wouldn't have come this far if it wasn't for Jesus, my Lord and Savior. You've tried everything else on your own since you got out, so it won't hurt if you try Christ. Trust me, baby, you know in your heart I would never tell you anything wrong."

Audumn's last words ended as soon as she placed the car in park in the grass on the back of the parking lot. Tree got out feeling a little better, but it still didn't shake the fact that he is broke. As they closed the doors, a parking lot director pulled up in a golf cart and asked if they needed a ride to the entrance of the church. Their lateness is what caused them to have to park in any of the open spaces that were still available.

"Welcome to Let It Shine," a greeter said, handing the two of them a program. "Hey, you look familiar. Do I know you, or have I met you somewhere before?"

"Probably not, but I used to come here back when my dad became senior pastor."

"That's right, you're Pastor Wingate's son, Torrence Wingate Jr.," the greeter said with words of expression. "Praise God, and look at you! I haven't seen you in about four years. Your father said you'd be coming here soon."

"He did?"

"Yes, at least once a month for the past two years."

"It's nice to meet you," Tree replies, shaking the greeter's hand while feeling ashamed for being absent from his dad's church for so long.

"Enjoy the service, Torrence, and don't be so much of a stranger next time. Coming to church isn't going to hurt you in any kind of way."

Hand in hand, the two of them walk toward the male usher standing in the only open door to the sanctuary. A heartfelt smile is given to them as he directs them to the ushers working the floor. Following directions, Tree trails behind Audumn in awe on how much his dad's church has grown over the years. The nosebleed section is the only section with seats available, so Audumn and Tree have to climb to the top. When they got halfway up the steps, Tree looks over and sees a guy who he used to sell crack to. His eyes become wide-open as he slightly stumbles because the guy he is looking at has changed dramatically. *Rosco?*

"Are you okay, baby?" Audumn asks.

"I'm straight, bay. Why do you ask?"

"Well, for one, your palms are sweating like crazy, and two, you seem a little nervous."

"I'm good, Audumn, just thought I saw someone I knew."

Sitting back, Tree tries to find his mother in the congregation but can't because it's like searching for a needle in a haystack. People are everywhere listening to the praise team, waiting to receive the word in which God has given Pastor Wingate to deliver unto them. The last song begins to come to an end, and an uproar of worship nearly shakes the building.

Audumn stands and joins in screaming, "Jesus!" repeatedly with the rest of the church, but Tree stays seated, thinking about how all the old women in the church used to catch the Holy Ghost when he was a kid.

Pastor Wingate steps onto the platform and walks over to the podium in tears because the Spirit has touched him due to the love Let It Shine has for Jesus Christ. "Let all things be done in decency and in order" (1 Cor. 14:40 NIV) is a scripture Pastor Wingate truly upholds, so he motions with his hand to speak after looking at the time. Adjusting the microphone, he tries to contain what's inside of him, but can't and yells, "Let it shine, church! Let it shine!"

Loud claps, stomps, and hallelujahs travel from Pastor Wingate to the first row of people up to Audumn and Tree as if it's a ripple effect. This morning the church is on fire for the Lord with an unquenchable flame, and everyone can feel His presence in the midst of them as they fulfill the scripture in God's first Gospel in the New Testament. Matthew 18:20 in the NIV bible says, "For where two or three are gathered together in my name, I am there in the midst of them."

Slowly, the noise level came down enough for Pastor Wingate to begin his message. "Good morning, Let It Shine, and praise the Lord for the love we have for Jesus Christ." Pausing, Pastor Wingate grasps the spiritual high he is on and allows God's words to flow from his tongue. "Please bow your heads so we can pray before the word of God is brought forth."

The congregation bows their heads, and Pastor says, "Thank you, Jesus, for being who you are. Amen."

Amens comes from every pew in unison before he goes on to begin his sermon.

"Faith! Everything we do in Christ Jesus is done in faith. We believe Jesus is real in faith. We accept him into our lives in faith. As we sit here today in God's house, we sit here in faith. Faith that Jesus has risen from the dead on Sunday, the first day of the week, and so doing that we honor him by gathering in his name on that same day in faith. Amen."

An usher brings the pastor a glass of water when seeing the opportunity. "Today, Let It Shine, we are going to talk about a passage of faith. Please turn your bibles to the book of Daniel 3:1."

As the pages turned, Pastor Wingate spoke briefly on what his sermon is going to be about. "Shad'rach, Me'shach, and Abed'-Nego'," he said as he watches the congregation nod their heads as if to say they've heard the story before. "The scripture reads, 'Nebuchadnez'zar the king made an image of gold, whose height was sixty cubits. He set it up in the plain of Dura, within the province of Babylon.' If you may, please go down to verses 4–6. 'Then a herald cried aloud: "To you it is commanded, O people; nations, and languages, that at the time you hear the sound of the horn with all kinds of music you shall fall down and worship the golden image. And whoever does not fall down and worship shall be cast into the burning fiery furnace."'"

Everyone listened to the legendary story of Shad'rach, Me'shach, and Abed'-Nego.' Pastor Wingate spoke from the wisdom of God as he revealed the faith of the mighty men's steadfastness in not bowing to the king's idol. Men and women throughout the structure begin to examine themselves when hearing how these great men were willing to die for their beliefs than bow down to a golden image.

"Let It Shine, the Bible says we must walk by faith and not by sight [2 Cor. 5:7]!" Pastor Wingate shouts while pounding his hand on the podium. Going on, he continues in preaching today's text. "These men of God had so much faith in their King that they believed their Lord could do anything and everything possible. Including saving them from the fiery furnace."

Tree thought about how he turned his back on God when he was set up in TDCJ by Blake and thrown into Ag-Seg for something he didn't do. That day, he wavered in his faith in God and took matters into his own hands. Glued to his seat, he feels his dad has chosen this sermon because he knew his son is in the audience.

"Daniel 3:24 and 25 says, 'then Nebuchadn'nezar was astonished after giving the order for the three men to be thrown into the fire for their disobedience. When Nebucadn'nezar looked, he saw four men and not three.' The miracle led him to say, 'The fourth man had the form of the Son of God.' Jesus said in the New Testament, 'If you have faith the size of a tiny mustard seed, you will say to the mountain, move from here to there and it will move' [Matt. 17:20]. These mighty men of God of the Old Testament had so much faith in the Father, they moved more than a mountain, the king said. What they moved was Jesus. Are we allowing Jesus to move in our life today, people, through faith because, church, it's time to stand up and stop playing with our Lord and Savior. Tonight, Let It Shine, I want you to meditate on today's message and ask yourself, 'Do I have the faith the size of a tiny mustard seed to move a mountain, or do I have the faith of these mighty men of God to move Jesus?' I pray something was said here today to give you insight on who you are in Christ, and with that in mind, I leave you with Luke 9:62: 'No one, having put his hand to the plow, and looking back, is fit for the kingdom of Heaven.' Shad'rach, Me'schach, and Abed'-Nego' didn't look back on their decision to obey the Father and persevered bringing glory to the one and only true King. Where is your faith, Let It Shine? Where is your faith?"

Tears began to fall from Audumn's eyes as she reflected on the sermon Pastor Pender preached at Fallbrook on "Where is your seed?" two and half years ago when she first heard and understood the word of God. On that day, the seed of the Holy Spirit was planted inside her heart, and since then, her whole demeanor on life has changed because she started to look to Jesus for the answers.

Tree's mom appeared out of nowhere from the audience because the Spirit of the Lord is upon his father, and Pastor Wingate's love for God has caused him to become mute. Stepping onto the stage, Momma Love joins her husband to assist him in closing the service. All the guests are asked to stand so that they can receive a proper welcome and a gift basket. Those who desired to join church, refurbish their relationship with Christ, or give their life to the Lord were asked to get with any of the staff in front of the altar. After the benediction, more than half the crowd exited, pondering on the message and praying for God to add to their measure of faith.

"Tree, is that you?" the guy who he noticed earlier on the way up to his seat said.

Tree looks the guy over and shakes the thought that this well-groomed man standing before him is the guy who would spend his newborn baby's milk money for a ten-minute crack high. "How do you know my name?"

"Tree, it's me, Rosco from Chicago."

"Rosco! I thought that was you when I was trying to find a seat! Boy, you look brand-new compared to what you used to be."

"God is good, Tree. One day I decided that enough was enough, and I came to church beat up from what the world calls life. I remember I was asleep at the entrance of this church one Sunday morning, and Pastor Wingate let me take a shower in the gym and gave me some clean clothes out of the donation box. On that day, I heard a word from God that I'll never forget. It was called the Beatitudes, and the first scripture the pastor read from the Beatitudes said, 'Blessed are the poor in spirit, for theirs is the kingdom of heaven' [Matt. 5]." Rosco pauses and looks up, thinking about how far he's come in the past three years.

"Rosco, I don't know what you've been doing over the years, but keep doing it because you look great."

"What I've been doing is Jesus Christ, and once you take a hit of him, there's no other substance that can replace that feeling."

"That's what's up, and I'm proud of you. By the way, Pastor Wingate that preached and helped you that day is my father," Tree said proudly, happy to see how much of a blessing his dad is being in the community.

"Word! Well, praise God for your father. When did you get out, and what have you've been doing these days?"

"I got out two weeks ago, and it's been hard to find some honest work. If it wasn't for this beautiful lady standing beside me, I'd be back in the streets of Northborough doing what I know how to do best."

"I can get you a job with me at the Port of Houston. I'm a foreman out there, and I get ex-offenders jobs all the time. I look at it as a ministry of giving back so that others can someday do the same. It's a temporary job, but it pays well enough to get you by until you find something steady."

Audumn is ecstatic when hearing Tree's old buddy can help him get a job. She's ecstatic because she listened to her Spirit and brought him to church this morning.

"Thanks, Mr. Rosco. You don't know what this means to us."

"Please, miss, you can call me Mr. Stevenson or just plain old Rosco. Here's my number, Tree. Call me in the morning before five, and I'll give you the directions so you can start tomorrow. God bless you, and your dad is awesome."

"Thanks again, Rosco," Audumn and Tree said at the same time as they waved good-bye. The church became scarce as they stood and waited for his parents to come out of the pastor's study. The stillness of the sanctuary starts to set in, and the only thing they can hear is a door or two closing every now and then.

With her hand clenched in his, Tree meditates on how today is truly a blessing for him because God works in mysterious ways sometimes. No one, including him, would have thought that a crackhead would change his life and help him in the long run. As he replays Rosco's testimony in his hard head of his, he realizes Rosco had something he didn't have. What he had is a smile of peace and a smile of joy. What he had is Jesus Christ.

13

The sun is hot and the wind is not answering anyone's prayer for a cool breeze. Workers are everywhere, but only a few can be seen because the rest are hiding from the heat. Rosco came through on his word to get him a job at the Port of Houston a month ago, so Tree's complaints of being jobless are replaced with body pains, headaches, and heat rashes between his thighs.

It's twenty minutes until lunchtime, and he feels like he's about to pass out. Waves of heat rose from the steel tracks as sweat ran from his hard hat down to the tip of his nose. After strapping the military Hummer down to the train transporting it, Tree tells himself lunch is going to come early today.

No one is looking when he jumps down and stashes his Crescent wrench in the rocks underneath his workplace after seeing the coast is clear. The closest shade to pacifying today's daylight torture is a cargo cart, so he decides to hide in it until he hears Rosco's whistle for lunch. The only thing is, three men have beaten him to the punch and are already inside the portable cave, fleeing this year's record-breaking 102 degrees' heat.

"Sorry, player, but this cart is taken!"

"Man, I'm not trying to hear that shit today, homeboy. I feel you but I feel this heat a lot more." Tree jumps inside the cargo door quickly.

"Hold up, I know that bullheaded voice anywhere," a second voice said from the shadows. "Torrence Wingate Jr., a.k.a. Tree."

"Huh? Boy, you must know me real well to be blurting out what's on my birth certificate."

JU appeared from the dark corner as if he is Chris Angel performing a Las Vegas magic trick. One minute he wasn't there, and the next minute he is. JU didn't know what to expect from his jailhouse friend when he walks over and apologizes for the deal he'd made with Blake before he left the Wells Unit.

After Tree remembers the emotional pain of not knowing if he was going home or not, he pushes JU up off him and punches him in the face.

"I can't believe you played with my life like that! I trusted you, and you betrayed that trust by making me Blake's bitch. And to think, I had your back as if it was my own ass, but too bad you can't say the same, Texas City."

"Okay, okay, I deserved that," JU said, wiping the blood from his bottom lip while waving his other hand to keep Tree from finishing what he started. "But I had to do it, Tree, because Blake had a price on your head from the time you were processed into the Wells Unit. I'm sorry, Tree, but I rather see you alive doing a life sentence then shanked in a bathroom stall lifeless. If I had to do it again, I would because your life is worth too much to be dead over not saying excuse me."

Tree walks over and stands over JU with his fists balled up so tight that his fingers are causing his palms to change colors. "I don't care what you say, JU, because you and I both know you were wrong. I'm a grown man, and I can handle my own, and whenever I die, I'm going to die like man. And as long as I have breath in my lungs, I'm going to live like a man. You got that, Texas City! You're lucky I'm at work, or I would have whipped your ass like you stole something."

"I feel that, Northborough," JU replied as he is helped to his feet from a guy he was chilling with in the corner.

The cargo cart is divided in two because the Wells Unit reunion between JU and Tree was enough for all four guys. With conversation completely out of the way, all they can hear is the sound of the wind circulating throughout the cart as they waited patiently for the whistle to blow.

Lunchtime came, and everyone hiding made it to the tree safe without being caught in their secret game of hide-and-seek. Some of the men rested in the grass, and some turned over buckets and crates for chairs. Sandwich baggies fell to the ground as paper bags missed the trash barrel in the garbage can basketball game they were playing.

After everyone had eaten, JU walks over and sits next to Tree at the far end of the lunch area. "So what's been up with you since you touched ground, big homey?"

"Ain't nothing been up, partner! What, you think I'm friendly or something?" Tree asks with fire in his eyes.

"Hell naw'll, I don't think you friendly because you and I both know you're definitely not that."

"Then why, JU?" Tree asks, feeling disgusted that he trusted him as his friend.

"I know Blake, and I promise he would have did you in. I know because he wanted me to do it for him. That's until I told him you would take my place when I left."

"Damn, homey, he really was trying to put me to sleep over nothing, huh?"

"Yep, and was serious about it too."

"Well, I'm not gon' say thank you for setting me up with the police, but if it was what you say it was, I feel where you were coming from," Tree said as they grabbed hands to help each other up.

"Once again, I'm sorry, Tree, and thanks for understanding."

Getting back to work is easier said than done because almost everyone besides the foremen is moving sluggishly from the forty-five-minute lunch they took. For the past month, Tree has worked by himself and has trusted no one to partner up with, but going back on his words, he allows JU to partner up with him while they worked the remaining hours.

The day went on, and the two of them talked about old times in cell 16. They both laughed as they remembered all they had seen and encountered on the Wells Unit.

From the time they returned from lunch, the two of them did nothing but talk, play, and act like they were doing some work. Layoffs for the month are today, and work is declining by the day. Rosco's assistant noticed the two of them standing around with their hands in their pockets and decided to let Rosco know about it.

A loud horn blares over the Port of Houston, and everyone from all trades began to make their way toward the exits. Everyone in Tree's group knows that today may be their last day, so Rosco tells them not to leave until checks and layoff slips are handed out. The mixed culture of men he works with are tired as they stand in a line outside of his office, going in one by one to retrieve their checks. A few men came out with a clearance to come back the following week, but the majority of the crew came out with sad faces.

Tree is next in line, so he turns to JU and tells him that they have nothing to worry about because he is cool with the head foreman.

"What's up, boss?" Tree asks sarcastically as he closes the door behind himself.

"Tree, I'm sorry, but work here is coming to an end shortly, and I'm afraid I'm going to have to let you go."

"Let me go! What do you mean you're letting me go?" Tree yells in fury.

"Calm down, son, because this is not the end of the world. When something comes back up out here, I promise to give you the heads-up on it first."

"That's cool, Rosco, but why can't I finish this job with you?"

"You can't because for the past two weeks, you've been hiding in cargo carts throughout the yard, and I've been taking up for you with my foremen underneath me."

Tree is flabbergasted to all that is happening to him and steps backward, bumping his back against the door. "Rosco, give me another chance. This job is all I got."

"I can't go over my assistant's head anymore because supervising the yard is what I pay them for."

"What you really mean is that you can, but you won't!"

Rosco walks over and places his hands on each one of Tree's shoulders while looking him in the eyes. "Son, I promise that the next job I'm running, you'll be the first to know about it. Take this time off to get your mind set for working a full eight hours on the next job God blesses you with instead of playing and hiding for the majority of the day. Honestly, Torrence, did I lie to you before?" Rosco asks, handing him his last check and a layoff slip.

Tree walked down the steps and left the door wide-open. His face is gloomy as he walks past the rest of the guys in line with his head down because he knows he's always trying to take the easy way out. After crossing the last set of train tracks in his steel-toe boots, he opens the gate, disenchanted for always allowing his old ways to get himself into trouble. A bus stop is across the street, so he decides to ride it instead of calling his mother. Flopping down onto the curb, memories of the day he lost his job at the supermarket for stealing a pack of gum and turned to the streets for stability began to replay in his mind like it happened yesterday.

"What's up, homey? You need a ride or what?" JU pulls up to the curb of the bus stop.

Tree is sitting, staring at his last check for $685, when JU's horn jolts him from his shame and disappointment. "My bad, JU. I don't know what came over me."

"What came over you is that boot we both just got for horseplaying on the job today."

"Rosco laid you off too?"

"Man, screw this working bullshit, Tree! I've been out almost six months, and every job I've worked on has laid me off. If it wasn't for my block, I'd probably be sitting at that bus stop next to you looking stupid," JU exclaims, tapping the outside of the driver's door of his pearl-white Navigator. "Hop in, man, and let's roll up out of here."

The passenger door slammed hard when he jumped inside, but JU knew Tree is angry, so he let the door slamming slide this time and puts an uncensored video in his touch screen Blu-ray player. The leather seats, sunroof, music, and wood running through the dashboard gave Tree a high he hasn't been on in a long time. He made good money working at the Port of Houston, but there's no money like dope money in his book.

"Damn, Texas City, when did you get this 'Gator?"

"Last week for about five bands on the southwest side of Houston."

"Man, $5,000 ain't bad for this mothership." Tree looks around the inside, missing the days when he had money to play around with.

The two of them drove through the streets of Houston, hitting all the spots they both knew women were going to be at during Friday evening's happy hours. No introduction is needed because JU's chrome twenty-four-inch rims did enough talking for the both of them. Six thirty is on the digital clock on the dash, so Tree tells his friend he needs to cash his check on the north side by 7:00 p.m.

"I got you, homey. Ms. Pearl will get you there on time," JU said, rubbing the wood-grain steering wheel of the mother ship.

Standing in line at the corner store, Tree looks at the time and sees it's 6:50 p.m. *Damn, that boy can drive,* he thinks. The check in his hand causes his layoff slip to reenter his mind, and he wonders what he is going to do next for income. Working at the Port of Houston was convenient for Audumn and him because a bus stopped was in front of it, and his mother didn't have to go too much out of her way to pick him up from work.

After cashing his last check, he counts out today's pay and puts the money in his wallet. *Thank you, Lord, for the job you blessed me with and the jobs to come,* he prays while he is leaving the neighborhood corner store.

"So what you getting into tomorrow, Northborough? I mean, it ain't like you got a job or something," JU said jokingly.

Tree cracks a smile and answers, "Just chillaxing, I guess."

"If you want, you can roll with me tomorrow."

"Nah, I'm good, JU, because tomorrow I'm going to relax and make some phone calls so I can find another gig before my mom starts tripping about me not working."

"Well, you got my number, so hit me up whenever you're ready," JU replies as he drives down the driveway to the guesthouse.

Tree hops out and thanks his old celly for the ride home. He is about to go inside until the sun gleamed off the chrome grill of the Navigator in his eyes, making him stand still like a deer caught in the headlights. *I got to step my game up, or I'm gonna be in last place,* he thought before turning around to go inside.

Pacing throughout the guesthouse, he can't stop moving because being still makes him think about his earlier conversation with Rosco. All his options are right before him, and the only ones that's seem beneficial for his current dilemmas are the wrong ones. Nothing seems to be going his way today, so he entertains himself by thinking about JU's decked-out Navigator.

The phone rings as he is fantasizing about counting wrinkled hundred dollar bills from his shoebox stash he had in the attic back in the day. Standing in the middle of the floor, the phone rings again, and he realizes that he really needs to get himself together before he gets a one-way ticket back to the state penitentiary.

As he took it off the receiver, he looks at the caller ID and doesn't recognize the number. "Hello," he said to the sound of a click from answering too late.

Pausing before calling the number back, Tree notices the number's area code is 409 and presses Talk in haste because Beaumont's area code is 409, and it might be Audumn. The number rung and rung until Tree's patience for holding the phone to his ear ceased. Right before his index finger is about to press end, a familiar voice came from the other end of the line.

"What's up with you, Mr. Tree? Did you miss me?"

"Blake?" Tree asks hesitantly, pondering on how Blake seems to always cross his path. "Blake, is that you?"

"Shhh, before someone hears you say my name," Blake replies, hinting that his phone may be tapped.

"When did you get out?"

"Yesterday, and I'm ready to get back to work with a new crew I can trust."

"When did you move to Beaumont?" Tree asks, thinking about the area code.

Blake chuckles because this is a business call, and Tree is asking too many unnecessary questions. "We have all day for you to play Inspector Gadget, but we need to talk in person about some things I got planned to expand my family business. Tomorrow I want you to meet me on Galveston Beach at the Seahorse Inn in room 222 at one thirty. I know I owe you $1,300, but since I'm in a good mood today, I'll go ahead and shoot you $2,500 for keeping your mouth shut while we were on lock. You did good up in there, Northborough, and I need *locos* like you to take my empire to the next level."

Tree listened to Blake's Hispanic accent and remembered the power he had on the Wells Unit. Blake did what he wanted, when he wanted, and to whom he wanted to do it to. No one tested his authority out of fear of what he could do to you from simply sitting in his cell. Inmates and guards gave anyone Blake associated with a pass because none of them wanted to be responsible for his money coming up short. Even to this day, Tree is still awestruck on how the inmates and officers respected him because of Blake, so he agrees to meet him at the set time.

"I don't know about the business end of the meeting, *vato*, but I will meet you to pick up that money you owe me. Hopefully that change you got for me will get me by until I find another job."

Blake laughed at his response but didn't take any offense to Tree's rejection. "Money is the root of all evil" is his favorite scripture in the Bible, so he tells Tree the offer will always be on the table because of his ability to keep his mouth shut. "If you need anything, Northborough, don't hesitate to call me. It's only a few people in the world that can say I've told them that, so please feel privileged to hear it."

Sweat ran down Tree's armpits as he hung up the phone because it's every hustler's dream to be plugged in with a drug lord, and here he is turning one down to fly straight. Once again, the devil has presented himself to him at his weakest moment, but this time he recognizes it, and yet he is still unsure if he can continue resisting temptation to prevent his own self-destruction. The grass he is eating is green, but the grass on Blake's side of the fence is looking a lot greener. Concentrating on longevity, he thinks about his family, but when he concentrates on the present, he thinks about his pockets.

Sitting in the recliner, he kicks his feet up and prays to God for an answer. After waiting for a voice to speak to him miraculously from the sky, he hears nothing but *chi-ching* chiming in his ears. As he closes his eyes again, he forgets about today's layoff and takes himself to a faraway land where girls are everywhere, willing to do whatever he desires for money. The limelight shines on him from out of nowhere, so Tree digs in his pockets and makes it rain one hundred dollar bills all over the women while screaming, "Money's not a thing!"

He is still dreaming when two angels came and sat on each side of his shoulders. The angel of death is to his left, and the angel of light is to his right. As he looks around at everything pleasing to the eye, Tree shakes the angel of death off his shoulder and wakes up. *Lord, help me,* he thinks as he lies in a pool of sweat, but in his heart, he had already made his decision.

14

Audumn is at Tree's house bright and early Saturday morning. To tell you the truth, Tree called her every hour on the hour Friday to make sure his point was clear about her coming. As the morning dragged on, he went left when Audumn went right. He didn't have the courage to tell her he'd lost his job because he didn't want her to feel sorry for him. Shutting himself off to the world, he avoids her questions on why was it so important for her to come so early in the morning.

The time of 12:00 p.m. came, and the shadows in every corner of the guesthouse have shifted due to the sun ascending on its axis throughout the sky. Audumn is taking a nap from her drive during the night, so Tree takes the keys to his car quietly, hoping she doesn't wake up. His mind is made up on what he wants to do, but his secrecy lets him know his mind is not operating correctly. All he knew is that the cards in his life have changed dramatically, and since he's not a poker player, he doesn't know if he's won or not. Oblivious to what he plans on accomplishing by meeting Blake, he looks at the sweet beauty of Audumn resting before locking the door.

Tree backs out the driveway and knows there's no turning back when he puts the gearshift in drive. As he accelerated onto I-45 South, he looks at himself in the rearview mirror and presses the gas pedal to the floor while merging far left across the lanes. Adrenaline causes his heart to beat rapidly, and for once he feels like he's in control of his destiny and not his dad, mom, or Audumn. *This is my life, and I'm tired of everybody telling me how to live it,* he thinks as he passes a sign that read he had forty-five miles to Galveston.

Traffic is backed up from Houston's city limits to Galveston's city limits this afternoon. The speed limit is 75 mph, but all the vehicles are poking along at 30 mph because of the sunny summer weather. Galveston Beach is a great tourist attraction, so everyone and their mommas decided that today is a great day to go for a swim. Finally, the traffic picked up to 50 mph in La

Marque, and Tree floors the gas pedal, crossing over the lanes, doing some of his best driving.

Police are in all their hiding places governing the expressway today. Some were under trees along the feeder roads, some were under overpasses, and a couple of them were in unmarked cars communicating with the local police on which cars were breaking the Texas highway laws. Tree is not a rookie behind the steering wheel, so he knows what areas to slow down in to stay off the cops' hidden radars.

The sign "¾ miles to Seawall Blvd" is going over the roof of his car, so he slows down to get in the correct lane to exit. As his speed declined going down the exit ramp, he notices officers are at the light, directing all vehicles down the Seawall at its appropriate time. A click from the buckling of his seat belt sounds lightly through the car because the power on his radio is off until he makes it past the police up ahead. Coming to a complete stop, he makes a left turn under I-45, headed toward the Seahorse Inn after being pointed at by the traffic cop and waved to go.

The shape of a seahorse grows bigger and bigger as his eyes spelled out the letters of Seahorse Inn over the gigantic object. After looking into his sideview mirrors for eyes that may have been trailing him, he sees nothing but people enjoying their Saturday at the beach.

It's exactly 1:28 p.m., and his back becomes moist as he stares at the numbers 222 on the faded green door. Tree knows that the man behind the door in front of him could change his life's circumstances for the better if he agreed to the terms Blake desired of him. But his plan is to get the money owed to him and be on I-45 North before he can think about the lifestyle he could've had if he'd said yes to the drug lord's offer.

A solid knock is the code, so Blake opens the door as soon as he hears it, but Tree stands in the doorway for almost a minute. "So are you coming in or what, because I don't got all day, homeboy."

Tree looks down at the door ledge and then takes his first step over the threshold into his new fate. As the door closed behind him, Blake told his old employee to take a seat after shaking his hand.

A dining room table is in the corner, so Tree pulls a seat from underneath it with a look of uncertainty on his face when Blake opens the second drawer to a dresser. Thirty crisp hundred dollar bills are in his hands when he turns around and begins counting each one of them out on top of the table in front of him. Blake tells Tree, "$2,500 is what I owe you, and $500 is for the drive down here."

Benjamin Franklin's face reflects off his eyes as Tree uses his inner calculator to add up what he can't believe is true. "Is this for real, Blake, or are you playing with me because I told you I'm having a hard time right now?"

"Stop insulting me, loco. I always pay my dues."

"Thanks, Blake, because Lord knows I need everything right now."

Blake excuses himself and goes into the bathroom. When he reenters the room, he places two kilos of 85 percent pure cocaine right before Tree.

Tree's eyes become wide-open as he looks at the most cocaine he's ever seen at one time.

"I want $33,000 for the both of them, which is $16,500 apiece. Whenever you're finished with those, I'll front you two more. Now if you want to continue doing business this way, I don't mind, but if you want to buy some coke for yourself, I'll sell you the kilos for $14,500 apiece. I like you, Tree, and if you want to walk away from this business deal, now's the time," Blake said, pointing at the door.

Tree heard everything Blake said except for his last statement about leaving the Seahorse Inn. With his eyes glued to the powdery substance on the table in front him, he remains quiet and lets Blake finish talking.

"I guess you are accepting my job offer then," Blake replies to Tree's body language of not leaving. "You know how I am when it comes to my money, so don't play with me, homeboy. Here's a beeper, and no one is to have that number but me. When it beeps, you call."

Tree sits and listens to Blake's employment requirements while thinking about how it's about to go down as soon as he sets foot on the streets of Northborough.

"$33,000 is a lot of money, loco. Do you think you can handle it?" Blake asks with a cutthroat look in his eyes.

"I can handle whatever. You just be ready to count up all the money we are about to make."

"Now that's what I want to hear, Mr. Tree. Call me when you're ready to take care of more business."

It's a quarter till 3:00 p.m., and the sun is at its peak when Blake's meeting is adjourned. When he exits, Tree looks left and then right as the vast shadows of the oversized seahorse gives him cover to open his car door. He tosses the backpack of narcotics onto the passenger seat and takes a deep breath before driving off onto the open road. And to think, in ten days he would have been out of jail for two months, and here he is back in the dope game. The young cats called the game Paper Chasers in the joint, but the old schools just love to refer to it as the Revolving Door.

The drive back home is very cautious because he did everything the law required from the time he turned on to the Seawall Boulevard until the time he made it into his driveway safe at home. After resting his nerves for a few minutes, he chuckles in unbelief because he realizes he now has one foot in the free world and one foot inside the Texas state penitentiary.

As he sits there, he also thinks about his new occupation and remembers how he hustled hard for Blake while on lock. Everything added up too easily, and he comes to understand that Blake was recruiting soldiers for his underground business while doing his bid for manufacturing of a controlled substance. Not snitching on Blake was the application, hustling for him in prison was the interview, and today was the orientation so Tree can get started on his new career.

A tap on the window causes him to feel frantic because of the illegal passenger he has next to him. Pushing the backpack to the floor, he rolls down his window nervously.

"Hey, baby. Where have you been all day?"

"No-nowhere," Tree stammers, still trying to regain his composure from being caught off guard.

"Nowhere? It's a quarter till five, and I haven't seen you since I fell asleep. I tried calling you, but you left your phone on the charger. I'm not trying to be in your business, but that tells me you left here kind of quickly."

Patting his pockets, he feels that his phone is not on his person. "Sorry, baby, I must have forgotten it."

"Yeah, I bet you forgot it," Audumn said in a way to let him know she knows when he's lying. "Baby, whatever you're doing, it better not be nothing stupid because I don't have time to be driving back and forth to those prisons in the middle of nowhere again."

"Baby, it ain't even like that. I got everything under control this time, promise."

"Whatever, Tree, I'm not crazy. You forget, I know you like the back of my hand. You're lucky I got to meet my friends Kizzy and Diana at the hair store on Veterans Memorial, or I'll be asking you what you got in that backpack you pushed to the floor when I walked up."

Audumn raced in the house to get her purse and keys while Tree hurried inside the guesthouse through the side door from the driveway. He quickly stuffs the backpack underneath the bed before he rushes back outside to talk to Audumn, only to see her backing out in anger. He knows that he's hurt her by lying to her, so he hurries back inside and gets his phone to call her, but before he can dial the number, the phone chirps from a text message in the inbox.

"Baby, I trust you with all my heart, so please don't ever lie to me again. Ttyl. Love You! Audumn."

The text message caused a sharp dagger of guilt to pierce his heart, and before he knew it, he is sitting in a chair holding his chest. As he sits there, his heart begins to shrink, and he feels like Fred Sanford about to have the big one because he vowed before getting out of jail that he is going to always keep it real with Audumn this time around. Finally, his love for her gave him the initiative to tell her the truth when she got back. *At least the half truth*, he thought.

Tree dozed off shortly after his heartache and awakens to Audumn, Kizzy, and Diana coming through the door. The guesthouse is dark because not one light was left on before his nap, so he has to squint to get his full eyesight back while trying to figure out what time is it. He sits up when the light switch is turned on and sees Kizzy and Diana dressed to impress for the night.

"What's up, bay? Where are you beautiful ladies going tonight?"

Kizzy and Diana paused when hearing the compliment because they both know Tree doesn't like them at all. Diana is in shock and thinks he is up to no good, so she steps outside to look at the address on the door to make sure that she isn't dreaming.

"Audumn, what's wrong with your hasbend? I mean husband," Diana said jokingly but with a straight face.

"Diana, please don't start. It's been a long day, and I don't need you two fighting with my man. I'm only here on the weekends for the summer, and I want to enjoy it with the people I love before school starts in August. Besides, ya'll gon' have to get along when we get married anyway." Audumn thinks about the day she would walk down the aisle to take Tree's hand.

"Honey, I'ma have to see it to believe it."

"You can say that again, Kizzy." Diana gives Kizzy a high five.

"When are you girls going to realize that I love Tree and Tree loves me?"

"Love, we both know you have for each other, yeah. The problem is the pain that comes with that love," Kizzy said in her New Orleans accent while giving Tree a beady eye.

Standing to his feet, Tree towers over Kizzy and Audumn while stretching his long arms. Diana has on heels, so he's able to look her in the eye because of her height. With a devious smirk on his face from ear to ear, he says, "Thanks for being a hater, Diana, because without you, there would be no me. Don't hate the player when you need to be hating the game."

Audumn disregarded his comment about being a player because Diana had it coming to her. Following Tree into the room, she goes into the closet and takes out one of her sexiest outfits for her night out on the town. Tree tries to lie back down, but before he can get comfortable, she asked him to go to D-1 Sports Bar with her on Kykendaul.

"Baby, can you go to D-1 with me and my girls?" Audumn undresses to take a shower.

"I don't know, baby, because I got some business to take care of tonight."

"Well, I'm so sorry that your business is going to have to wait. Unless you want to tell me what was in that backpack earlier, I suggest you find something to wear before we have to pay to park at the club."

Going to the sports bar seemed a lot easier for him than explaining two kilos of cocaine underneath the bed. Sliding the closet door back, he grabs an outfit he hasn't worn from the cleaners yet.

"Uh-uh, that was too easy," Audumn said, watching his every move. "Tomorrow after church, we're definitely going to have a long talk."

Cars are lined up along the streets around D-1 while tow trucks circled, waiting for the right time to snatch the cars that were parked in tow-away zones. Parking spaces are limited, so everyone in the car gives five dollars to park in the VIP section. As they stepped out of the car, Tree looked over the hood and smiles at how stunning his love looks. Her beauty makes him walk around the front of the car and caress her hand.

"Audumn, you are too beautiful, and I'm honored to have you for my girl."

"Thanks, baby, and we still going to have a long talk tomorrow."

Diana and Kizzy go in first because its 9:54 p.m., and they want to get in free before ten. After stepping inside, Tree pauses because he hasn't been to a club in almost two and a half years. His gut tells him to leave, but since Audumn wanted him to come, he decided to stay and watch over her.

The club is fired up, and the men are on the prowl trying to pick up women who are insecure or vulnerable from drinking too much. Audumn and her girls are on the dance floor doing the pretty girl walk while secretly watching Tree's wandering eyes. Tree is not stupid, so when he does look, he looks discreetly and at the appropriate time. People are everywhere, and the women are looking sexier and sexier each time a different face passes by. Looking to the dance floor, he sees Audumn has turned her head for a brief second, so he blends into the train of people passing in front of him.

"Finally I shook her," he said while looking at the ladies dressed in some of the tightest outfits he's ever seen.

The crowd gets thick as he ventures off in his sightseeing quest. Weaving through the small openings given to him, he brushes his hand against a few ladies' backsides but then sees a familiar face out of the corner of his eye. He tries to avoid trouble as much as possible, but the person he noticed is persistent and calls his name over the music.

"Chikora," Tree said, stepping back to the wall under the lights.

Chikora is Tree's old fling and side chick who is from the streets who's down to do whatever necessary to make Tree happy.

"Come on, Tree, that's how you're going to do your girl? I know you not acting funny since you're out now," she said flirtatiously while rubbing her hand across his broad shoulders.

"Chikora, what's up? You know it ain't nothing between us, and I told you while I was on lock that I'm gon' be with Audumn." Tree realizes Audumn is in the club, so he runs his eyes through D-1, looking for anyone who might see him talking to Chikora. "I got to go. Audumn is in here, and I don't need no unnecessary drama tonight."

"Boy, I don't know why you fronting. You know where your true love is at," she said while tucking her phone number into his back pocket as Tree exits.

Feeling guilty from talking to his old fling, he makes his way to the dance floor to be with Audumn. As he walks sideways through the crowd, he divides everyone like he is a razor blade because of his wide frame.

Damn, Chikora still fine as hell. I ain't gon' lie, she's truly a "bout it bout it" chick and has always been down for me like four flat tires, he thinks as he makes a mental note to keep her on his team for his new business plans with Blake.

The dance floor is jumping, and the ladies are practically throwing themselves at him because he is a new face in the club. As he approaches Audumn, Diana is the first to throw her two cents at him on where he's been, but Tree tunes her out because he knows he's been out of sight and out of mind for no longer than a few minutes.

"You betta watch that boy, yeah," Kizzy said, tapping Audumn on the shoulder.

Tree acts like he doesn't hear the comment and begins feeling the music as he does his same old two-step. Audumn's face starts to glow under the disco ball as she grinds on the one man who's always had her heart.

"Baby, do you love me?"

"You know I love you, Audumn, and that's the silliest question I've ever heard."

"Then don't lie to me again," she said, pounding her finger into his forehead. "Because if you can't tell me the truth, we don't have nothing."

"Audumn, a lot of crazy stuff happened on Friday at my job that I don't want to talk about, and as for that backpack, baby, that's just me making sure we gon' be all right."

"We are already all right, baby. We just got to take baby steps until we reach our goals."

"I'm sorry, Audumn, but baby steps ain't fast enough for me."

"So that's it. Just that simple, you're back in the dope game," she replied, staring him in his eyes.

"Two months, baby, and I'm through, promise."

"I love you, Tree."

"So that's it? Just that simple, you cool with me being back in the streets." Tree stops dancing.

"Your mind was made up when you went and got it, baby. I love you, Tree, but I don't think I can go through seeing you behind bars again."

"So what you saying?"

"What I'm saying is that you're here, so stay here."

Audumn's sweet voice wouldn't stop rolling around in his head for the rest of the night. He hoped that everything he's told her comes true, but he knows that what he's about to do is a road that leads to nowhere.

As the people vanished one by one, he is left in the middle of the dance floor by himself in deep thought. The light turned on shortly after the last song is played, and DJ Chris begins to shout out all the after-hours spots that will be opened for the remainder of the night. Suddenly, he snaps out of his daydream, feeling how he felt in jail before Audumn's first letter.

Diana and Kizzy are outside flirting with the guys when Tree steps outside the tinted doors of D-1. Audumn is standing on the passenger side of his car, so he rushes over and gives her a kiss on the lips while his enemies are occupied. As he walks around the rear of the car to go to the driver's side, Tree places a single bullet in an imaginary gun because he's about to play Russian roulette with the love of his life. After spinning the barrel, Kizzy and Diana opens the back doors of his Cadillac and jumps in. His index finger is in the shape of a hook on the trigger as he squeezes, only to hear a click from the chamber. A sigh of relief spews from his mouth because this time he is very lucky, but his gut tells him that he doesn't have too many more chances left with playing with Audumn's feelings.

15

JU is back in the picture, but Tree's in charge this time around, and Blake only deals strictly with him. It's the exact opposite of the operation they had back on the Wells Unit, but that was then, and this is now. Tree only felt it right to bring JU in on his new game plan because he knew Blake better than he did, and two heads were better than one. Together they were a force to be reckoned with, and the streets hated them but accepted them due to their low prices.

The Pyrex cup is spinning, and light brown bubbles are popping inside the glass jar while they evaporate from the waves of heat surrounding it. The powdery substance inside the steaming-hot water transforms into a gel as Tree stares through the glass of the microwave, waiting to hear a beep. Baking soda is the secret ingredient, and it is the reason why the bubbles are dancing so merrily in the hot water. "JU, get ready to put another one in the microwave because this pie is about cooked!"

Steam burst from the microwave's door when Tree pushes the button to open it. He quickly places the Pyrex on the counter and takes his hands off the handle because of how hot it has become. His only tools for his new job are an old fork, dishwashing liquid, and some table salt for when the gel doesn't want to act right. Clockwise and counterclockwise his wrist spins in haste until he can get the perfect circle before it locks up and turns into crack. *That a girl*, he thinks as he looks at it form into the circled shape he desires.

Cold water from the faucet is run over it, and a slight rattle comes from the bottom of the jar. Reaching inside, Tree pulls out the devil and places it on a napkin with seventeen others. As he wipes his face, he gets another batch ready because JU only has nine seconds left on the microwave's time clock.

"It's on you now, Tree," JU said when the microwave beeped for them both to repeat the whole process over again.

Thirty-three white pies sit on the countertop, and Tree has whipped up nineteen of them. Tiny sweat beads are across his forehead as he spreads his fingers wide-open, trying to work out a cramp. "If there's no pain, there's no gain," he said out loud as he crowns himself Iron Chef of the day.

Chikora comes through the door as they are bagging each cookie individually up for shipment. When all the necessary steps are complete, he tells her to clean up the kitchen while he places his pharmaceutical product into a shoebox for distribution.

"Chikora, did J-rock give you that $2,300 he owed me when you brought him that nine pack he ordered?"

"Oops, my bad! I don't know how I forgot about that," she said with a smirk while digging into her bra for the money.

Chikora hands Tree a knot of twenties, and he replies, "Yeah, I bet you did forget. I probably would've forgotten $2,300 stuffed in my pants too."

"Say, Tree, we need to get up out of here because the block is calling my phone like crazy."

"That's what's up, JU. It is getting late, and I ain't trying to be out all night. Grab that shoebox, and I'll meet you in the car in five minutes."

JU exits the apartment while Tree goes into the room with Chikora. As he is walking over to the bed, he sees her eyebrows are pointed toward her nose, and the tension in the room is rising each step he takes toward her.

"Baby, I just got here, and you already running back to that tramp! Tell me, Tree, what she got that I don't got? I mean, it can't be much if your ass is always over here screwing me."

"Chikora, don't play with me. You knew what it was since day one, so don't even go there. Audumn is me, and I am Audumn. You can't have one without the other, so don't let me hear you call her out her name again. What we have is business, and whenever you get that through your head, we can take this empire I'm trying to build to another level."

"That's all you think about is your money and Audumn when I do everything for your black ass!" Chikora snaps back while pouting.

Tree gets up and kisses her on the forehead while rubbing his hand across her left breast. "I got to go make this money, boo, so here's $400 to get yourself something nice."

Ms. Pearl is sitting outside purring, waiting to make some rounds throughout H-town and Texas City. JU is behind the wheel smoking some weed when Tree jumps inside and taps the outside of the door. As they backed out, JU puts in his new *Hustle Harder* CD in the radio and uses his remote to turn the volume up to its max. "Damn, homie, what you got back there, a jackhammer or something?" Tree asks because his back is vibrating in the seat.

Northborough's street economy has risen drastically since Blake's first phone call to Tree thirty-two days ago. The tennis shoe hustlers are wearing every pair of new Jordans, the block hustlers are balling, and the smokers are having a field day. Whatever fixes the streets desired, the streets had because JU and Tree didn't miss anything from $500 and up. Hard or soft, they had it, and the quality of their product traveled from Texas down to Louisiana. Not one important dollar was missed.

The sun went up and the sun went down while Tree's time on the streets was starting to show some progress. His mind told him to keep going, but his heart yearned for peace with Audumn because every day that he walked inside the guesthouse, it felt colder and colder. The smiles were there because of all the money they had stashed in his mama's house, but their love life was another story at hand. Each time he walked out the door, it was as if a piece of Audumn walked out with him. She wanted to leave him, but her love for him always stopped her at the door. Audumn came too far to turn back again, so she decided to take her baby up on his deal and just spend as much money as she can. The day school started back up is his deadline, and the sand in the hourglass is slowly seeping to the bottom.

Every day she reminded him about their agreement because in two months, she was leaving—no ifs, ands, or buts. He hoped that she would open her eyes to what he is trying to do for them, but nothing he gave her or said could change her mind. In a way, that's what he wanted, but in a way, her constantly being on him is what he needed to stay grounded. Besides, her caring is what he loved about her the most because that's what she had that Chikora didn't.

Trap houses were set up throughout the city of Houston. His homies who ran them were legit, so if anyone needed some drugs, they had to go through them to get it because Tree didn't meet anybody he didn't know personally. His freedom, money, and losing Audumn is on the line if he got caught slipping, so he kept his eyes open at all times for the snitches.

Snitches come with money, and so do jackers, haters, and a whole lot of controversy if you want to cross Go in this game of monopoly.

There's one stage on the board that's hard to succumb because male tendencies are so prone to mischief. This is the stage in which the opposite sex is involved.

"Women! Can't live with them, and you damn show can't live without them." Girls love money, and money loves girls, so Tree only felt it right to explore this phase on the board. Especially since he had Mr. Casanova sitting to the left of him at all times. JU is a true ladies' man, and he attracted women with his pretty-boy swagger. Every day he would have on a different outfit while Tree would only wear red T-shirts and Dickies.

Strip clubs awaited their presence because money wasn't a thing, so they splurged to the utmost. Tricks spent numerous dollars in the Mr. G's for five-minute table dances while Tree and JU would wait to the end of the night to leave with the club-preferred choices. You should have seen the women they had in their company during the after hours. The word *beautiful* couldn't come close to explaining the faces they were hanging out with because *perfection* is the only word that can be said to give you a visual.

Life is good, but Tree's upbringing and incarceration have shown him that everything of this world can vanish in the blink of an eye. He couldn't remember the scripture in the Bible, but he knew it read something about our life being like a vapor. Here today and gone tomorrow (James 4:14).

Laying his seat back, Tree stares out the window at the stars passing by. As he zones totally out, he remembers how the heavens reminded him of Audumn while he was on lock. The thought of her caused a smile to grace his lips, but the giggling of the girls in the backseat brought him back to date. The Navigator came to a stop at a two-hour hotel on FM 1960, and Tree gets out, promising himself that tomorrow he'll go to church with Audumn.

Sunday morning came and Sunday morning went, and his promise was broken when his two-hour stay at the hotel extended on into the evening. It wasn't like he didn't remember to go or wanted to go, but it was the fact that church made him feel guilty about the way he is living. Also, for the past month, he's been dodging his mother because no matter how much he lies to his mom, she always knew when Torrence Wingate Jr. was up to no good.

The next day, Audumn went back to Beaumont pissed after church. She usually stayed until Monday morning, but the empty seat next to her during service set a fuse off that she's been keeping out the past few weeks. She allowed Tree to do whatever he wanted during the time frame they agreed on, but part of that agreement was for him to go to church with her on Sundays. Since the day they made a pact, he's only been once, and that was the first and last Sunday he had owned up to their agreement.

After Audumn left, the week flew by, and Tree enjoyed every minute of it because of the peace that came with it. It wasn't the peace he was looking for with Audumn, but her not being in his ear helped him focus on moving the ten bricks of cocaine Blake dropped on him at the end of last week.

Friday is tomorrow, and this week's week of hard work has paid off because he's down to two of them. With all the dope almost sold, Tree's thorn in his flesh started to resurface, and it showed through his actions. Audumn didn't call not once during the week, and it ate him alive from the inside out.

JU told him the streets will always be there, but true love is for a lifetime. After a few minutes of discussion on Tree's love problems, JU's solution is to the take two remaining bricks of cocaine back home to Texas City with him.

"You need a break to get your head screwed on straight. We made a lot of money this week, so take this weekend off and spend some time with your lady. Audumn loves you, and this lifestyle we're living is not her anymore. I don't know what you two got going on, but if you don't do something soon, you're going to lose a good person in your life."

"JU, you don't know what you're talking about. Look at all this money." Tree opens one of many paper bags full of cash. "Audumn ain't going nowhere. She just tripping because I'm not going to church with her."

"Don't tell me what I don't know, big homey, because I remember the letters that lit up cell 16 with its sweet fragrance and put a smile on your face to the next mail call. And if you think money is the reason she's down with you, then you're crazy as hell because you didn't have shit back on the Wells Unit."

Today is the first time JU spoke something positive to him since the day they hooked back up in the free world. Even though half of the conversation fell on deaf ears, Tree at least heard what his partner had to say. As he shrugged off the guilt he's put his girl through, JU's statement of losing a good person begins to echo in his brain. *Tomorrow night when Audumn comes back to Houston, I'm going to take my baby out to eat and to the movies,* he thinks, not wanting JU to think he's the reason for opening his sensitive side.

Love is in the air Friday night, and it's the first time in weeks that Audumn has had her hubby all to herself. Tree bought her some perfume to wear for the evening, so the enticing smell coming from the back of her neck has his hormones about to jump out his skin. As they walked through Woodlands Mall, her beauty reminds him of the first day they met.

"Six years, baby." Tree wraps his arms around her from behind.

"Six years?"

"Yes, my love. It's been a little over six years we've been together now," Tree replies, knowing that there's no other woman better he could trust his heart to.

"Dang, it has been that long, huh, baby?"

The movie theater inside the mall had a diner inside of it, and since everything was going his way, Tree just brought Audumn there instead of a restaurant. It was like everything was unreal for the both of them because the night was magical as they entered the double doors into pitch-black darkness.

"Baby, I love you," Audumn said softly as they took their seats.

It's Audumn's night tonight, so she picked the movie they're seeing while he ordered some spicy hot wings for the both of them.

As the movie came to a close, Tree has no doubt that Audumn is his soul mate, and this is the best night to get off his chest what's in his heart for their future. *I hope Audumn don't be tripping on what I want her to do for me,* he thinks as he waits patiently for the words "The End" to come across the big screen.

Finally, the credits begin to run down the vast projection screen, and people start to leave one by one. Tree knows it's now or never, so he blurts out in a low tone, "Baby, I want you to move back to Houston."

"Move back to Houston?" she replied, releasing his hand. "What about my mom, and what about my school?"

"Baby, we both know that your mom is in remission and is doing great. Not only that, but she has your dad and four brothers if she needs any help."

Audumn knows he's telling the truth because her mom is doing better than what most people thought since her hair started to grow back. "What about my school?" she said, wondering what answer Mr. Smarty Pants is going to come up with next.

"Baby, the month is July, so you still got time to transfer!" he exclaims, stopping her on the steps before entering the lobby. "Audumn, we have $140,000 put up in my mom's house. We can move wherever you want to move."

"Tree, you're not ready to give up all this, and you know it. The only reason I play this game with you is because I love you. Every day you come home with more money, I see your promise getting harder and harder for you to keep. Honestly, Tree, do you think you can walk away from what you've accomplished in two months for me?"

"Baby, I can and I will! I love you, Audumn, and you're the best thing that has ever happened to me. Promise me you're going to at least consider it," he said, softly pulling her chin to his lips for a kiss.

"I promise," Audumn replies, putting her sole trust into him again.

Entering the lobby, the two beers and two cups of water begin to tug on his bladder. Excusing himself, he goes into the bathroom to release the extra water weight he is carrying. Audumn doesn't go because the guesthouse is not too far, so she decides to wait. When he came out, Audumn is talking to a guy standing with two kids, and her skin becomes pale as Madonna's when Tree walks up.

Interrupting their conversation, Tree asks, "Audumn, are you ready?"

"Yes, I'm ready, baby, and this is my old friend, Secorion. Secorion, this is my boyfriend, Tree."

"How are you doing, Tree? It's nice to meet you." Secorion said, releasing his niece's and nephew's hands to extend it in friendship. Secorion is Audumn's friend/ex-boyfriend who was there for her as a shoulder to cry on when Tree got locked up. He is a true gentlemen and only wants the best for Audumn.

Tree shakes his hand and answers, "Sorry, but I never met you or heard about you until now."

"He's just somebody from my past," Audumn answers quickly because Tree is a very jealous-hearted person.

"Oh, well, it's nice to meet you too, Mr. Secorion," he retorted with a little humor. "I'm sorry we can't talk longer, but it is getting late."

"Yeah, you're right about that," Secorion replied, putting the kids' hands in the air. "Audumn, it was nice seeing you again."

"Same to you Secorry," she answered as they went their separate ways.

Stars are scattered throughout the dark skies tonight as they walked to the car. Audumn is silent and feels sad because she could see the pain in Secorion's eyes when she left with Tree. Secorion really loved her, and she cut him deeply when they called it quits between the two of them almost a year ago.

On the flip side, Tree watched her every move and felt the coldness of her hand when he grabbed it in the lobby. *His name was Secorion, but Audumn called him Secorry,* he thought. Wrapping his big arms around her, he puts two and two together and realizes that Secorion is the other person that holds a key to her heart.

"I'm sorry for everything I put you through, Audumn," he whispers in her ear with compassion.

"Everything's going to be all right, baby, and I forgave you the first time I saw you through that glass in visitation," she said as reminiscing tears of Secorion's love for her rolls down her cheeks and onto Tree's shoulder.

16

"Get out, Tree! Get your shit and get out of my house now!"

"Momma, what's wrong?" Tree asks, walking to the kitchen of the guesthouse, wondering why his mom is cursing.

"What's wrong is that I trusted you, and you still slapped me in the face with your drug-dealing lifestyle again! I knew you were doing something you had no business doing, but I didn't know you were doing it to this extent!" she yells, throwing a duffel bag full of money to the floor.

"Momma, I'm sorry," Tree pleads.

"Sorry! I can't believe you have the nerve to say 'I'm sorry' after using me and your father's house in your street crap!"

"Momma!"

"Get out!" his mother yells sternly. "The devil has no place in this house!"

XXXXX

Tree awoke in the hotel room heavily panting. If it wasn't for his heart beating so loudly, he'd probably still be asleep on Nightmare on Elm Street.

Audumn feels she heard a noise, so she pokes her head out of the shower curtain. "Tree, did you say something, baby?" Audumn ask as she listens for anything out of the ordinary. *That boy done really messed up with his parents this time,* she thinks, returning to her shower.

The temperature in the room is almost eighty degrees because Audumn turned the air off until she is finished showering. To Tree, it feels like a furnace as he sits up from the man-shaped wet spot underneath him. As he wipes his forehead, he stands in disgust for hurting the one woman who's always loved him unconditionally. "Damn, Tree, you really screwed up this time," he mutters while staring at the four tubs of clothes along the walls.

It's been fifty-four hours since his mother gave him the boot, and he can still feel her size 9 like it happened a couple of hours ago. Tree knows what his next move is going to be, but in order for him to checkmate on it, he must calculate it down to the tee because of the $157,000 that's at stake. For the past two days, he's had Audumn missing work so she can find them an apartment, and since then, they have found nothing worth renting. Today is the last day she can be absent from work again, so today is the day she has to find her and her baby a new safe house.

Everything is moving so quickly for Audumn as they drove from apartment to apartment through the suburban areas of Houston. Her plan was to transfer her classes to U of H and find an apartment at the end of August, but Tree's eviction has changed her plans and has pushed everything up tremendously. She didn't mind helping him because truth be told, he stopped selling dope shortly after their romantic night at the movies.

"Baby, it's getting late, and we need to find an apartment or get another room until I get back Saturday." Audumn looked at the sunlight growing dimmer.

Ironically, Autumn Lakes is the last apartment complex on her list. A man-made lake sits in the front of it, and the sunset's reflection off the surface is mesmerizing. As they walk inside, Audumn takes a floor plan for a one-bedroom off the console while Tree goes to the window to look at the beautiful pool.

"Welcome to Autumn Lakes. My name is Therresa, and how may I help you today?" the leasing agent asks, shaking Audumn's hand.

"It's nice to meet you, Ms. Therresa, my name is Audumn, and I am interested in a one-bedroom apartment."

"I guess you're in the right place, Autumn," Therresa said, hinting that her name is the same as the apartment complex.

"Oh, my name is Audumn with a *d*, not a *t*," Audumn replies, correcting her.

"That's different but pretty." She thinks, replacing the *t* with a *d* in her mind. "I can honestly say I never seen *autumn* spelled that way before."

The scenery is breathtaking as they walk past the lake, pool, and tennis court. Tree has nothing to say as the two women converse about the perks Autumn Lakes has above other complexes in the vicinity. When asked if he is going to be on the lease, Audumn answers no because she knows Tree never puts his birth name on anything.

Audumn walked inside the apartment first, and the smell of fresh paint opened up her nose as she stood in awe at how much space the living room has. A red wall is in the dining area, so Tree smiles because that's his favorite color. The leasing agent notices the change in his facial expression and tells Audumn she has to see the view from the bedroom.

"Isn't this beautiful, baby?" Audumn asks, looking down at the pool from the balcony. "What do you think about it, Tree?"

"It's straight. I mean, I do like the red wall and the plush white carpet."

"Can I get it, baby? Please say yes!"

Therresa interrupts the two lovebirds' moment in the sun and tells them before they make a decision she has to show them the bathroom. Tree decides to finishes his own tour while Audumn and Therresa go explore the apartment's luxurious bathing area. As he is standing in the kitchen admiring the black appliances and wood floors, he hears a high-pitched shriek from Audumn.

"Baby, you got to see this!" Audumn exclaims, pulling him by the arm into the bathroom to see the garden tub and his and her sinks.

Audumn is happy, so Tree is happy. With that being said, it isn't hard for him to say yes when the leasing agent asked if the floor plan of Autumn Lakes is what they're looking for. While walking back to the office, Tree decides to lag a little to take a deep breath of the fresh air because he can't believe he's made it out of the dope game.

A jingle from the apartment keys in Audumn's hand brings him out of his trance, and he sees that all his hustling is starting to pay off.

"Snap out of it, baby, and let's go get your stuff so we can move in our new home," Audumn said, happy that her prayers for stability is finally being answered.

The two of them put Tree's clothes inside in haste because the daylight is not on their side. When the last tub of clothes is placed in the center of the floor, he grabs the duffel bag of money and stashes it in a storage compartment underneath the water heater after taking out $10,000.

"Here you go, baby."

"What's this for, Tree?"

"Get us some furniture, pictures, curtains, lamps, and a bed because we ain't got shit."

"Boy, you're crazy, and watch your mouth," she exclaimed, kissing him on the lips.

The kiss led to a touch, and the touch led to them rolling around on the floor. His hands are rough, but Audumn loves when he takes his index finger and gently drags it down to her stomach. After hearing a soft moan, Tree knows she is ready for him to unlock her chastity belt, so he slides her shirt off and quickly becomes aroused when seeing her perky breasts are staring at him. He kisses them one by one and says, "Everything I have is nothing without you," before diving into Audumn's waterfall of love.

Audumn awoke at three thirty the next morning because she had to be at work in Beaumont at seven to open the store on time. Before leaving, she writes a note and leaves it on the marble counter. It read, "Sex was great. Putting in for a transfer at work today. Be back in two days. Love you. Mwah!"

Tree's eyes opened later than he had expected because last night he gave Audumn his all in the battle of the sexes. If it wasn't for the sunlight shining through the curtainless window and heating up his face, he probably would have slept past noon.

Standing to his feet, the sheet that covered him falls to the floor, leaving him naked. As he steps out the sun's rays, the coolness from the shaded parts of the apartment causes chill bumps to form down the sides of his arms and legs. Audumn's note is on the counter under a fruit basket that came with the apartment, so he grabs it and begins to read while sticking his chest out. "Tell me something I don't know," he said, dropping the note while heading toward the shower.

JU knocked on the door around two with a toothbrush, toothpaste, and deodorant. When he walked inside, he looks around and says, "You need some furniture, curtains, pictures, lamps, and a bed because ya'll ain't got shit."

"Fool, tell me something I don't know!" Tree shouts, snatching the bag of hygiene, laughing.

Fresh, dressed, and smelling like a million bucks, Tree steps out of the apartment and brushes dust off the toes of his Gucci loafers. His Gucci shirt and shorts still have the tags on them, so he rips them off and tosses them over the railing.

JU sees that Tree is clean from head to toe and asks, "Why the change in fashion all of a sudden?"

Tree hears him but doesn't answer until he puts on his expensive sunglasses. "Because I'm on vacation. Now let's go."

Audumn was right when she said Tree is out of the dope game, but being out the game doesn't necessarily keep him away from the streets. Everyone respected him because of his money, and that respect made him feel like he is on top of the world. JU, on the other hand, has picked up a new trade because he didn't like going through Tree all the time to get cocaine from Blake.

"What's that I smell?" Tree asks, already knowing what it is.

"PCP, why, what's up?"

"That's what you on now. What happened with the weed connect in LA?"

"I touched bases with him yesterday. I bought fifty pounds, and he fronted me five gallons of water [the code name for PCP] to see if I can get off of it."

"Water!" Tree exclaims, thinking about his good and bad days with the addictive drug. "Why you moving water when you know I can call Blake whenever you need me to?"

"Just decided to change it up, I guess. Besides, with this water I can make three times the profit instead of double. Plus, it goes just as fast as crack do. Hell, to tell you truth, I prefer to call it liquid crack."

As the day went on, JU made his money quick just like he said he would because people from all over scored PCP to smoke and to sell. All Tree could do is sit back and watch as the smokers' faces turned zombielike after hitting the wet substance on a cigarette. The strong stench starts to open his mind each time JU dipped a cigarette or joint inside the bottle that contains it. *Chill out, Tree. You bigger than that,* he thinks, secretly wanting to smoke a dipped cigarette for himself. Ignoring his hidden desires, he tries to bury his addiction by telling JU to put the drugs up for a minute so they can get something to eat.

JU agrees and tightens the top on the bottle before stashing it in the steering wheel. As soon as it out of eyesight, Tree feels better already and realizes that PCP is still a demon in his life.

"What's up, Tree, you all right?" JU asks because his friend hasn't said too much of nothing all day.

"I'm straight. Just didn't take you for a PCP hustler."

"This is a one-stop shot because if you want it, I got it," JU replies with hunger in his eyes.

"I feel that, but watch yourself when selling that water because them wetheads will do anything when their funds ain't looking too good."

"That's what up. After these five gallons are gone, I'll chill out for a little while. All I need you to do is be ready to get back on this cash with me when I do."

"I got you. Just give me some time to get everything in order with Audumn."

They both get out at Popeyes Chicken, which is the one place they both always have agreed upon. JU is on the phone with someone who wants a half gallon of water as they go through the doors to stand in line. The special for the month is a three-piece meal with a two-piece meal for free, so Tree orders it and adds an extra wing to the two-piece meal because every extra dollar counted in his book.

As they turned around, a beautiful girl bumped into JU, and he recognizes who she is and gives her a dirty smile. The diamonds and gold in his teeth makes her remember him as well after they sparkled in her eyes. A few words are exchanged, and before you know it, Mr. Casanova is throwing the keys to Tree, not worrying about the food they ordered.

"I'm out, Tree. Call me when you get to the house because I'm about to go kick it with my old friend, Antoinette," he said, giving his boy a wink while throwing his arm around the girl's shoulders.

Tree sat in Popeyes thirty minutes after eating his food. He prayed JU would call soon, but he knew that wasn't going to happen by a long shot. In his mind, he felt he could handle the pressure of being around the PCP, but his body's cravings spoke something different. Nervously, he gets up and walks to the Navigator like a sheep heading to the slaughter. Unlocking the door, his phone rings, and its JU wanting him to bring two ounces of water to BJ's spot off Richey Road for him.

Tree doesn't want to comply, but he agrees to the request anyway because JU would do it for him if the shoe was on the other foot. As he drives to make the delivery, he thinks about everything he has and dupes himself into thinking it's okay to tap the bottle one time for old time's sake.

A pack of Newport cigarettes is on the dashboard, so everything he needs to get high is within arm's reach. Ducking off, he pulls inside a parking spot at the flea market on Airtex. The tinted windows give him cover as he looks around to see if anyone's watching him. His mind is made up when he pulls a cigarette from the box and loosens the top of the bottle. His hand starts to shake because of all the bullshit the drug has put him through, but he balls his fists up to stop it. Before dipping the tobacco into the watery substance, he thinks about his downfalls of being on the drug again and then shakes the thought by saying, "No one will ever know. It's only this one time."

With his seat laid all the way back, he anxiously waits for the car lighter to heat up and push out. Finally, a pop sounds throughout the silent SUV, and Tree must confront what he's been running from since the day he got out of the state penitentiary. At least that's what he thought he was going to do until the heavy smell traveled up his nostrils and ignited his old behaviors.

As he takes a hit, his pupils become the size of tiny moles, and the old Tree is back. The Tree that loved to get high, the Tree that didn't give a damn about nobody but himself, and above all, the Tree that Audumn promised to never be with again.

17

Dark clouds covered the city of Houston throughout the entire last week in August. Showers from the east have caused the water to flood the drainage system and overflow the curbs exceedingly. Tree opens the blinds to his new apartment and stares at the raindrops falling to the balcony while listening to the skies cry continuously, hitting the roof.

Yesterday he promised to stop smoking PCP, but all the water surrounding him from nature is starting to make that promise null and void. He tries to numb his body to the itch that wants to be scratched by eating some leftovers from Timmy Chan's, but after three bites of the Chinese food, his stomach sends a full signal back to his brain. Lately, his appetite has been gone, and his face is starting to look drawn. The candleholder in the hallway has a mirror on it, and for some reason, every time he passes it, he tends to glance at himself to see if his countenance has changed within the last hour or sometimes minutes.

Ten days he's been on the drug, and he's already tightening his belt a notch from the unseen weight loss around his waist. The side effects probably wouldn't have come so fast, but being that his money is unlimited, Tree has smoked as much as he could whenever he has gotten the chance to.

Audumn noticed the change in his behavior and asked questions about it, only to get excuses after excuses. She tried to listen to her woman's intuition, but Tree knew she had to be at work in Beaumont every Monday morning, so he did his best to keep her from prying over the weekend until then.

Friday, which is tomorrow, her job transfer will be complete, and Audumn will be living in Houston again. Since she didn't have to start school at U of H until September 1, Tree knew if he wanted to get high without being bothered, now is the time. With that thought popping up in his mind more than once, he makes a phone call to his dealer, Baby Boy.

No one knows about the thorn in his flesh that he can't seem to pull out to find relief because he's been very secretive and hasn't allowed anyone in his presence. JU has been constantly calling him, but he only allows his calls to go straight to voice mail. It's not because he didn't want to be bothered or anything, but because he is ashamed of what he knows deep down inside he is slowly becoming. Maybe if he would have allowed someone in his inner circle, Tree wouldn't have been as far gone as he presently is.

The worst kind of smoker is a closet smoker because a closet smoker knows right from wrong and doesn't allow anyone but people of their kind to know they're getting high. When asked if anything is bothering them, they tend to answer no, and then shy off before someone eventually sees through the mask they're hiding behind. They think their actions are invisible because they feel they live normal lives, so the only thing that one can do for them is pray that God will send someone into the closet to confront them about the strongholds restraining them from life.

A streak of light parts the clouds and causes the downpour to slack for a few minutes. Tree sees that this is his cue to leave and stuffs his pistol in his pants because the exceeding use of the drugs has his nerves bad, and he feels everyone is out to get him.

Before jetting out the door and down the steps, he snatches the rental car keys from off the key holder. Audumn doesn't know about the pistol or who rented the car for him because it's in Chikora's name, but that didn't stop her from being suspicious. If it wasn't for the month of August being so hectic for her, she would have been investigating the negative senses she's been having the past month. September is around the corner, so she promised herself that she is going to figure out what her man's been up to since she hasn't been around that much.

Baby Boy met Tree at the car wash next to the ExxonMobil off Beltway 8. He had enough money to buy his own ounce of PCP but never did because he knew that ounce would magically evaporate into his system. Baby Boy also told him that he'll come out a lot cheaper if he went that route, but Tree felt that if he bought individually laced cigarettes, his addiction wasn't as bad as it seemed.

Between the rainy weather, getting high, and driving through the streets of H-town, Tree begins to zone off into his own world while back-to-back thunder from the night-like skies sends roaring vibrations of sound through the air. He is driving at 15 mph, and yet he is still passing the cars that are creeping through the rising waters. At the stoplight, he pulls on the cigarette hard and exhales the excess smoke as lightning strikes the earth in the distance. *Damn, this is some good shit,* he thinks, remembering that his grandma used to tell him the old fable that lightning is God's finger pointing at you when you're doing something you have no business doing.

Feeling like he is on the moon, Tree's thoughts begin to drift while looking at himself in the rearview mirror. As he looks at his reflection, he notices dark circles starting to form under his eyes from his restlessness. A loud horn from behind frightens him as he is staring from outer space as the light changed from green to yellow.

It's 4:00 p.m., and he's finally starting to come down off the two-hour hiking trip he's been on. His hair and face hasn't been brushed or cut in over a week, so he decides to get cleaned up for Audumn tomorrow. Thinking about her makes him feel good inside because for the past two years, her being with him is all he's been praying for. He didn't appreciate when God turned his back on him when he was set up by Blake in jail and when Rosco laid him off his job, but he did feel that God shined his light on him and answered his most sincere prayer, and for that, he is very thankful.

The phone rings as he is turning on Antoine to go to the barbershop. Accidentally, he touches the face of the sensitive screen and answers the phone, but after seeing who it is, he straightens up and clears his throat.

"Son, is that you?"

"What's up, Dad, and how have you and Mom been doing?" Tree replies, pulling into the parking lot of Kingz of Kutz while trying to keep his cool.

"We've been doing fine, and how are you, son? Did you find somewhere to stay?"

"Yes, sir. Audumn and I got an apartment in Autumn Lakes. She's moving down here tomorrow."

"Son, I apologize for everything you're going through. All your life I've been busy tending to the church problems when I should have been more involved in yours. I thought that if I steered you towards God that you would eventually take the wheel and drive the car for yourself. What I didn't take into consideration is that the world we are living in was also steering you towards the devil. The neighborhood you grew up in didn't make it any better either."

Tree cuts him off because he loves his father and doesn't want him to feel his life as a drug-dealing thug is his fault. His childhood was above average, and every choice he's made in life was outside his father's teaching. He couldn't understand why, but at least at the end of the day, he felt the life he lives is by his choice and not anybody else's.

"Dad, stop," he said in sorrow. "You and Mom are not to blame for my mistakes. Yes, you are a busy man, but that comes with what God has called you to do. You change a lot of people lives every day, and I'm proud to be named Torrence Wingate Jr. The reason I go by Tree is because your name is too honorable to be caught up in the streets over my nonsense."

"Torrence, you don't have to live that way. All your mom and I ever wanted from you and your sister was to try. As long as you were trying, you know we would have gone to the ends of the earth for you two. You remind me so much of me because I was just like you when I was young. I felt I had to prove to my parents I can make it on my own, so I left home at seventeen. I went through a lot of ups and downs before I realized my parents were right. 'Trust God, and the rest of life will come easy for you,' they used to preach to me. I thought, 'God is not coming fast enough, so I'll just go ahead and do it my way.' That thinking was my worst thinking, but due to my everyday life, it seemed like my best thinking. Am I wrong, son?"

Tree sat and listened to his dad tell him everything he's been battling within his conscience. To Tree, it feels like his dad is a physic consultant mimicking his exact thoughts that only he knows about. He always wondered if it was God giving his father that insight concerning him, or was it the genetic pattern between the two of them.

"Are you still there, son?" his father asks because the other end of the phone line sounds dead.

"I'm still here, Dad, and I hear every word you're talking about," Tree replies, ready to get off the phone so he can get high before he gets his haircut for the weekend.

"I guess what I'm trying to say is we love you, Torrence, and at the rate you're going, your mom and I are very worried about you. Please understand that God didn't give us life to live it only for ourselves. Always remember that, Torrence, and don't never forget it."

No response came from Tree because he was inhaling the first hit off his dipped cigarette when his father was looking for some feedback.

"I see you're busy, so call me back, son. No matter where I'm at, I'll always answer."

"Yes, sir." Tree softly coughed. "I promise, Dad, I'll get it right. Trust me."

Kingz of Kutz's crowd today is at a minimum because of the weather conditions, but since the day is starting to look better, Tree knows he must go in quickly before business picks up. When walking inside, all the barbers tell him what's up because of his status in the streets. Shorty is one of the owners, and he is the only person that Tree trusts to cut his hair. The two of them go way back, and they have been keeping it real with one another since they met in 2005.

"What's up, Shorty Low, what it do?" Tree shakes his friend's hand.

"I can't call it. Just taking it one day at time on this million-dollar goal I got in my head," Shorty replies, edging the back of a customer's neck.

"Where's Rob G?"

"He'll be back in about thirty minutes. He had to take care of some business."

"That's what's up. Tell that boy I said to holler at me whenever he takes a pit stop."

"Have a seat in the waiting area, and give me about ten minutes to get to you."

It's his turn for a cut, so Tree takes a seat, enjoying the high he thinks no one knows about. The PCP is overwhelming, and Shorty smells it rising from his hair but doesn't say anything because the barbershop is a place where you can speak your mind and be yourself. Shorty and Rob G strongly believed in these concepts and felt this is how their barbershop should be run no matter what.

Halfway through his haircut, Tree starts to think about his conversation with his dad, his love for Audumn, and his drug addiction that is growing by the day. As he is meditating, Shorty finishes putting the finishing touches on the back of his neck and then tells Tree to lay his head back so that he can shave him.

Tree closes his eyes while Shorty rubs white shaving cream all over his face. He knows that the shaving cream has to sit for a few minutes, so without knowing it, he begins to open up to his longtime friend and barber.

The conversation they have is genuine except for the sugarcoating of his PCP addiction, but Shorty understands his embarrassment for smoking the horrible drug and acts oblivious to what he is talking about. A hot towel is placed on his face to take away the excess shaving cream, and soon after, he edges his mustache and beard while telling Tree he needs to slow his roll before he ends up in a place in life that he doesn't want to be at.

His barber's words didn't fall on deaf ears because Tree always listened to Shorty for some reason. He probably didn't use his advice wisely, but he always at least heard what his friend had to say to him. The reason being is because Shorty is just like him in a way. An ex-street thug who has made it out the hood successfully, and for that reason, everyone respected him.

"Good looking out, Shorty Low," Tree said, looking into the mirror at his fresh cut before leaving. "And thanks for those words of wisdom. I really needed to hear that."

Kingz of Kutz barbershop is located in a shopping center with four or five small businesses occupying it. The rain is gone, and since the day has turned out to be a beautiful day, people from the surrounding neighborhoods started to come out and enjoy the rest of it. Tree is not in any hurry, so he turns his ignition switch on and glues his eyes to the windshield because of all the girls that are walking in front of the car in their Daisy Duke shorts. An urban clothing store is located two doors down from Kingz of Kutz, and its business is just as good as Shorty's and Rob G's.

As he places the car in drive, a familiar face catches his eye out of his peripheral vision. *This must be my lucky day,* he thinks, watching Blue with a hawk eye leaving the urban clothing store.

Slowly creeping through the parking lot, Tree stalks the one guy he used to trust with his life. That same trust he trusted Blue with is what sent him back to the county on a new charge. Blue set him up with some undercover police officers a while back to save his own ass, and today Tree is seeing him enjoy the fruits of his labor by walking the streets freely. For some reason, snitches tend to forget that this is a small world, and the people they've crossed the wrong way might possibly bump into them again. Payback is today, and nothing he could say or do will give Tree back the time he's had away from his family.

Tree follows two cars behind Blue, smoking a laced cigarette while waiting for the right time to turn him into the color red. As he turned onto Aldine Bender, Blue catches wind that a car has made all the exact turns as him from the time he's left the urban clothing store on Antoine. Haverstock

Projects are up ahead, and Blue knows a few people who stay out there, but Tree makes the turn behind him too quickly and almost hits the back of his bumper. The side-view mirrors give Blue a clear glance at the person stalking him, so he speeds off over the speed bumps as fast as he can. Tree's mind is made up as he pursues vigorously, not caring how this sense of revenge is going to end.

The chase is on, and Blue is driving through the maze of Haverstock Projects, trying to find his way out. Residents who see the high-speed chase turn the other cheek as if to say it is nothing because crime is something these projects are used to. A substation is on the back of the complex, and the two Nascar drivers fly past it, disregarding the Harris County sheriff cars parked in front of it. An officer getting ready to make his rounds drops his doughnuts when seeing the unbelieving act being committed on his beat.

Finally, Blue has made it to the exit gate and skids as he is turning back onto Aldine Bender. Shots rang out from behind him because Tree is right on his bumper, remembering the day Blue made the phone call to the undercover police officer to confirm the transaction. His anger has given him tunnel vision because in the distance from behind, he doesn't notice the red-and-blue lights closing the gap between the two of them increasingly.

Tree fires another shot and blows out the back of Blue's back window, causing him to swerve across the lanes over the curb into an old wooden fence. *Did I get him?* he thought as the loud sirens bring him up-to-date.

"Oh, shit! What was I thinking?" Tree screamed as the car screeches around a sharp corner onto Airline Drive.

His foot becomes a piece of steel, and the gas pedal feels like Tree is trying to step it through the floor as record speeds are reached, and he gets a blind spot for a quick second. Another sharp corner is up ahead, so he grabs the pistol off his lap and tosses it out the window shortly before the patrol car can come back into sight. The on-ramp to Highway 59S is to his left, so he decides to bring his game of cops and robbers to a higher level as cars begin to part his way, not wanting to be hit by a reckless driver.

Twenty minutes into the chase, and he realizes that this is not going to end well. Cell doors closing begins to ring in his ears because his parole officer is cool, but even so, she is still going to have to violate him for this new charge. As he presses the gas pedal harder, all he can think about is what his time on the streets has added up to. Church, his job, the money, drugs, Audumn, and now this runs across his brain as if it's on a teleprompter.

His dad and his mother are last on the list of things in his life. When thinking of them, he thought about how his mother only wanted the best for him and how his dad only wanted him to know Jesus Christ for himself. Sorrow pierces the abundance of his spirit, and the earlier conversation with his dad starts to take root because his father's name is at stake with this fiasco he's gotten himself into.

His foot eases off the pedal, and Tree looks to the heavens and slows down. "Lord, watch over me," he silently prays as he brings the car to a complete stop onto the shoulder of the highway.

HPD attacks the car from all directions with their cross bows locked onto their target. Adrenaline is pumping through the officers' veins, and their fingers are steady on the triggers, awaiting the slightest movement from their suspect. Tree knows they have the clearance to shoot if the situation doesn't go according to plan because of the gun he shot at Blue in front of the officer in pursuit of him.

"I'm coming out peacefully!" he shouts, slowly placing both hands out the window.

"Don't move again, boy, or we are going to blow your god-damn head off!" an officer shouts, approaching cautiously.

Tree becomes a statue as soon as he heard the fierceness in the officer's voice. He feels like he's watching *Gunfight at the O.K. Corral* in 3-D, but that thought vanished when he is snatched through the window by two heavyset officers. The pavement doesn't give an inch when his faced is forced into trying to make it move as words of anger are tossed into the air of how he could have killed someone with his stupidity. No one is on his side, and everyone looking on feels that he should get what he deserves. His mouth is shut because fighting or talking back can only give an excuse to get his ass whipped by the officers. Besides, he's far from stupid. His actions may have been stupid, but he's fully comprehensive to everything that has happened in the last thirty minutes because right from wrong was instilled into him the day the doctor smacked him on his bottom. All he can do is accept the consequences like a man and move on to the next chapter in the book of Tree.

A slam from the police door vibrates the frame of the car from being closed so hard behind him. Tree can only look at his lap because his heart won't allow him to pick his head up. Life has come to an end in his eyes, and he knows he's going back to the penitentiary. The restraints wrapped around his wrist won't allow him to move freely, and he remembers how this same incident happened two and a half years ago with Audumn in the car. A police chase leads to him going to jail, and going to jail leads to him losing Audumn. The thought saddens him tremendously as he stares through the gated front seat at the officer speeding off in the direction of Harris County Jail. "Damn, I'm having déjà vu," he said aloud, wishing he could wake up and start this day all over again.

18

A small gust of wind blows the back of Audumn's pressed hair as she is getting out of Tree's car. It's the perfect time for a morning surprise because the night is currently winning the battle with light, but daylight can only be beaten for so long, so Audumn hurries up the steps and to the door. The sound of her key going through each groove of the Brinks lock echoes off every piece of furniture throughout her vacant home.

As she is slowly opening the door, a slight squeal comes from the hinges, so she steps inside and bites her bottom lip. *So far so good*, she thinks before placing her bags on the floor in front of the sofa.

Quietly she walks to the bedroom door and opens it, only to find the bedsheets ruffled from the last time Tree slept underneath them. Audumn is shocked to see her future husband not in the bed and begins to worry, which in turn overcomes every bit of joy left in her spirit. The surprise is over because now her gut is telling her that this is not going to turn out the way she hoped and prayed during the long week of saying her farewells in Beaumont.

Meanwhile, in the Harris County Jail, an officer is waking the pods up one by one for morning chow. "Breakfast at the door!" he shouts as he unlocks the thick piece of green-painted steel that separated him from the hungry inmates.

Orange scrub-like uniforms began to stand up and stretch from almost every bunk in the twenty-four-man cell. Normally, Tree wouldn't have gotten up to eat the county breakfast if his life depended on it, but the last thing he ate was the few bites of Timmy Chan's yesterday morning.

As he goes to the back of the breakfast line for a tray, Tree avoids eye contact as much as possible because he is ashamed of what the so-called good life has bought him.

If he could give it all back, he would, but even Moses didn't get to see the Promised Land because of his disobedience.

Bright yellow powdered eggs are on the poorly washed reusable trays, and no matter how dirty the trays were, the one handed to you is the one you keep. Faces of disbelief are on each of the offenders' faces as they pick smashed peas from yesterday's meal from off the sides of them. Tree notices how dirty the breakfast trays are and pauses in disgust of what he must eat from. His stomach doesn't see what his eyes sees because all they can see is a full-course meal, so Tree's hands are forced into taking the portion due to its owner.

One tray is given to each offender, but cartons of milk are unlimited because half the inmates drank it, and the other half didn't. Tree's mouth hasn't had any fluids, and anything will help the void of liquids in his mouth. Plus, everything added up when it came to his hunger pangs, so he sucked down as many cartons as possible until his stomach felt like a cow's. It wasn't the fullness he is looking for, but for the time being, it pacified the empty feeling inside of him.

As he got up to stack his tray in the corner with the rest of them, he wonders if Audumn made it back to Houston yet. The time is a quarter till 6:00 p.m., so he silently prays for God to bless her for all she's done for him over the years. He knows that it's over between them because he's made a conscious decision to let her be free from the nuisance he constantly afflicts on her. At the end of the day, he understands it's time to uproot the old Tree from Audumn's pastures and move on with his life.

It's Friday, and this is supposed to be the happiest day of his life. Today was a day he was going to bask in Audumn's love and do anything her heart desires because money isn't a thing when it came to his true love. By the time nightfall came into play, he wanted her to know she had made the right decision in moving back to Houston. Now, he wished she would have followed her first mind from the beginning and moved on with her life.

The thought of her face, pain, and heart being broken again made him feel worse than Judas in the Bible. Guilt and more guilt begin to poke at his soul, and he remembers how Judas hung himself after betraying his trust to Jesus. The feeling is mutual, but taking his life will never become an option. All he can do is lie down and cover his head until Harris County is ready to decide what they are going to do with him.

Houston's population is over three million people when you include the small towns surrounding it. For that reason, court usually comes as soon as or before you get your red-and-white housing bracelet in book-in. At least that's how it usually works, he thought as he wakes up to see a bright star sitting high over the earth through a barred window.

"Excuse me, homey, but did anyone call Torrence Wingate, bunk 7?" Tree asks a guy watching *Family Guy* at the aluminum table.

"Not that I know of, but I can be wrong. Why, what's up?"

"I don't know because I got here late last night, and they still haven't taken me to arraignment to let me know what I'm being charged with."

"Ask the guard to look it up on the computer for you. They should be able to tell you something."

Tree pressed the intercom button next to the door and asked to go to the picket. A loud buzz unlocks the cell door, so he steps out and closes it, leaving it slightly ajar. As he puts his mouth to the speaker, he speaks with his most polite voice. Before, he would have talked to them any kind of way, but trouble is not something he is looking for, and trouble is not something he is trying to find.

"Sir, can you please check the status on my case because I don't know what I'm being charged for."

"Don't give me that BS, inmate. You know what you did to get yourself in here," the guard replied, emphasizing yourself.

"Yes, sir, I do, but I would like to hear the way it's going to be presented to me in court so that I can be prepared for it."

The tapping of the keys from the computer sounded through the two-way speaker for almost two minutes. Most of the time, all the guard had to do is type your name, and your entire criminal history would pop up, but today the computer is not showing his current offense. A letter is next to Tree's name, and the CO isn't familiar with the code because he is from another department. After making a few phone calls to headquarters, he hangs up with the answer Tree is looking for.

"Mr. Wingate, your case is under investigation."

"Investigation? Did they say what for?"

"I'm sorry, but I don't have the authority to give you that information."

Investigation is all he can think about when walking back inside the tank because up until now, he's blocked out all of his actions that happened yesterday. The officer told him he knew what he had done to get himself in jail, so with that in mind, he allows his brain to remember all his mischievousness. His face is full of anxiety when he thinks about Blue falling over after he'd shot out his back window, but nothing can undo what he has done, so he begins to open his eyes to the fact that he can possibly never be going home again.

Dear God, I'm sorry for taking all of your blessings for granted. As I look back, my heart becomes saddened because from the time I came into this world, you've watched over me during my good days and my bad days. Nothing I have done has been pleasing unto your eyes, and yet you still allow me to open my eyes each morning. Today I bow at your feet, not on behalf of myself, but on behalf of everyone who's wanted nothing but the best for me. I thank you for Audumn, my parents, my sister, and everybody else I missed for standing by me, even when I was doing things that wasn't worth standing by. I know my current dilemmas are very upscale, so I'm willing to suffer any consequences that come with my absentmindedness. I promise to do better when it comes to the gift of life in which you've given me twenty-eight years ago, and whatever is to become of my wrongdoings, I accept full responsibility, without any excuses. Please, Lord, I pray that Blue is okay, and he can forgive me for trying to take the life in which you've blessed him with. I love you, Lord, and if it's not too late, please forgive me for all my sins. In your precious and gracious son, Jesus's name, I pray. Amen.

Tears roll down Tree's face as he got up off the hard-cemented floor. His prayer was sincere, and it's the first time he prayed for anything or anyone other than himself. Even though God is all things and can do all things, today he and his son stopped all what they were doing to listen to him. For the word of God says that sometimes God will leave the flock of sheep to go back for one that is lost (Matt. 18:12–14).

Tree looks around before lying back in his bunk. The lights are off, so no one noticed his waling because everyone is trying to fall back to sleep. Not that he cared what anyone thought about him or anything, but because before he fell to his knees, everyone was still awake from the early morning breakfast. It's odd because during the time of his prayer, he felt like he was in a quiet place, one-on-one with the creator of all things, and most importantly, he felt God actually listened to him this time. His tears stopped, and finally he finds the peace of rest he's been looking for since the day he was laid off from the Port of Houston.

A loud yawn with a sigh came from Tree's enlarged mouth late Saturday morning. His back is hurting, and his joints feel like the Tin Man on *The Wizard Oz*. When he stands to stretch his stiff bones, he hears a small pop from his left knee and wishes he had a can of oil to lubricate it. Three inches is the thickness of the mattress in which he slept on, and three inches of compressed cushion is how it felt. As he tries to plump the mattress up as much as possible, he sees that what he is doing is to no avail because a Tempur-Pedic mattress is what he desired, but that is at Gallery Furniture off 45N.

Shaking his head to what his 6'4" frame must lie upon, the smell of musk rises from his armpits because Thursday is the day he came to Harris County Jail, and Thursday is the last time he attended to his hygiene. He thought if he had slept long enough, God would allow him to wake up Wednesday and do it all over again the right way, but since that hasn't occurred, he asks a guy named Duck for his shower shoes so he can get himself together.

Duck is cool and does so without any hassle. As he hands them to Tree, he also hands him a bottle of used deodorant and says, "I'm no saint, but God is good."

Tree slides the shower shoes on and replies, "God is good, Duck, and thanks for keeping it real with me."

Tree steps into the shower and crosses his fingers in hopes of hot water when he pushes the button underneath the showerhead. The water is warm as it runs over his head onto his frail body, and he sees that his physique has changed tremendously since his last shower behind bars. After ten minutes go by, the last of the dirt he had left on him from the free world finally runs down the drain.

Before getting out, he recalls how his mom used to baptize him and his sister in the tub as a kid. "Lord, I baptize myself in the name of the Father, Son, and Holy Spirit," he said aloud as the water comes to a complete stop. It wasn't much, but to him it was a start in the direction of change on the path he is about to walk.

"Torrence Wingate Jr., come to the picket!" the guard yells over the loudspeaker, interrupting the inmates' movie, *Gladiators*. An uproar comes from the pod because of the rudeness of the officer, and Tree almost joins in but doesn't.

"Yes, sir, I'm Torrence Wingate Jr."

"I don't know why, but pretrial court is calling for you for some reason."

"Pretrial court?" Tree repeats.

"Yes, pretrial court. Now stop busting my balls, and get your ass down there before I call and say you refused!"

Pretrial court is not your real court date, but it is helpful in numerous ways because if there's no probable cause presented, the judge can throw your case out of court and release you. If probable cause is presented thoroughly through the police report, he or she will tell you what you're being charged with and what sentencing the case carries. Basically, pretrial is the beginning of Tree's fate in the remainder of his stay during his incarceration.

Usually there's a gang of offenders going to pretrial court, but his case is an exception because of the investigation and extent of the offense. Murder, evading arrest in a motor vehicle, endangering of others, and God knows what else is on the list of crimes he's committed on the worst day of his life.

As he walks through the winding halls toward the jailhouse courtroom, Tree looks into the faces of men and women in the holding cells and wonders if their crime was as stupid as his. *No,* is the only thought that pops up in his mind when replaying the whole incident again and again from the time he saw Blue at Kingz of Kutz barber shop.

Before entering the jailhouse courtroom, the CO escorting him briefs Tree on the do's and don'ts of pretrial court. Tree listens carefully because he doesn't need any misunderstandings in what he is possibly facing. After everything said is understood, he steps inside the red box imprinted on the tile floor and faces the camera.

The honorable Judge Judy appears on the two-way flat-screen monitor and begins her speech on the rights of any offenders appearing before her. Tree answers, "Yes, ma'am" when asked if he understands what she has just told him, and she replies, "Court is now in session."

"Torrence Wingate Jr.," Judge Judy said into the microphone, "on Thursday, August 27, 2011, Harris County apprehended you for shooting at an unknown suspect while pursuing him at unlawful speeds through the streets of Houston. An officer from the Harris County's Sheriff Department witnessed the high-speed chase between you and the unknown suspect and then joined in the pursuit, in which you knowingly evaded arrest in a motor vehicle trying to elude the officer from bringing you into custody. After being pursued by the Harris County Sheriff Department for over twenty minutes, finally you came to a halt on Highway 59 South and therefore were retrained before any innocent bystanders were injured."

Tree holds his head up high when hearing all what he has done because nothing can change what he did. All he can do is pray that God's light shine on him one last time.

"Torrence Wingate, this month is an amnesty month for the city of Houston, and today I'm going to show some compassion on behalf of lack of evidence due to the gun was not found and the perpetrator in which you were pursuing fled the scene shortly after his or her accident. Everything presented before the courts today is hearsay, and therefore, I have no choice but to charge you with evading arrest in a motor vehicle. You are currently on parole, so no bond will be set because of the parole hold that has been placed on you. Your court date is September 13 in Judge Beverly's courtroom 101. Do you wish to hire an attorney or have a court-appointed represent you?"

"Court-appointed, ma'am."

"Please, Mr. Wingate, don't take your blessings for granted because this is a once-in-a-lifetime decision that has happened here today. I promise you that if you come before me again with your extensive background, amnesty will be the last thing on my mind when it comes to judging any offense that is presented before me on your behalf. Good day, Mr. Wingate, and court is adjourned."

Tree begins to high step out of the courtroom. "Thank you, Jesus, thank you, Jesus, thank you, Jesus," is all he can say and think about all the way back to his tank. Even the guard escorting him is surprised at what he's just witnessed because he thought for sure this unknown fellow he'd brought before Judge Judy was going to get the book thrown at him.

Before closing the door behind Tree, he tells him, "Mr. Wingate, you've been given a second chance at life as a free man, so please, for your family's sake, do the right thing when you get out next time."

Everyone is still awake when Tree enters the pod. A smile is on his face, and no matter how hard he tries, he can't seem to make the curves on the corners of his lips straight. Street Flavor begins to play late-night videos, so the tank's attention is glued to the television for the next hour. Usually tonight is a night that he would be occupying a space on the hard benches, but the joy that's inside of him causes him to head straight for his bunk.

As he takes a seat, Duck walks up and hands him a pocket-size New Testament Bible. "I don't know why, but something told me to give this to you."

Nothing came to mind at first because he hasn't held a Bible since he was granted parole in TDCJ. The only scripture that he can remember is John 3:16, so he flips through the pages and runs his index finger down chapter 3's fine print. It read: "For God so love the world that He gave His only begotten Son, that whosoever believes in Him shall not perish but have everlasting life."

Meditating on the scripture, he decides to let God's word sink into his brain and closes the Bible, vowing to read as much as his spirit can handle until the time he is released from prison. Today is truly a blessed day, so he kicks his feet up over the towel rail and closes his eyes, thanking God for the continuous prayers his parents has prayed over him since the day he came into this world.

As he fades from light to total darkness, a faint smile on Audumn's face is the last thing that flashes before him while tears of missing her love are caught by his eyelashes.

XXXXX

Audumn's heart, on the other hand, is stuck in her stomach because she gave up everything to be with Tree. *Lies! It was all lies!* is what her heart kept telling her. After coming to the realization something was definitely wrong with this picture, she made some phone calls and did her own investigation because the streets had ears, and if it had ears, it had a mouth as well.

Northborough told her everything that she didn't want to hear. What she found out was devastating, and she couldn't believe the Tree she'd grown to love would try and take someone's life. Tree made his choice when it came to their relationship, so when it came to deciding whether she should stay or go, it wasn't hard by far. "I'm through with these childish games," is all she could say in tears as she leaves the parking lot of Fallbrook Church after Sunday morning service.

For the past few months, she's been attending Tree's parents' church, but this morning, she decided to attend Fallbrook because she didn't want anything to hinder her decisions. All through church, she prayed for an answer, and all through church, she received nothing. Nothing is her answer, she thought, because nothing is what she now has. She tried her hardest to find some light in all this mishap, but for some reason, the sun feels like it's shining on everyone but her.

Tree's Cadillac came to a complete stop two inches from hitting the curb in front of his mother's house. Her nose is red from all of the sniffling, and tears won't stop falling from her eyes. The driver's door opened after she sits for a minute, and Audumn steps out, holding a duffel bag full of money. She knows in her heart that this may be the last time she could possibly come to his parents' house, so that thought made all of this even harder for her. Reason being is because Audumn loved his parents, but for the past six years, she and Tree has been on this roller coaster of trials, and finally the ride has come to an end.

"Hello, Audumn," his mother said, opening the door after hearing the doorbell ring a few times.

"Hey, Mamma Love." Audumn barely looks her in the eyes. "I'm sorry about your son."

"I'm not sorry, sweetheart, and you shouldn't be either because sometimes God will let a person go through the same thing over and over again until his chosen vessel gets it right."

"Well, I'm sorry because I can't keep going through the same things over and over again." Audumn burst into tears.

"I know, honey," Tree's mother replies, hugging her dearly. "I don't blame you. A woman has to do what a woman has to do."

Audumn released Tree's mother after that statement and placed the bag of money on the steps because no longer could she look into the eyes of the adopted mother she had grown to love through the years. As she turned to walk back to the car, she says, "Tell Tree I will always love him." She then gets inside and drives off.

Mamma Love's heart went out to her once so-called daughter-in-law. She didn't say anything, but when Audumn turned to walk away, she noticed fresh letters on the small of her back spell out her son's nickname, Tree. Love is something hard to get back after it is broken, so she knew that tattoo on Audumn's back is a tattoo her son will never get to see.

"Good-bye, Audumn," she whispers as she closes the door on one of the best persons her son has ever had in his life.

19

"Mail call! Mail call! Everyone listen up for mail!"
No one said a word as the officer stood over the aluminum table because receiving mail is something well respected behind bars. All the offenders of all races agreed to the respect of mail call, so letting one hear if their name is on the lottery pick of envelopes is something inmates will always allow until the end of time.

As names begin to be called off the envelopes, inmates looked on at the letters growing shorter in the hands of the officer and returned to whatever it is they were doing. Tree's nose is in the Bible, and he isn't expecting anything because his court date was yesterday, and no one showed up from his family on his behalf.

"Torrence Wingate!" the CO shouts before placing his envelope on the table.

"Say, Tree, you got mail!" Duck yells across the pod, interrupting Tree's study.

Tree's mind is full of question marks as he dog-eared the page he is reading and closes the Bible. Up until today, he hasn't heard from anyone who he'd at least thought that might care whether he is alive or dead, so when he heard his name, he thought that it was a mistake.

When he approached the table, he sees that all the envelopes are gone except for his sitting solely by itself. After picking it up, he reads his mother's name in the top left corner and feels like Charlie when he found the last golden ticket in *Willy Wonka and the Chocolate Factory*.

I love you, Momma. I knew you wouldn't let me down, he thinks, showing all his teeth as he walks back to his bunk, savoring all the love he knew his mother has for him.

Hello, son,

I love you, and I hope this letter reaches you in the best of health. Please forgive me, but I won't be attending your court date tomorrow. I'm sorry, but I'm very disappointed in you for allowing yourself to fall back into the lion's den God has already delivered you from numerous times before in the past. It hurts my heart to know what you're in there for because you are a part of me, and I thought you could never do such a crime. I've tried all that I can think of throughout the years to help you overcome the stumbling blocks that are on your path, and I understand now that if you don't want to overcome them, then all that I'm doing is wasting my time.

Your father says to let you do this time in jail on your own so that you can find out who Torrence Wingate Jr. truly is. Out of respect for my husband, that's what I'm deciding to do this go around with you, Junior. I will write you once every two weeks to see how you are doing, and as far as visits, I'll come and see you when I find time.

By the way, Audumn bought your dope money by the house and said she's through with you, so don't bother to try and reach out to her. Your drug money added up to be about $111,000. She also said she kept some of the money to help her get by until she finds out what she's going to do with herself. I put $500 on your books, so you don't have to worry about commissary while you are in there. I hope that your precious money was worth losing the essential things worth living for in life because your money is all that you have now. You really hurt me, son, and you make me feel like I failed as a mother. I love you, Torrence and it's time to get your life right with God.

Love,

Momma Love

PS: "Resist the Devil and he will flee from you!" (James 4:7).

The letter was read numerous times after he had opened it, and no matter how he tried to rearrange her words, Tree felt sadder whenever he read that his mother felt she had failed as a mother. His mother's point is clear as each letter, each word, and each period stood out more and more each time he examined the pain in his mother's handwriting. Her heart is broken, and he isn't there to assure her that the roots of the Tree he is becoming are alive again. In fact, his roots are as strong as they've ever been because he has planted himself by the life-giving rivers of water, which is the Bible. All he could do now is stay focused on the task at hand and keep moving forward until he reaches the finish line of change.

Tree didn't know where he is going in life, but what he did know was his past. The last sermon he could remember his father had preached said something about putting your hands to the plow and not looking back. Many times before, he has done just that, and each time he's always fell short just as the word of God promised. Also, this time it's different for him, so he doesn't have to tell anybody about the quickening in his heart because God and his son are the only two people who need to know right now. Everyone else will have to see it in his new walk he is walking from this day on.

Yesterday's court went according to God's will, and since his case was only evading arrest in a motor vehicle, he didn't bother in trying to obtain an expensive attorney. The court-appointed lawyer he was given presented to the DA a sentencing of one year county time running concurrent with the three years he has left on parole. The judge granted it without any questioning because he knew that his prior conviction would swallow the new sentence up without a shadow of doubt. Now that the hard stuff is behind him, all he has left to face is his parole hearing, which will be at the end of September.

Caught up into the word of God, the minute hand seems to tick like the second hand on the clock, and the days seemed to disappear as fast as the sun woke up the world. It's exactly one month from the day he stepped foot back into the state's correctional system, and Tree's whole demeanor has changed because lately he finds himself sitting by himself, reading the Bible day in and night out. He wants to play dominoes with the guys, and he wants to watch television too, but for some reason his soul has joined to the owner's manual of life.

Everything he is studying is causing him to mature mentally and spiritually each time he stares in the face of God. His growth in God's word is growing rapidly because God the Father has separated him to receive some one-on-one time with his son Jesus Christ, his personal savior. The scales over his eyes are beginning to fall away slowly each time a Bible verse is imprinted on the face of his soul. At the rate he is reading, Tree will have read the Bible in its entirety by January 1, 2012.

Sunday morning woke up everybody today because the guard over the pod thought every offender should be mandated to go to church. Tree didn't agree with his way of thinking, but got up anyway to go to the room assigned to be the sanctuary on the floor he is on. After brushing his teeth and throwing some water into the corners of his eyes, he waves to the CO in the picket to open the door for him. No one is in front of him or behind him when he steps into the vacant hallway. The only people that are around are a few trustees who are like road signs giving directions for anyone seeking help from a higher power.

Tree follows their directions carefully, and when he gets to the door in which they are meeting for service, he hears "Amazing Grace," being sung in all the wrong notes. The preacher for the day welcomes him as he walks inside to find a seat, but the only seats available are the one's up front. When the song is over, all those who had opened up their voices unto the Lord felt good inside because they gave God all they could give at the present time.

The word is brought forth shortly after a prayer is said for anyone present who had a prayer request. Minister Anthony Lewis isn't the best speaker the county has to offer, but his ferventness made him the easiest to relate to. Every offender opened up to him because he reminded them a lot of how they viewed themselves someday. The reason he came to the county jail so much is because mostly all the offenders wanted to do right, but it's like every time they're released, attending church doesn't go with them. Minister Lewis knew this, so most of his messages focused on being steadfast when the devil tries to detour you from fellowshipping with other believers.

"And that concludes our message for today," Minister Lewis said after saying amen. "Before we leave, guys, God has put on my heart to do something different this morning. Starting at the back from left to right, I want everybody who wants to join in to tell God thank you for something in their life today."

Inmates on the back row begin to look at each other as if to say, "You go first," because no one wanted to stand and start the chain of thank-yous out of fear that they would be the only one to participate. Finally, a small Hispanic guy in the left corner stood up with his head down and says shyly, "Thank you, Jesus, for giving me three meals a day." Small giggles begin to come from around the room as soon as he had spoken, and also a few jokes were blurted out for what he was thankful for.

Mr. Lewis noticed how the crowd's attention was deviated so easily and got his service back in order by explaining how some people are less fortunate than others. "Do we have anyone else that's thankful for anything today?"

After the short comedy show is over, one by one, orange uniforms started to stand and thank God for whatever their minds could think of. Some offenders thanked him for their families, friends, and cars, but some offenders still wanted to laugh at the guys' comments, so Mr. Lewis had to tell them that God smiles when we thank him for everything in our lives.

The majority of the small church's thank-yous were for waking them up this morning, and that made Tree recall in his readings of the Old Testament that God desired the children of Israel to honor him with their firstfruits of each day. Being that it's 2011, Tree thought that being thankful for waking up each morning is a way of giving God our firstfruits.

"Next please!" the preacher exclaims, pointing at Tree while looking at the time over the blackboard.

Tree stood hesitantly, but when his knees locked in place, he realized the bars he is currently behind wasn't anything to be ashamed about and that he had everything to be thankful for. As he stood there, so many things came to his tongue to say all at once, but not one word could find its way out of his mouth. Mr. Lewis thought he had frozen because of shyness, so therefore he told him to take his time. The only thing is, shyness wasn't the problem, and unspeakable joy is. Finally, the most important event ever done throughout the ages and the ages to come came spewing out his tongue, along with some tears traveling down his cheeks.

"Thank you, Jesus, for stepping off your heavenly throne to walk as a mere man and dying an unworthy death on the cross for our sins."

Everyone became silent again and stared at Tree as he sat down because the small congregation felt the sincerity in his words and made those who were playing throughout the morning take an outlook on their thankfulness. Even Mr. Lewis didn't have anything to say to follow such a powerful statement, so all he could do is let the words linger through the spirits of every individual there, including him.

"I pray something was said here today so that we can move forward in our lives as better men, and next time we meet, I want to try this thankful session after my sermon again. I think next time most of you, if not all, will have more to be thankful for than what was said here today. Thank you, and have a blessed month of October."

Walking down the halls of the county jail, inmates from church told Tree thank you because they needed to hear that. A few of them also said that they wished they had somebody like him in their tank whom they felt really knew God or at least was searching for him with a sincere heart.

Before reaching his pod, their words begin to poke at his soul along with the words of God he's been studying every minute of the day.

As he pondered on what the Holy Spirit is trying to tell him, he walks inside and sees inmates playing dominoes, checkers, watching television, reading the newspaper, books, and even flipping through the pages of the Bible. Then you had those who were sleeping their time away, and the rest were indulged in conversations about nothing. *WWJD? What would Jesus do?* he wonders while taking a seat at an empty table.

A sense of peace came inside the twenty-four-man cell throughout the day because the TV's volume is low from not fighting with the noise level in the cell. Also, the guards are not over the loudspeaker being disrespectful, so the tank is being respectful by not giving them any unnecessary strife.

As the man in the moon starts to show his face, Tree looks to the star that's always shining over him and says, "Amen," for his steadfastness in prayer during the day. From the time he sat at the table this morning, he's been praying earnestly for his pod because when he came back from church, all he saw were a lot of lost sheep in his cell without a shepherd.

"Excuse me, but are you Torrence Wingate?"

"Yes, may I ask why?"

"The guard wants you. I think you have a parole visit."

"On a Sunday?" Tree asks, wanting to complete his day in God's presence.

"Parole doesn't care because you never know when they gonna show up on you."

Parole is the last people he wanted to see today. Approaching the officer in the hallway, the officer tells him to stand on the wall until his name is called. While standing there, he rubs his back pocket to make sure his Bible is by his side because he never goes anywhere without it since Duck gave it to him after pretrial court.

"Torrence Wingate?" a beautiful black Ethiopian woman said, stepping out the door with *parole* painted on the header above it.

"Yes, that's me," Tree answered, extending his right hand. "Where's Ms. Liberty?"

"Hi, I'm Ms. Dobbins, and I'll be giving you your parole hearing today because your file has made it to Austin, Texas, and is no longer under her review."

"I understand, Ms. Dobbins. Well, I'm ready whenever you are."

"Great, so have a seat, and we will begin to go over your file."

Ms. Dobbins presented to him his whole past from the day he started to get into trouble as a teenager. His repetitiveness of misdemeanors and felonies is very shameful, so he turns his head after she reads over his four pages of criminal history. He knows that there is nothing he can do to tone out what he used to be, but listening to her made him look forward to rewriting his future.

"So what do you have to say about all this, Mr. Wingate?" Ms. Dobbins asks, kind of horrified to be reading his background.

"I'm guilty of all what you have before you, and I thank Jesus for giving me the opportunity someday to try things over again the right way."

"What kind of answer is that?"

"It means that when those steel doors open for me next time, I'm flying straight as a Robin Hood's arrow, Ms. Dobbins," Tree clarifies, pondering on that glorious day.

"Well, I'm sorry, but with everything I'm reading and the new offense you've been convicted of, I have no other choice but to recommend to the Board of Parole that you be violated and sent back to the state penitentiary."

"Yes, ma'am, I completely understand."

"You do?" Ms. Dobbins replies, caught off guard by his response.

"Yes, ma'am, I do. I understand you're just doing your job."

"Oh, okay. Well, normally you would have to wait for an answer, but since you understand what is going on here today, I'm going to speed your process up so that you can get to TDCJ and make it back home as soon as possible. Good luck, Torrence, and stay out of trouble."

"Thank you, Ms. Dobbins, and God bless you." Tree shakes her hand and exits into the hallway.

Parole went well, he thought as he stood at the door to his pod, waiting for the door to buzz open. It's been a long day for him, but most importantly, today he has owned up to his responsibility as a man and accepted all what he's done over the years without any excuses. *No more running from my mistakes or my responsibility to God,* he thought, stepping inside, remembering how earlier his fellow brothers were seeking reassurance but had no one to reassure them.

Back at his bunk, he sees his study Bible at the foot of his bed and realizes that everything that has happened through the years was to get him to this precise place at this precise time in his life. When I say this, I'm not talking about the things he has done to get himself into jail, but what I'm talking about is the calling God has had on his life since the day he placed Tree in his mother's womb.

We are all here for a purpose, and whatever that purpose may be, it is going to be fulfilled whether we like it or not. We can either do it the easy way, which is God's way, or we can do it the hard way, which is our way. Tree chose his own path in his life, but being that God has had a predestined purpose over him since the beginning of time, today he is stepping up to plate instead of continuously hiding in the dugout.

"Prayer call! Prayer call! Please feel free to join me in prayer and a small word from God before the lights go off," Tree shouts in faith, ready for the fiery darts the devil is about to start throwing at him, starting with the Texas state penitentiary.

20

Orange and brown leaves fluttered through the endless acres of land on the Preston Unit, causing the naked trees to shiver at the cool winds that have taken their green covering away. Summertime is over, and today marks the official one-year anniversary of Audumn leaving Tree in Harris County. The season doesn't make him feel any better because each year autumn comes around until his days on earth end, he would have to relive the pain of losing the one person who he truly cared about.

Tobacco rolled in toilet paper wrapper clouded the air on this sad day for Tree as he tries to smell nature's fragrance of the new season. Some cars are passing far in the background, so Tree finds a corner and stares at them through the barbwire fences on the recreation yard. Hypnotized from all the beauty of colors surrounding him, he praises the Lord for Audumn giving him nothing but her best during the years they spent together.

Every day his mother's first letter from the county seems to conjure its way out of the hole he's dug and buried it in and makes him want to tell Audumn he's sorry face-to-face. He knows that's not possible, so he indulges into his Bible daily for comfort, and he finds an eternal filling and the essence of his being is complete again. But he couldn't lie to himself; he still loved her deeply.

Walking in God's favor the past year has truly blessed him in many ways on defining his potential character. It is as if someone finally pulled the chain on the lightbulb over his head when it comes to living life because his eyes are now keen to the carnal man inside him. "Do unto to others as you would want done unto you," is a scripture he says during the times when he desires to embark in something he has no business doing.

TDCJ has also opened his eyes to other things that he didn't see when he first came to the penitentiary and played jail until he was released. This time around, he decided to utilize everything and everyone around him for the good of his rehabilitation because coming back a third time would make him a fool. Last time he did his time to himself, but this time, he's interacting with the fellow offenders and guards so that he can learn about people in general.

Interacting with those around him has taught him that most people feed off what is given to them, so they tend to become someone they're not because of what's fed to them each day. In the case of the offenders, it's gangs, tattoos, mischief, and fights. In the case of the guards, it's inmates masturbating while staring at the women officers, inmates cursing every time an officer asks them to do something, and having family problems at home that leads to them bringing their anger back to work with them. All these circumstances and more gives the wicked one an opening to do what he pleases in the enclosed world of the penitentiary. Therefore, Tree constantly engages himself with the officers and offenders to show that you can be happy and content in any state that you're in if you trust God to see you through.

Between the Bible classes, going to church, and the Bible studies Tree holds at the peak of each day, everyone on the unit knows that his lifestyle is the truth when it comes to church. Every time he steps foot outside his tank, offenders from all over the facility tip their hats off to him because you can't help but feel the power of the Holy Spirit when he comes around you. That's why he's thankful for the job God has blessed him with because he started out in the fields, but since he's blessed and highly favored in the eyes of the Lord, he's now a third-shift warden floor waxer. Meaning, he gets to move around freely to wax the floors of the entire Preston Unit and sometimes other units that are maximum security in the surrounding areas.

Being a man of integrity and a third-shift warden floor waxer has given him a lot of freedom throughout the unit because the guards on every shift have started to allow him to go and come as he pleases as long it is not count time. Whenever he's in between waxing the floors, the warden has granted him a clearance to help with the chain going out and coming in for the unit. All the offenders who arrive at the Preston Unit must follow Tree's instructions before standing in front the officers to be processed in the unit and also before being transferred from the unit.

Things are definitely looking up for Tree, and having to wax the floors and work the chain has helped the days practically fall off the calendar before him. From the time he opens his eyes until the time he closes them, he says breath prayers for strength in bearing the cross that he nailed himself to. At the end of each day, all he wants is for anyone who comes into his presence is to know that when you fall down, don't be ashamed to get back up again.

After completing his jobs at the end of each weekday nights, Tree gathers all the bibles that have been thrown away from the offenders leaving the unit and places them in a wool laundry basket. Other commodities he retrieves on his escapades are pens, paper, envelopes, shoes, and boots that are in better condition than some of the boots the offenders are currently wearing. All these things and whatever else he can get his hands on are given to anyone who lets him know what they are in need of before he goes to work the outgoing chain each night.

"How are you doing this morning, Ms. Garrett?" Tree asks, tired because last night's chain was over 150 inmates.

"I'm okay, as long as I got this steam coming from my coffee mug."

Tree chuckles and replies, "You're crazy, Ms. Garrett, but I feel you."

"I'm not crazy, Wingate, just prepared for this double I got to work today. You know we're shorthanded."

"Do you mind if I bless a couple of guys in tank 1 and 3 with a Bible and some boots they asked me for yesterday?"

"Yes, you may, Mr. Wingate, and keep up the good work because unlike us, God doesn't sleep."

Tank 1 pops opens, and Tree pushes the buggy in quietly because inmates are still asleep, and everyone needs their sleep for when it's time to go to work the following day. Walking over to a fellow inmate, Tree taps his shoulder to let him know he got the boots he needed for work.

"Say, Snoop, I got your boots you asked me for."

"Word," Snoop replied, wiping the corner of his eyes. "Damn, you fast, preacher."

Tree laughs at the comment because *preacher* is what a lot of the offenders have been calling him lately. "It's not me, it's God who blesses me so that I can be a blessing to others."

"That's what's up, preacher. Thanks, because my big toe is hanging out of these." Snoop holds up his busted left boot.

"I'm glad I can be of some service. By the way, I need your olds ones if I want to keep helping our brothers around here."

"No doubt, here you go, right here."

"Thanks, Snoop, and God bless you. Holla at me if you need anything that I can be of some help with," Tree said, shaking his hand while going to another guy's bunk who needed some envelopes and a pair of shoes.

"Two down and one to go." Tree closes the heavy steel door to the first tank he entered and goes over to the third tanks door that Ms. Garrett buzzed for him earlier. Ms. Garrett is in the picket looking on behind the tinted glass with great spirits because it's not every day you see offenders going out of their way to help other offenders who don't care about anything but themselves. None of her fellow coworkers knows this, but Tree's giving has inspired her to start a fund-raising organization for the needy at a community center in her neighborhood. She has been doing it for the past six months, and the only person who helped her get it off the ground was God.

"What's up, Tree?" a Caucasian offender by the name of Clint says, walking up as Tree entered the fifty-four-man cell. "Did you find me a Bible with the Old and New Testament in it yet?"

"Whiteboy Clint, can't you see a brother trying to catch some z's before all the lights come on?" a husky guy complains, poking his head from under his cover.

"That's my bad, Mike Z, I should have waited a little later to bring him this Bible," Tree replied in Clint's defense.

"Tree, is that you waking me up this early in the morning?" Mike Z ask, squinting, trying to focus on Tree's face. "Don't even worry about it. You know you good, preacher. Oh yeah, next time you in my neck of the woods, bring me a Bible too."

"I got you," Tree whispers so that none of the other offenders will wake up.

Clint takes the Bible and tells Tree he needs another favor before he can turn around and leave. Tree doesn't want to break Mike Z's rest again, so he calmly grabs his friend's arm and sits him down at one of the tables away from the bunks. Clint is not a real big guy, and Tree knows that his pale skin color causes some of the guys on the unit to pick on him from time to time. Even though Mike Z let it slide about interrupting his sleep this go around, some of the other offenders may not do so easily.

"What is it, Clint, and hurry up because I got to get back to my tank before 8:00 a.m. count."

"I'm sorry for holding you up, but word is that you are a very smart brother. I hope I'm not asking for too much, but I really need some help with my math and reading sections of the GED because three times I have taken it, Tree, and three times I have failed," Clint said, a little ashamed.

"Why don't you ask your teacher to help you? I mean, of all people, she should know what areas of academics you are struggling in."

"Don't get me wrong, Mrs. Petry does help me a lot, but she is only one person, and there's other inmates who need more help than me."

"Let me pray about it, and tonight I'll ask the lieutenant if I can tutor you for a few weeks. He shouldn't have a problem with it because while you are in school, I'm always across the hall in the law library anyway. Now if that's it, I got to go before that loud horn blows across the yard for count."

"Thanks, Tree, for the Bible, and tonight I'm going to pray about you tutoring me too."

"Now that's the faith God loves to hear, Clint. Don't worry because God will figure something out."

The loud horn sounded as the door to his tank closed behind him. A small sigh comes from his panting lungs as he catches the little wind he lost moving down the bowling alley so swiftly. Morning count is here, and if he wouldn't have made it back to his tank, he would have had to stand wherever he was until the horn sounded counts clear.

After a few minutes of catching his breath, Tree is tired, so he heads for the shower and cleanses off yesterday, looking forward to tomorrow. As the warm water runs over his bald head, he thinks about how far he's come when it came to befriending people because all his so-called friends has hurt him or possibly played a part in his incarceration. Since the day he started to embrace the man he is today, he vowed to choose his friends wisely and that being a positive individual in this world is what life is all about.

While thinking, he hears what his heart is telling him to do and agrees with himself to help Clint as best as he could.

Count cleared right after he put on his state-issued boxers, so Tree goes to the window by the door to see if he has some mail from yesterday. Every day he checks the window when he gets out of the shower to see if anyone thought about him by mistake because once every two months, he gets a letter from his family, and once every two months he writes back. He prayed for the day his mother wouldn't think his rehabilitation is a hoax, but Tree has proven to be a chameleon too many times before.

Lovey Wingate is written on one of the envelopes in the window, and Tree smiles because he loves to read his mother's name on anything. After reading the letter over, he sees that his mom will be coming this Saturday to visit him. It's been one year into his sentence, and he hasn't seen his mother but once, and that was in the county jail. At that time her attitude wasn't good or bad, but a little suspicious to listening to what her son was saying has happened in his life. He hoped his letters would have touched her heart by now and made her receive the change that has occurred in him from the day he started to look up for the answers.

As he takes a seat on his bunk, Tree tucks the letter in his locker and dries off the inside of his shower slippers. Visitation hours is two days away, so he unfolds his best white uniform and places it between his mattress and hard bunk as if to iron them of some sort. If placed correctly, the day after tomorrow when he goes to see his mother, he would be wrinkle-free and possibly have a slight crease in his cotton pants and shirt.

Finally he's ready for bed, so he reads over a few scriptures before praying for Lieutenant Smith to saying yes to tutoring Clint. Amen is the last thing he remembers before falling asleep to recharge his battery for the next night of long hours he would have to work when he wakes up.

Last night's prayer proved to be promising because Lieutenant Smith said yes to the tutoring of Clint as long as it didn't interfere with his job performance. It's Friday, and Clint can't wait to get started on his first tutoring sessions. What's funny is that Clint didn't know the lieutenant said yes, but spoke it into existence until Tree walked into the classroom today to help him. The other student offenders were a little jealous because they felt like Clint is getting the extra help he needs to pass the GED but kept their comments to themselves in hopes of Tree might help them later.

"Ms. Guidry, is that you?" Tree asks, thinking how small this world really is.

"Torrence?" Ms. Guidry asked with words of expressions.

"I thought that was you, Ms. Guidry, and why are you way out here in Hondo, Texas?"

"Because I'm Mrs. Petry now," she replied, holding up her wedding ring. "What are you doing back in here? I thought you went home from the Wells Unit."

"I did get out, but now I'm back on a violation."

"Come on now, Torrence, you are too smart to keep coming behind these caged walls."

"I know, Ms. Guidry, that's why you better take a picture because this will be the last time I'll be in all white ever again."

"Don't forget, it's Mrs. Petry now, and it better be the last time I see you in here again." Mrs. Petry looks him over. "Why are you here? Because I thought you graduated from high school."

"Yes, ma'am, I did graduate from high school, but Lieutenant Smith told me it would be okay to tutor Clint so that he can get his GED."

Mrs. Petry remembers how bright Tree was and agrees for him to help Clint if he would also help her with the other students who are behind in their studies. The experience of becoming a part of someone growing in their education made him agree to what she requested to assist her.

"Thanks, Torrence, because I can really use the help in here. Also, I'm proud to have you on board, and I'm proud to see you are a different person from that thug you were back then."

Tree is a little rusty at first on his education skills, but as the hours went on, twelve years of school begin to come back to him, and he begins to show Clint where he is going wrong when solving equations. Clint's mistakes were that he's breaking down the problems the best way that suited him, and not the way the teachers have taught him in the past. Tree showed him a few shortcuts and some easier ways to find the solutions to the harder problems, and by the end of the day, Clint's work started to show some progress. As far as his reading and punctuation skills go, Tree wasn't the best tutor, but he did know enough to get Clint over the hump that was too high for him to jump.

The horn for evening count clearing is also the bell for school's release. When hearing it, all the students left quickly because of the two-and-a-half grueling hours of tiresome schoolwork. Mrs. Petry thanked Tree and told him she looked forward to seeing him Monday while Tree told her thank you for having him and that he looked forward to being there.

As he exits, he looks at the clock and notices he has exactly one hour until he has to report to floor duty, but seeing his mother tomorrow morning gave him the energy he needed to get it over with. Yes, working in GED is going to be hard for him because of his busy schedule, but being that his last name is Wingate, he promised not to quit until Clint achieved his certificate of completion on the GED final exam.

21

"'T is the season to be jorry, fa ra ra ra ra, ra ra ra ra!'"
Laughter and loud chuckles sounded off every brick wall of the vast enclosed cell. The movie *A Christmas Story* is on, and it's at the part where the Chinese are singing "Deck the Halls" to the main cast's family. Everyone who is anyone has seen the movie, and each time the Chinese restaurant scene comes on, the majority of the unit stops what they're doing for a quick laugh.

Green jackets are on the backs of the offenders on this chilly night. The heat is working, but because of germs, medical has the temperature set at 76 degrees. Today is the beginning of the three-week countdown until the day Jesus Christ was born, so inmates are paying the artist in the tank to draw art on handkerchiefs and envelopes to send to their loved ones. The days are going by as fast as they come, and some offenders are becoming uneasy because at midnight, they will only have twenty days left until the day of all days.

"I'm sorry, Joe C, but I had to color Minnie Mouse's dress red," a Hispanic guy by the name of Diablo said while delivering a handkerchief to Joe, who is in the gang called Crips.

"Red! What do you mean you had to color it red? Everybody on this unit knows what time it is when it comes to what color I'm representing, and here you are disrespecting me by giving me some bullshit that I hate with a passion!" Joe C points at Minnie Mouse's red dress. "I'm sorry, Diablo, but I ain't paying for that, so you might as well start over while you still have enough time to draw me another one the right way."

"I'll be damned if I start over after I've written your girl's name on it. It took me three days to draw this for you, and you gon' pay me, or we gonna have some problems!"

"I don't give a damn if we have a problem and some answers because I'm still not paying you for shit until you get my handkerchief done the way

I told your ass to do it! Capiesh?" Joe C thinks his Italian comment was Spanish.

Diablo and Joe C's words bounced off each other like a game of ping-pong with no paddles. One would think that the beef between them would stay between them, but as they got louder, members of each of their gangs started to pop up out of nowhere like weeds that you never thought was there until it's too late. The tension between the two of them started to rise like heat until Joe C got fed up with the air boxing and punched Diablo in his mouth to shut him up.

Diablo drops but gets right back up and drives his pencil into Joe C's chest, barely piercing his skin because of the cushion in the green jacket he is wearing. Before you know it, both parties are involved, and the fight escalated into a last-man-standing match on WWE.

Tree is at the table playing a friendly game of chess with his Hispanic Christian brother, chatting about the Christmas visits they were going to get from their families real soon. Suddenly, from out of nowhere, the day is interrupted, and from the corners of his eyes, the color green from the jackets seemed to be in more places than one. Not thinking, he runs over and tries to break it up, but before he can get there, a Hispanic inmate hits him across the back of his head with two bars of soap in a sock. The hard blow instantly knocks him out for the count and sends a stream of blood over the cemented floor.

A black offender watched Tree fall and stabbed the guy who did it in the back with something sharp he made out of contraband. Tiny drops of blood on the ground started to become bigger as more wounds began to be opened, but the more blood that was shed, the harder they fought. By the time the lights began to flash repeatedly, every offender of all races was fighting for their life.

It's a shame that such a great act of violence can blow up numerous of innocent bystanders' lives from such a small fuse over the color red. It seems like each year that goes by, a piece of our human morality goes with it. The world will come to an end someday, but if we as a people don't begin to work on our morals, that someday may be tomorrow.

Lying on the floor unconscious, Tree is stepped on and stepped over while the rest of the offenders tried to stay on their feet for survival. Enough is enough, so the guards are lined up in their nonpuncture uniforms, waiting for the word from their captain to go inside and contain the situation. The signal is finally given, and three pepper spray smoke bombs are shot from a bazooka-like launcher into the tank in three different directions. As the gagging smoke circulated throughout the air, inmates begin to choke and run for any source of water among them. A few of them looked like ostriches because their heads were in the bottom of the toilets, trying to stop their eyes from burning.

The captain waited for the pepper spray smoke bombs to take its full effect on the tank, but a guard who had some rank felt the inmates needed a fourth bomb to assure the guards' safety. After he launches the bomb, the captain opens the door on the count of three and signals for his tactics team to run in with their guns drawn. "Everyone down on the ground!" the captain shouts with muffled words because of the gas mask protecting his face. When they walked through to make their rounds on those who didn't comply with their demands, all they could hear is coughing and gagging in the fog-like smoke as the offenders stretched out across the floor so as not to be shot with the rubber bullets.

The bomb that was shot last somehow found its way igniting in Tree's face and caused him to awake from the earlier blow to the back of his head. His mind is still blank from all of the mishaps, so he jumps to his feet, feeling like he's been sprayed with a can of Mace. Hunching over, he coughs up last night's chow because of the dense smoke that is burning his throat and his lungs.

A guard with an AK-47 replica is parting his way through the heavy smoke when he sees an offender five feet away from him hasn't complied to the orders from his captain. Out of reflex, he feels Tree's hand gestures of waving burning smoke from his face are a threat and pulls the trigger, striking him two times in the chest and once in his rib cage. The powerful blows make him fall to the pavement again, but this time he is squirming on the floor, and his upper body feels like he's been hit with a missile from point-blank range. Everything is happening so fast, and his short-term memory loss isn't making anything better.

"I'm on the ground!" Tree yells as he sees the black boots of the guard approaching swiftly.

The officer hog-ties his hands to his feet and says, "It's a little late to be following orders, inmate. You should have thought about that, genius, before I put three hot ones in your ass."

Tree is left restrained and lying in a pool of his own saliva after the officer detained him and continued into the thick smoke, looking for any more troublemakers. Finally the air is starting to transform from dense white to clear in the tank, and the offenders see that the COs are in full control of the situation. No one in white is making any sudden movements because they heard the loud screams from Tree when he was shot three times from not listening.

"Now, you maggots listen up!" the captain yells. "I don't know what in the hell all this is about, but you have thirty-one days to think about it because this entire unit is on official lockdown until then. Jackson, call the infirmary for this idiot you had to put down for thinking he can disobey my orders. As for the rest of you dimwits, medical will be here shortly to see if any of you are hurt severely. By the way, Merry Christmas to the fool that started all this because I'm pretty sure everyone on the unit is going to tell them thank you when ya'll get off lockdown in January."

Medical showed up shortly after Tree is carried out like a coffin by the officers. Before the captain left, he told everyone else who needed medical attention to sit in their bunks until the nurses tend to their wounds. After the last injury is seen, only two of the offenders were escorted to the infirmary for further medical attention. The battle between the Blacks and Mexicans was horrific, but the green jackets they were wearing protected them from any major injuries.

As for Tree, his memory came back when he was getting eleven stitches in the back of his head. Also, his chest is badly bruised from when he took the three rubber bullets to the chest and caused his ribs not to allow his body to move the way he wanted to. X-rays showed that he suffered a hairline fracture on one of his ribs and wouldn't be able to resume his duties as a warden floor waxer for three to five weeks. Normally, he would have been sent to a medical unit for his injuries, but Tree asked the nurses could he stay on the Preston Unit because the work God has for him to do is not finished yet.

After about a week of resting, the doctors sought forth to agree to his recovery's request, and Tree knew in his heart that all his hard work with the offenders and officers was not in vain.

Recovery is a time of peace for him as he exercises his upper body every day so that he can get his health back to 100 percent. During his time off, he also researched subjects from all religions so that he could get a better understanding on why people followed the God they served. Every word that is soaked in from his research strengthens his beliefs in the one who was lifted up and drew all men unto him. He couldn't see the big picture, but all his studies were embedded in him for a greater purpose.

On his third week of healing, he had his mobility back, but a sharp pain still slightly pierced the inside of his chest. For three weeks, the unit has been under the torture of peanut butter and syrup sandwiches, but during that time, the inmates stayed inside the yellow lines throughout the lockdown. Since nothing else broke out to destroy the warden's holiday spirit, he allowed the Church of Jesus Christ to go to each building and pass out homemade Christmas cookies. Everyone enjoyed them and kept the peace because they knew that Warden Preston was deeply offended over the outburst between the rival gangs.

Disregarding the pain in his chest, Tree is ready to get back to work when the warden gave the clearance for school to resume at its normal schedule. Offenders who were not in school were still on twenty-four-hour lockdown for the fourth and final week or until the captain said something different.

Not thinking about the Christmas visit he missed, Tree regains his focus and asks the nurses to give the okay for light duty so that he can go back to tutoring the offenders in GED. Now don't get me wrong, missing Christmas did bring his spirit down a bit, but the delicious variety of cookies from the church was better than nothing.

Warden Preston said yes to his request to tutor the offenders when the nurses said he was able to perform light duty. Usually he sticks to his guns when making decisions on permanent lockdown, but Tree's case was an exception because he is a tutor. And since he started three and a half months ago, the unit's certificates of completions on the GED have gone up 12 percent, making the headlines in Hondo's November newspaper. No matter how the warden looked at it, Tree was special to the unit, and the entire staff saw for the first time that the warden wasn't as coldhearted as everybody thought he was.

"Torrence, I don't know what you did for the warden, but he said it's okay for you to go back to tutoring during the lockdown," Nurse Carolyn said.

"Praise God, because I'm not going to get to my best cooped up in this infirmary all day."

"So what you're saying is that you don't like my company."

"No, Nurse Carolyn, that's not what I'm saying," Tree replied with a grin. "What I'm saying is that I need to get out of here and stretch these long legs of mine, or I'm going to end up stiff as a board."

Week four took its time in coming, making the three weeks that just passed feel like they all added up to one. School started in twenty minutes, and up until now, Tree's patience has held up quite well. Twenty-four hours for the past twenty-four days, he has been locked down, and the time remaining for school to start has caused him to become a little tedious. Nurse Carolyn sees he is becoming anxious and tells him to relax before he bursts a major blood vessel in his brain.

"I'm sorry, Ms. Carolyn, but the worst thing other than being locked up is being locked up while you're locked up."

The horn sounded as soon as he finished telling the nurse how he is feeling about the twenty-four-hour lockdown stipulations. "You see, Torrence, waiting is not as hard as you thought it would be."

Tree walked inside the classroom, and Mrs. Petry is relieved to see he came back to assist her. Her passion for her students' education lifted because his presence helped the offenders understand that having an education can open endless doors for you in society. All the students were glad to see him too and thanked him for coming back as well. The students who were new to the class heard all what he had done for the previous offenders who had graduated and told him they appreciate the volunteer work that he's been doing each day for them.

"So how does your head feel?" Mrs. Petry asks at the end of class.

"I'm okay, Mrs. Petry, and thanks for asking."

"What about your chest? Are you still in pain from the gunshots?"

"A little, but I'm a big boy."

"Good for you," Mrs. Petry said, patting him on the back. "Please, Torrence, I don't want to hear about you being in the middle of a lot of mess you don't have no business being around because any day now, these doors are going to be opened for you."

"Yes, ma'am." Tree thinks about how he was shot three times. "You know what I just realized talking to you, Mrs. Petry?"

"What's that, Torrence?"

"That you can't save everybody."

"You are exactly right, Torrence. My husband told me that same thing one day when I was trying to cut corners for some students who were trying their hardest and still failed. After seeing my frustration, he came to me in love and said, 'I'm sorry, Devin, but you can't save everybody.' I know you had a lot of good intentions in whatever you did, Torrence, but running from stupidity gives you a chance to run another day. Think about that tonight when you go back to medical for your ribs you injured on behalf of someone else."

The conversation with Mrs. Petry made Tree ask himself what is it that he is trying to achieve during this span of life on earth. Before, he thought that if he walked according to what the Bible teaches that everyone around him would follow, but as he rubs the knot on the back of his head, he understands that if the people around him daily didn't follow him, then who will? *From now on, all I'm going to do is what God leads me to do because life is a gift, and I must cherish it.*

Being in the infirmary was better this final week of lockdown because tutoring school gave him something to do that was positive to pass time. Every day for the entire week, he gave his all in those two hours of class, and since he had so much free time on his hands, he studied writing and literature books to sharpen his English skills. His hard work pays off quickly because each day he studied, it seemed liked the student he was helping needed help in that area of their curriculum in which he brushed his skills on the night before.

At the end of the week, he thinks about the last few weeks while looking at himself in a mirror in the bathroom. As he stands straight up, he raises his shirt and stares at the three dents in his chest. His body is healing at an increased rate, but he still couldn't shake the thoughts from when the Hispanic guy knocked him out. A small tap on the door makes him jump out of the past and causes that painful day to fade away. Nurse Carolyn comes in and asks if he's all right because he is sweating while the temperature in the infirmary is low. At first he is a little ashamed to confide in her, but her kindness made him tell her about his dreadful visions. Her only answer is to pray because that's the only medication TDCJ has for those kinds of symptoms.

"Torrence, this came in the mail for you today from the Board of Paroles." Nurse Carolyn hands him a slip with the change of line class status across the top of it.

"Parole!" *What in the world is parole sending me when I haven't even seen them yet for my release?*

"What, you surprised or something? Whatever it is can't be bad because your line class has changed to a trustee status," she replied, pointing to the word *trustee* on the slip.

Looking at the words underneath the line class change, Tree zones off and forgets the nurse is still there. Nurse Carolyn sees that he needs some time to himself, so she walks off to finish passing out the rest of the mail.

"You are hereby granted to outside duty trustee status" were comments written by the Board of Parole in the state's capital, Austin. The comments also stated that due to the high volume of offenders in the state of Texas, the Board of Parole has decided to discharge a random number of offenders for good behavior. The excitement of seeing the word *discharge* rises from off the paper, and he barely finishes the rest of the notation that stated he has been granted a FI-6 with a release date of June 14.

"Mrs. Carolyn, I'm going home in June!" Tree exclaims, showing off his parole answer.

"That's great, Torrence, and don't forget that you are going to be leaving us soon too."

"Oh yeah, I forgot that being an outside trustee means I have to go to an outside trustee camp." Tree's excitement stops abruptly.

"Well, I think it will be good for you to get off this unit and be around inmates who care if they are going home or not."

"But I thought God needed me here."

"That what's wrong with people today, Torrence. For some reason, they tend to think they know what's best for them when God has something totally different for them to do," the nurse replied as she is paged over the loudspeaker to attend to another patient.

22

April 25 is Tree's birthday, and it's also the day he celebrates his second birthday as the new man the world has grown to love. Last year he celebrated his twenty-ninth birthday by praying and fasting the entire day to be closer to God. But this year he decided to start a one-meal-a-day fast on the first of April and end the fast on his birthday when his mom comes to visit him. His fasting is for God to chip away at his father's heart so that he can accept him as a changed man when he is released in two months. It's been almost two years since he last talked to his dad on the phone, and yet the sorrow in his voice still rang in his ears like it was yesterday.

"Happy birthday, Tree, and good morning."

"Thanks, Eric," Tree said, extending his hand as he walked to the entrance of his cubicle.

"So are you going to church today, or are you going to chill out and relax for your b-day?"

"Am I going to church? What kind of question is that? Do I ever miss church, E?"

"Not that I can remember," Eric replies, staring into thin air, trying to find that one time Tree has missed church.

"Well, that's your answer then."

"Good because it wouldn't be the same without you."

"Yes, it would, because only God can give the increase," Tree replied sarcastically as Eric goes back to his cubicle to get ready for Sunday morning service.

Church service starts at 7:00 a.m. and ends at 8:30 a.m., but Tree is the lead man of the setup crew, so he and his coworkers have to be there early to make sure everything's in order. Getting up in the morning isn't an issue for him because his mind-set alarm clock almost always wakes him up at 5:30 a.m. to breathe the crisp fresh air outside.

During the week, his daily routines are pretty much the same, but Sundays are different for him because before service, Tree likes to go into the chapel to be in God's house in secret.

Doing time on a trustee camp is a lot easier than doing time on a regular TDCJ farm because the offenders have a lot more freedom as an outside trustee. Within the gated trustee camp are three buildings with the letters A on one of them, B on the next, and C on the last. Inside of these lettered buildings are a hundred cubicles in which the offenders can go and come as they please on the camp's enclosed property as long as it's not count time or rack time.

Also on the trustee camp's facility is a massive dayroom so that all three buildings can interact with one another like normal people, and there was also a commissary that is opened throughout the day. Every morning Tree goes to the windows of commissary to buy orange juice to help start his day, and it is with these perks and more that helps an offender's stay on the trustee campgrounds go as comfortable as possible. But for Tree, he is just happy to be right next to Houston in Sugar Land and not in no-man's land like when he was out west in Hondo.

"That will be $1 for the orange juice, and will there be anything else for you today?"

"No thanks, Mrs. Jenkins, and good morning." Tree hands her his ID card so that she can retrieve the money from off his books.

"Good morning to you too, Mr. Wingate, and God bless you on this beautiful Sunday morning."

"Ain't it beautiful out here today?" Tree asks while looking at the dew melting off the blades of the grass. "Sorry I can't stay and chat with you, Mrs. Jenkins, but I have to get ready to set up the chapel for service."

"Well, I guess you better be on your way because you only have one hour left until church starts."

Tree is behind on his Sunday morning schedule, so the orange juice he bought he gulps down at the doors of the chapel. Everything is pitch-black as he walks through the sanctuary to the chaplain's office to let him know he's there. While walking carefully, all he could see is the light shining through the blinds of the office as he approached slowly. His ears can't hear a thing except for the rubber on the bottom of his canvas shoes, which sounds a little creepy after each step he takes across the tiles. Before he opens the door to the office, he knocks softly just in case the chaplain is praying or studying the scriptures. As it opened wider, a yellow note is on the desk next to the telephone stating that he had to leave on a family emergency and that the guest speaker will not be coming today.

Tree looks at the clock change from 6:20 to 6:21 and falls into the office chair, not knowing what to do next. He rubs his forehead in frustration and says a quick prayer for guidance in what to do on behalf of church service this morning. As he is opening his eyes, he notices that Chaplain Brown's Bible is opened, and there is only one scripture highlighted on the pages. The scripture read, "How then shall they call on Him in whom they have not believed? And how shall they believe in Him of whom they have not heard? And how shall they hear without a preacher?"

Romans 10:14 struck him in the depths of his spirit. *Is it truly my time to speak, Lord?* he thought as he read the note for a second time. "I don't know the first thing about preaching Jesus. Praying for somebody or reading a scripture here and there, yeah. But preaching, Lord, I don't think I can do that."

His team for the setup crew began to come in while he is contemplating with himself and God.

"Where's the chaplain, Tree?" Eric asks.

"He had to leave on a family emergency, so we need to pray for him."

"Well, do you want to pray now or during altar call after service?"

Eric's question is a question he has to ponder on for a minute. As he is thinking on what to do about service, the lights in the sanctuary begin to be turned on, and the setup crew is starting to line up rows of chairs in front of the pulpit.

"I'm sorry, E, but the guest speaker isn't coming today either, so tell the guys that it's on us today to hold service and that I will be preaching the Word of God."

"Why don't we just cancel? It's only one Sunday."

"Because how can the lost souls hear the word of God and believe if there's no one there to preach?" Tree replies, knowing that this is what God has been conditioning him to do from the beginning of his sentencing.

Within the hour, the chapel reached its capacity of 120, and extra chairs had to be placed along the walls because the trustee camp came out to show their support. A few guards Tree knew heard that he is preaching and decided to stand in the back so that they wouldn't be a distraction. The different colors of faces blended together beautifully in the rows of chairs and gave him the courage to stand firm in what he is about to do for the first time. Church in the past TDCJ units was segregated, but here on the trustee camp, all the offenders look at each other as they are all in white uniforms, so why fight with one another?

The microphone is all Tree can see as he walked up to place his Bible on the podium. When he grabbed it, suddenly everyone appeared to have a look of suspense on their faces. A small pause is taken so that he can take a deep breath because he hasn't had any time to prepare for today's message. As he stood there, he searched throughout his brain, and the words "Choosing your friends wisely" slips out the back of his throat from out of nowhere.

"Hello, church, and I'm sorry that our guest speaker couldn't be here today, but before I go any further, I would like to thank all of you for coming out to hear what thus says the Lord despite the absence of our guest. By the way, my name is Torrence Wingate for those who don't already know me, and today I will be preaching my first message for the Kingdom of God."

No one said a word after his response, but that didn't stop him from going on with the message God put on his heart for the trustee camp to hear. "The topic for today is entitled 'Choosing Your Friends Wisely,' and to elaborate on our subject, I am going to tell you a story from a Jesus perspective so that everyone can have a better understanding on how we should choose our friends."

Everyone's ears are opened and their minds are receptive when hearing that Tree is about to tell a story.

"Today's scripture will be coming from the NIV John 15:14–16 for those who have brought their Bibles with them."

A short flutter from the pages of the Bibles sounds in the quiet church then stops when Tree begins to read the scriptures. "The scriptures read, 'You are my friends if you do whatever I command you. No longer do I call you servants for the servant does not know what his master is doing; but I have called you my friends, for all things that I heard from My Father I have made known to you. You did not choose Me, but I have chosen you and appointed you so that you may bear fruit and that your fruit shall remain.'"

Eric walks up with a clear glass of water after the scripture reading, and Tree feels like his father preaching at Let It Shine. After taking a sip, the

Holy Spirit takes over him, and his voice begins to sound as if he's preached a thousand times before.

"Today, church, I want you to listen carefully to the story of a man named Jesus who came to this earth and walked amongst us as God wrapped in flesh. A lot of people may agree to disagree, but whether we like it or not, Jesus was a man just like me and you are.

"He also was a man who had to endure everything we as human beings could possibly have endured so that he can fulfill God's Law of the Old Testament and abolish it. This would, in turn, bring in the New Testament of grace on the day he would offer up His sinless sacrifice on the cross. Please, congregation, I want you to open your imaginations to the story 'A Typical Day with Jesus' as I tell the unseen things people tend to forget about the disciples who later became the pillars of our church. Amen."

"Amen!" an old Chinese guy blurts out from the right in a squeaky voice. A little laughter started to conjure up after the Chinese guy's response, but Tree raised his hand, and everyone became silent again.

"My story begins on the banks of the Jordan River, and the disciples are worried because two days ago, a heavy storm has pounded the surrounding areas of the Jordan and has caused the crossing to overflow to eight feet. The horses and mules can make it across on their own only if they didn't have to carry anyone, so out of respect for Jesus Christ, the disciples began to talk amongst themselves to see what is best for their Master. The only solution they came up with is to keep walking until they found another crossing, but no one asked Jesus what he wanted to do, so he kept quiet.

"As they started to continue on their journey up the banks of the Jordan, John, the disciple who Jesus loved, spoke up, 'Jesus Christ, thy Son of God. If it be thy will, why don't you command us to walk on the water and cross the Jordan River just as you commanded our brother Peter to walk on water when we crossed over to the land of Gennesaret in the boat?' [Mark 6:45–53)].

"Jesus turns and says to him, 'I'm sorry, John, but my father did not send me into the world to overcome the obstacles in life for you, but he did send me to go through them with you. I say, let us cross right here before night catches up with us.'

"'Yes, Master,' they all said in unison as they watched Jesus take the first step in the deep waters."

Everything that was just said, the inmates saw in their minds clearly, and they began to focus more as Tree went on to speak. Tree, on the other hand, felt his mouth become dry after allowing the Holy Spirit to capture the fullness of a day with Jesus Christ, but the water Eric brought him gave him the nourishment he needed, and he went on to preach in honor of his father.

"Crossing the Jordan was very tiresome for the thirteen men, including Jesus. The destination they are trying to reach is two days away, so Matthew suggests that they camp along the shore and start their journey in the morning when they are fresh. Nightfall came faster than they expected, and the river begins to send a cool breeze from off of its surface. Jesus, wanting to be of some help, goes and collects some twigs to start a campfire while Peter, the experienced fisherman, goes out to fish. Finally, the fire is started, and everyone is warming themselves, waiting for Peter to come back with tonight's meal.

"After they waited for about an hour, Peter appeared from the dark night with seven small fishes on a string. Anger is all over his face because he knows that what he has caught is not enough to sustain them for the night or tomorrow's journey.

"'Jesus,' Peter said, holding up the string of fish, 'if it be thy will, could you bless what we have and feed us like you fed the five thousand in that deserted place?' [Matt. 14:15–20].

"'I'm sorry, Peter, but my father did not send me into the world to overcome the obstacles in life for you, but he did send me to go through them with you. Come, let us eat what my father has provided for us and be thankful.'

"'Yes, Master,' they all said in unison as they watched Jesus cook the fish over the open fire."

Listening to himself, Tree is surprised that he's made it this far without Sandman from the *Apollo* booing him off the stage. It was like he is sitting in the audience and watching himself speak because the things he is saying, he didn't even know he knew.

"The next morning, the group of men went to wash in the river, and Jesus slightly cut his foot on a rock, but Luke, the physician of the bunch, noticed the blood in the sand as Jesus walked along the shore and went over to help him.

"'Lord, are you okay?' he asked with great concern.

"'Yes, Luke, I'm okay, but could you please bandage my foot so we can be on our way? Besides, it's only a small cut, and daylight waits for no man.'

"'My Lord, if it be thy will, why don't you heal yourself like you healed the man with leprosy back in the city we just left?' [Luke 5:12].

"'I'm sorry, Luke, but my father did not send me into the world to overcome the obstacle in life for myself. But He did send me to go through them just as you do. Please, Luke, could you bandage my foot just as you would bandage anyone else's?'

"'Yes, Master,' Luke replied as they all watched him tend to Jesus's foot.

When Tree finished his story, he looked up from the podium, and all of the men were in awe. Even the guards in the back were talking to one another on how Jesus lived a life on earth just as we do today. The story caused everyone in the chapel to ask themselves whether or not they were praying for what they needed from Jesus or for what they wanted to help pacify their everyday life.

After allowing everyone in the building to devour the dynamics of the story about Jesus, Tree went on to explain and close his sermon.

"I pray that what I have spoken to you today fell in the depths of your hearts just as it fell in my mind as the story unfolded. There are many ways one can interpret the story 'A Typical Day with Jesus,' but today, I am going to explain to you how Jesus chose his friends wisely."

Tree pauses to think about the best way to expound on the story so that everyone can understand.

"The reason why I chose this topic is because of the bars we are currently behind. Yes, I know that these bars have turned into barbwire fences now that we're on a trustee camp, but at the end of the day, we are not free like the average citizen. Before I go any further, I want to ask all my brothers present a question. How many of you here today are in here because of their friends or the company they kept around them?"

One hand came up on the first row as soon as Tree asked the question, and then a second hand went up shortly after from along the walls. Offenders who saw some of the barbaric inmates participating raised their hands as well, and before one could blink his eyes twice, the entire chapel had their hands raised.

"Today, church, is a glorious day for me because it is my thirtieth birthday. The sad part is that during these thirty years, I find that most of the time I've been in trouble, it was because I was with my so-called friends. It's been almost four years total I've been incarcerated, and since the day I entered TDCJ's system for a second time, I realized that I must choose my friends more wisely. What I've also learned over the years is that in order for two people to become true friends, they must first be on the same page.

"To give you an example, think about a banker and a bank robber being friends with one another. Now honestly, church, can these two people be friends?"

"No!" the church said all at once.

"And you are exactly right, so please keep that in mind as I tell you how the story 'A Typical Day with Jesus' compares with our topic for the day. Now, church, on the day Jesus spoke in John chapter 15, he knew that his death on the cross was on the road up ahead of him and was in great anguish because of what he had to endure for us. I believe that when Jesus looked back on his three years of ministry that it uplifted his spirit because of the ups and downs the disciples had to endure to follow him. Or shall I say how the men he had chosen to be in his presence was on the same page as him. Such as the eight-foot Jordan River they had to cross or the seven pieces of fish they had to divide amongst thirteen men. Not only that, but how they slept together, bathed together, ate together, and mended each other's wounds together. These things and more are the things that made Jesus say to his disciples, 'Today, I call you my friends.'

"You see, church, Jesus called them his friends because the disciples stood by his side when he wasn't doing anything miraculous and when he was only being an ordinary man just like them. With enough said, I ask you, who are we calling our friends today, and are we choosing them wisely just as Jesus did after testing their faithfulness and friendship for nearly three years? John 15:13 says, 'Greater love has no one then this, than to lay down his life for his friends.' Like I said before, Jesus loved his friends so much that later on in the scriptures, he ended up dying for them.

"I'm sorry, but our time is about up, and I pray that the story 'A Typical Day with Jesus' will be of some help when choosing your friends more wisely in the future. Please pray for Chaplain Brown, who is out on a family emergency, and if there's nothing else, Eric will close us out so we can be dismissed. Thank you, and be blessed."

Eric came up to the pulpit and hugged Tree while whispering in his ear he has a visit. As he stepped down to exit, a few claps begin to sound from different corners of the chapel until a standing ovation nearly raised the roof. Almost half of the church shook his hand and told him "Thank you" for preaching in a way so that they all can understand. The guards that were there told him to keep up the good work and that they never heard the word of God preached that way before in their entire life. Tree wished he could stay to fellowship, but rules are rules, and if he didn't make it to visitation on time, it would be like he denied his visit for the day.

Visitation is in the building adjacent to the chapel, so getting there isn't any problem for him. While standing in line to be logged in by the officer, Tree sees a rainbow in the clouds and thinks about the covenant God made with Noah when the water receded off the face of the earth (Gen. 9:13). The rainbow was to show God that he would never destroy the earth again with water because there are always people out there like Noah and Tree who truly loved him for who he is.

"Torrence Wingate," Tree said to the officer behind the desk.

"You do know you are late and I can cancel your visit?"

"Yes, ma'am, and I apologize for my tardiness."

"Please don't let this happen again because I will have no choice but to do my job next time. Now go on in, you're at table 12."

Table 12 is around the corner, so he couldn't see who had come to see him. He thought it was his mother, but as he came around the corner, the only person he saw is his father standing with open arms behind the table he had to sit on the opposite side of.

"Happy birthday, son, I love you," his father exclaimed, giving Tree a hug for nearly a minute.

"I love you too, Dad, and thanks for coming to visit me because we have a lot of catching up to do."

23

Every year that passes has different seasons because in life, we are going to go through seasons that change according to how we live our lives. Either we can become complacent and accept the season that we are currently in for what they are, or we can step out on faith and move forward into the next season God has prepared for us. Whatever we decide, we must understand that yesterday is not going to be the same as today and that God knows what is best for us.

Finally, the month of all months has come, and any day now, Tree will be called out for the chain going to the Wells Unit in Huntsville. It's been twenty months and twelve days he's been behind bars, and even though he can't wait to be released, Tree feels that the season he is in now is the best season he has ever experienced in his life. As he thinks back on how he left God in jail when he got out the first time, he becomes a little scared because he knows that's what brought him back to the penitentiary a second time. *What is freedom?* is all he can think about because in his heart, he knows he is free already.

Tonight, is different for Tree because the feeling of suspense is covering him like the blanket of the dark black skies. Tree is still a little troubled as he lies on a small hill by himself, but the glowing of the moon shining down on him slightly uplifts his spirit for the time being. Everything in his life at this present time is better than ever, and Tree couldn't ask for anything even if he wanted to. God has been good to him since the day he stepped foot back into the system, and he didn't want the cares of the world to detour him from what he has accomplished in the Lord. Doubt of what is to come when he steps outside those gates slowly lurks throughout his inner being until his friend Eric interrupts his thoughts and tells him to join the rest of the guys in the dayroom.

"Surprise!" every man in the dayroom yells as Tree and Eric walked through the side doors together. Tree looks around and wonders why all the offenders he has befriended have come together under one roof tonight. His mind continues to be blank, but seeing all his friends together at one time made him not care what the special occasion is for.

"Aren't you surprised, Tree?"

"I mean, I guess I'm surprised, E. But I don't know what for."

"Tonight's your night, H-town. Officer McDaniel let us know you were on the chain tonight, so me and the guys wanted to throw you a going-away party."

"How am I on the chain when I don't go home for another two days? If anything, I should be on the chain tomorrow night."

"Oh yeah, Officer McDaniel said TDCJ is honoring Flag Day this year as a holiday, so the Wells Unit won't be releasing anyone on June 14 this year. And since they can't release you a day late, they have to release you a day early."

Before he could respond to Eric, a couple of guys walked over and handed him a big bowl of chili noodles with all kinds of different meats in it. Everybody who is there has pitched in to help make the meal so that everybody can eat. As Tree sat down and took his first bite, he realized that tonight may be the last night he probably will see this special group of guys again.

"Can I have everyone's attention please?" Tree shouts while tapping his plastic spoon on the steel table as he stood up. "Before I came in here tonight, I was outside beating myself up on what am I going to do when I get out in a couple of days. But as I see all of you guys sitting here tonight, supporting me on my release, I want to say I apologize for thinking so negative on what we all pray for every day. There's no reason I should be afraid of what's on the other side of these walls because I have people like you who only wish success in my life. When I came back to the penitentiary, I didn't know what to expect in here, but here I am twenty months later, about to go home a day early. Thank you, guys, for helping me overcome my fears, and thank you, guys, for this party tonight. I love all of you and pray that your day to go home will be just as blessed as mine. I promise I won't let you down this time."

Tree's eyes begin to water as he ended his small speech, and since he is around a bunch of guys, he turned his head to wipe his face. His friend Julio came and brought him a piece of cake he made from four packs of cookies, a jar of peanut butter, and six candy bars after he saw Tree gained his composure. The starch and sugar content in it is very high, so the inmates could only eat a little bit of the homemade cake, or they could get sick.

As the night started to show some closure, Tree stood by the door so that all of his friends can shake his hand for the last time on TDCJ's property. All their bellies are full from all the food they had eaten as they passed by and told him, "Good luck and God bless you out there."

"Thanks for everything" is all he can reply because he never thought he could grow so attached to the brothers he would encounter in jail. Officer McDaniel taps him on the shoulder around 9:00 p.m. to get his belongings together for tonight's chain, so Tree departs after one last wave to all the guys left in the dayroom.

Back in his cubicle, Tree passes out all of the food he had in his locker to the inmates who were not as fortunate as others to go to commissary. Anything that had the state of Texas on it, he gave away except for the white jumpsuit on his back. The study bible and concordance he studied out of he gave to Eric so that he can grow in his studies just as he did during his walk with Jesus Christ. The only thing he kept to be processed for the chain was his mail and the bible his mother sent him a year ago for his last birthday.

"I'm ready, Officer McDaniel."

"Are you sure because it looks to me like you don't want to go home?"

"Well, maybe you need to clean your glasses because it seems to me that your perception is off tonight."

"Naw'll, Mr. Wingate, I think my eyes are just fine." Officer McDaniel laughs out loud as he hands Tree a name tag to tie around the red meshed bag he is allowed to take to the Walls Unit. "You be careful out there, Torrence, and don't let your past affect your future."

"Yes, sir, and thanks for being one of the good guys around here. God bless you, Mr. McDaniel."

"God bless you too, Mr. Wingate."

The bus for the chain came during the middle of the night. It usually comes early, but Sugar Land is not too far from Huntsville, so the trustee camp is the last stop the bus makes on its way to the Walls Release Unit.

Everybody is still asleep when Officer McDaniel wakes Tree and shuffles him to the bus with the six other inmates who are going home. All the inmates going are half-asleep, but the excitement of being free in a couple of days causes their legs to high step to the bus instead of drag their feet like they wanted to.

Three officers are their escorts on this last trip for the inmates on their way to the house. One is the driver, and the other two are the overseers. A caged door in the middle of the aisle is locked, and the guns they have on their sides are placed in a metal box with the officer who is going to sit to the rear. Everything is checked on the outside of the bus with round mirrors strapped to four-foot poles as all precautions are taken highly because of an escape. The gear is placed in drive, and Tree looks at the trustee camp through the caged window go in the opposite direction the bus is going. "Thank you, Jesus, for peace and tranquility while I was in this place," he prays as he cracks a smile for the friends he is going to miss.

Nothing has changed since the last time he was released from the Walls Unit. The same guards that took him off the bus last time are the same guards who took him off the bus this time. Two by two, Tree had to walk to the same holding cage he had to sit in for nearly a day two years ago. Attitudes were at its highest level because of the sleep no one was allowed to get during the night, and processing didn't start until six, so that didn't make anything better.

Tree and the passengers on his bus lucked out this morning because it's a quarter till six, and today's show is about to get on the road in a few minutes.

Fifteen minutes flew by, but during those fifteen minutes, more and more white uniforms were piled on top of each other in the small enclosure. Some of the offenders started to push, and some threw a few elbows to keep others from invading the little space they had. Gay slurs begin to be tossed in the air randomly as the men inside the gate had to back up to let more offenders in. The guards that are working this morning shift tried to make someone get out of line with them so that they can make an example out of him for anyone else who might want to try something funny. No one there fed into the guards' games, so the offenders kept their words of anger among themselves in hopes of making it inside as soon as possible.

Suddenly, a loud horn sounds over the unit approximately at 6:00 a.m., and the shadows from the sun start to form along the ground as daylight peeks over last night's skies. Everyone inside the holding cell stands and is ready for the guards to call off the first group of men's names, but Tree is in no rush until the jingling of keys causes his eyes to eyeball the holding cell door like a hawk.

"Okay, now listen up if you want to make it inside the building with no delay. Rule 1 is be quiet!" the officer shouts. "Rule 2 is when I call your name, I want you to step outside the gate and show me your wristband! And rule 3 is I don't give a damn if we do this today or tomorrow, so please obey rules 1 and 2! Now, are we clear on these rules because I can show you better than I can tell you!"

No one responded to the officer's questions because the only answer the offenders gave him were blank stares of men tired of being cooped up in a cage.

"I guess those dumb-ass looks on your faces mean ya'll understand. Oh yeah, I forgot to tell you not to let me repeat myself twice." A second officer walks over and hands him today's list. "Sugar Land and Jasper, come to the gate and show me your wristbands as I call off your names!"

Time is no longer an essence after Tree leaves the last stages in the gym from processing all his belongings he is going to take home with him. Relief of walking through the fifteen-foot gate tomorrow falls upon him as a guard directs him to the last cell he is going to stay in behind bars. Step by step he walked up the stairs to level 2, savoring the learning experience he's had the past twenty months in the penitentiary.

As he sat down in his cell, no one is there to greet him, so he closes his eyes and remembers the powerful words of Old School from the last time he was released. "Never play another man's game because he didn't invent it for you to win," he recalls when thinking how he ended up back in jail just like the old man said he would if he went back to the dope game.

Light is something not found tonight as Tree looks through the bars over the gym down below. No one is there for him to talk to, so the stillness of the dark cell causes him to fade in and out for brief moments during the night. Each time he dozed off, the dreams he had picked up right where they ended. The first time he dozed off, he heard wedding bells. The second time he dozed off, he heard vows. And the third time he dozed off, he saw Audumn and Secorion standing at the altar, waiting for the preacher to put the finishing touches on their marriage so the two lovebirds can go live happily ever after. Everything he's witnessing is unreal as he listens for the preacher to say, "If anyone here has an objection to the holy matrimony of

Audumn and Secorion Woodson, let them speak now, or forever hold their peace."

Tree burst through the double doors of the church still in his white TDCJ uniform. His hands and feet are shackled together as he hops down the aisle toward Audumn with the look of disbelief on his face. "I have an objection!" he yells while looking into Audumn's eyes.

"Torrence, what are you doing? I told you that if you smoke that mess again or go back to jail that I was going to leave you."

"But—" Tree said, trying to think of something to say.

"But nothing because we're through, Tree! Besides I'm in love with Secorion now."

Beads of sweat were all over his forehead as he awoke with Secorion's name echoing in his mind. His neck and armpits are soaked as he rises up quickly out of his dream, nearly hitting his head on the top bunk. Everything up until this moment has been like a dream come true until the dream he just had felt more real than the present time he is in now. He thought he had buried being with Audumn once and for all when his sister answered his letters regarding her. Gayriale wrote, "I'm sorry, big brother, but Audumn is with a guy named Secorion, and she looks happy, so please let her go."

After reading what he feared the most, he wished the once love of his life the best and pushed her to the back of his mind as best as he could. In doing that, he forgot that his heart will never forget the passion they shared for nearly seven years.

"Torrence Wingate, get ready because you're on the first release of the day," an officer said into his cell while going on to the next man who is going to be released.

"Dang, I can't believe it's morning again already." Tree stands to stretch his cramped bones from sleeping in so many awkward positions. "I'm sorry, Audumn, and I wish you were here to see the miraculous work God has done in me. I will always love you, and thanks for everything."

Stepping outside the cell, he takes a deep breath and begins to follow the crowd of men to the far side of the unit. This morning, everyone is following directions carefully because none of the offenders want nothing to come between them and the door they are about to walk through. From a window, a trustee hands Tree an old pair of black church pants and a faded yellow shirt that smelled like it has been in a box for a decade. Tree says, "Thank you" and moves on to the next window, which is the clerk. A check for $50 with his name on it is given to him for all his hard labor, and after he finished signing for it, the lady behind the glass tells him that he has to report to the parole office on West Thirty-Fourth at 8:00 a.m. on June 15.

"Everyone who is finished, you are free to leave. The Greyhound bus station is two blocks down and to your right," an officer shouts, pointing toward the door. "If anyone is caught in Huntsville after three hours of being released, we will have no choice but to detain you for another day or until you can find some means of transportation. Good luck, and please let this be the last time you pay the Texas Department of Criminal Justice a visit."

Today is a good day for Tree to walk beyond the fifteen-foot gate that separated inmates from citizens. The two blocks they had to walk to the bus station felt more like one because the streets were a lot shorter than the ones in Houston. As they all sat and waited on the bus, Tree feels born again as he turns down cigarette after cigarette from the guys who cashed their checks and bought a pack. Just think, last time he got out, he smoked until he couldn't smoke no more, but this time the only thing he wanted in his lungs is the breath God has given him.

The bus pulled up and stopped abruptly right in front of the bench he is sitting on. After the bus driver swung the door open, the line everyone is standing in grew shorter as everyone rushed inside to find a seat near a window.

Tree steps onto the bus last and glances down the street toward the Walls Release Unit before sitting in the first seat that is available. "It is finished," he mutters as the door closes behind him and the wheels begin to roll out of the bus station.

Life is a lesson that we learn each day as we live it. Sometimes the days that we think that are good are really bad, and sometimes the days that we think that are bad are really good. There is no one on this earth who can grade us on the lesson of life, so we as people must learn to grade ourselves to the best of our ability. It took Tree forty-two months of incarceration to take an outlook on his life until he changed into the man he is today. As he sits back, he looks around at the twenty-six men that were released with him and contemplates on how statistics show that more than half of them will return on a new charge or violation. Finally, today, his heart has no worries because June 13, 2012, is the last time he would walk out of bondage again.

The End

CPSIA information can be obtained
at www.ICGtesting.com
Printed in the USA
BVHW051001210821
614134BV00004B/13

9 781947 247642